PUT OUT

—TO—

Pasture

A FARM to TABLE MYSTERY

AMANDA FLOWER

Poisoned Pen
PRESS

Published by Poisoned Pen Press, an imprint of Sourcebooks
P.O. Box 4410, Naperville, Illinois 60567-4410
(630) 961-3900
sourcebooks.com

Library of Congress Cataloging-in-Publication Data

Names: Flower, Amanda, author.
Title: Put out to pasture / Amanda Flower.
Description: Naperville, Illinois : Poisoned Pen Press, [2022] | Series: A
   farm to table mystery
Identifiers: LCCN 2021014774 (print) | LCCN
2021014775 (ebook) | (paperback) | (epub)
Subjects: GSAFD: Mystery fiction.
Classification: LCC PS3606.L683 P88 2022 (print) | LCC PS3606.L683
   (ebook) | DDC 813/.6--dc23
LC record available at https://lccn.loc.gov/2021014774
LC ebook record available at https://lccn.loc.gov/2021014775

Printed and bound in Canada.
MBP 10 9 8 7 6 5 4 3 2 1

For my favorite farmer, David

Chapter One

It was a crisp mid-October afternoon. The weather was perfect for sweaters, light scarves, and riding boots. The air smelled of apple cider, hay, and pumpkin spice. It was my favorite time of year. Autumn in Michigan was something I had missed the fifteen years I lived in California. Despite the beautiful day, a knot was pulled as tight in my stomach as the ropes that tethered the boats to the dock on Lake Michigan.

Cars, minivans, and pickup trucks lined the half mile-long driveway as they waited to park in the open pasture next to my barn. When I came up with the idea of Fall Daze, I never for a moment thought I would have this level of response. It was overwhelming, and worse, I was underprepared.

I wasn't the reason all these people were here either. I had done my part by putting flyers up around town about the event, made an event post on social media, and bought a tiny ad in the local paper. However, my best guess was seventy percent of the hundred-some vehicles in my pasture were there because of my best friend, Kristy Brown. When Kristy endorsed something in Cherry Glen, people listened and lent their support.

Kristy managed the Cherry Glen Farmers Market. It was

one of the most popular farmers markets in the region outside of Traverse City. She scored a spot on the local television station to plug the market, which she did, but she also
spoke about Fall Daze at Bellamy Farm, calling it the best
fall festival of the season. By the looks of it, people listened,
and now I had to live up to her claim. That was a tall order.
Fall in Michigan was serious business. It seemed that every
town, city, and farm had a festival, and every weekend until
the first snow was packed with autumnal activities. If everything went well, I had a real chance to save my family farm.
If it went poorly, I might drive the farm further into the hole.
No pressure.

When I was a child, Bellamy Farm was composed of four
hundred acres. When my grandfather died, he divided the
farm in half between his two sons. Years after my uncle died,
Stacey, my cousin, sold the half of the farm she'd inherited
from her father so that she could pursue her real passion in
local theater.

She sold the land to a developer for a pretty penny, but
then the development company landed in some trouble. As a
result, that portion of the old Bellamy Farm was left to waste.
As far as I knew, the development company still owned
the property but had made no changes to the land. I wondered if it was just biding its time until the housing market
boomed again and the second half of Bellamy Farm could
be transformed into a subdivision. A subdivision on our
family's land would make my grandfather do somersaults in
his grave, and it made me a bit queasy just thinking about
it. Ideally, I would have the money someday to buy the land

back and put Bellamy Farm together again. However, since I didn't even have enough money to replace the shutters on the farmhouse, it wasn't looking good.

My father, Sullivan "Sully" Bellamy, stood next to me, gripping the arms of his walker. In his early eighties, he was perpetually cold and had a sour disposition that occasionally the right person could crack and make him smile. I was rarely that person. At the moment, he wasn't pleased with me at all. There were very few things my father enjoyed less than being around large groups of people. Hundreds of people invading his sleepy farm was his worst nightmare.

My father wore a black stocking cap that was pulled down over his bushy, gray eyebrows. The cap gave him a bandit-like appearance. He glowered at me. "How on earth are you going to feed all these people?"

It was a good question. My fawn-colored pug, Huckleberry, stood at my father's feet and cocked his head as if he considered this too. Then he glanced around with his wide-eyed pug stare. It looked like his round, brown eyes might just pop out of his head. I leaned over and scooped up the pug and hugged him close. I knew when my dog needed comfort. Maybe I needed some too.

Dad shook his head. "You've turned the farm into a circus."

"Dad, this is great PR." My voice was a tad shaky.

"Not if these people go home hungry. I'd say that's terrible PR. In fact, that's the worst PR that you can get. I don't know what it's like in California, but when someone shows up at an event in Michigan, they had better not leave with an empty belly or there will be hell to pay. I can tell you that!"

I glanced at the food table that was becoming sparse. When the festival began two hours ago, it had been piled high with plastic containers and bakery boxes of my organic baked goods. I used the festival as an opportunity to test my organic recipes. I had always loved to bake, especially with my Grandma Bellamy while growing up, but when I had been in LA, I had little opportunity. Too many people in the Golden State avoided carbs, myself included. Since returning to Michigan, my passion for baking had returned and I had wild dreams of someday having a bakery and café on our property that would serve real, organic farm-to-table fare that was produced right here on Bellamy Farm. The dream was a long way off, but the festival was a start, and I had truly believed it was a good start until it began.

I thought I had baked enough for the two days of the festival. There were over three hundred items ranging from cookies to muffins to cakes, but it would never be enough.

My assistant, Chesney Stevens, made a face at me. She was a tall and strong woman in her late twenties with brown hair that just brushed the top of her shoulders. She always wore a cloth headband to hold the hair back from her face. Chesney was a graduate student whom I had hired a few weeks back when I realized I couldn't do everything I needed to at the farm myself. She only worked as much as I could pay her, which admittedly wasn't a lot, but having her help for the ten to fifteen hours a week I could afford made a huge difference.

She was the perfect candidate for the job. She was getting her MBA with a concentration in agricultural business at my old alma mater in Traverse City but lived right here in Cherry Glen. She rented a small house in town with her younger sister. The little money I could pay would help her get by and supplement the stipends she received from the university for her graduate program. It all sounded too good to be true, so being me, I expected that it was.

Imagine my happy surprise when she turned out to be just who she said she was. There was no way I could have pulled off Fall Daze without Chesney's help. The last few weeks we worked tirelessly to make the worn-down farm presentable for this big event, and now it might be ruined because people would go home hungry.

I swallowed. "I have enough apples to make more apple cider," I told my father. "And I've called in reinforcements. They should be here soon. There's more to Fall Daze than food. There's the corn maze, yard games, and the hayride—plenty for everyone to do while they wait to eat. Don't worry, Dad. I've got this handled."

"Looks like you do," he muttered and shuffled away.

I sighed and went back to Chesney at the food table.

Chesney handed a customer her change. "Enjoy your cherry strudel!" she said with a bright smile.

The customer walked away, and while the next person in line considered what was left on the table, Chesney whispered to me. "We're running low."

"I know. I called a friend. She should be here soon with more food."

"You have a friend who is an organic baker?" Her blue eyes went wide.

"Not exactly…"

"Shi!" a friendly voice called to me from the pasture. Kristy Brown walked toward me, weaving in and around the people standing in front of the barn waiting in line for food.

Kristy pushed a double stroller. She was a new mom of twin girls, and she looked quite pleased with herself. "Look at this turnout! You did a great job getting people to come!" Her dark eyes sparkled. She wore a brightly colored handwoven scarf around her neck. The scarf was yellow, orange, pink, red, and lime green. The colors should have clashed with the rest of her outfit, but the intricate geometric pattern of the scarf just worked. I knew the scarf well. Kristy had had it for over twenty years, a gift from one of her aunts in Mexico.

My eyes went wide. "This is because of your spot on TV. I had very little to do with it."

"Don't be modest." When I didn't say anything, she studied my face. "What's wrong?"

I set Huckleberry on the ground. He walked over to the stroller, put his forepaws on the side of it, and peeked in at the sleeping twins. Huckleberry looked back at me with a whimper.

Kristy laughed. "Looks like he wants a little sister."

I frowned. "He has plenty of little sisters and brothers in the barn cats. There are the chickens too."

She rolled her eyes. "Your chickens do not qualify as siblings for Huckleberry. They are more like a street gang."

"That seems a little harsh."

"Shi, one of the chickens chased a woman through the corn maze until a volunteer caught the chick and locked it up," Kristy said.

I winced. "I thought they were all in the coop."

Hearing this news about the chickens, I was more grateful than ever for the high school volunteers who were helping Chesney and me out with the event. All of them were members of the high school's Future Farmers of America chapter. To be honest, they were probably a lot better at chasing chickens than I was. There were thirteen high school student volunteers in total. They guarded the corn maze—from wild chickens apparently—drove the hayride, supervised the pumpkin picking in the pumpkin patch, and helped park the long line of cars. I would be in a lot worse shape without them, including having to deal with a lawsuit over a chicken attack.

"I bet it was Diva," I said. Diva was a chicken who more than lived up to her name. "She's my most disobedient hen."

"I want you to take a moment and think about what you said just now, and then think back to six months ago when you were sitting in a fancy LA office."

I grimaced. The image was quite a leap.

"So what's wrong?" she asked.

I sighed. I had hoped she'd forgotten about that question. She shook her finger at me. "Don't lie to me. I know something is wrong. You made that same face in biology class when you let Mr. Donalson's rats out of their cage and they ran out of his classroom. They never did find Gertrude."

I still felt bad about that. Poor Gertrude. Mr. Donalson was never the same after the incident. "I just wanted to pet one. I didn't know it would try to bite me. I jumped back for half a second, and they made a break for it. How was I supposed to know they were going to do that?"

"They're rats. They bite. Have you never heard of the Black Death?"

"That was a mistake. Fall Daze might be a mistake too. I didn't bake enough for this many people."

She grinned. "Not to worry. Jessa is on her way with more food. She's bringing pies! Deep-fried Twinkies too."

"I feel terrible pulling Jessa away from her diner. The afternoons there are always busy. Not to mention there's the issue of her food not being organic."

"Organic is in the eye of the beholder." She grinned. Her daughters cooed and kicked their legs as if they were in agreement with their mother.

"No, it really isn't," I said and then added quickly, "Not that I'm not thankful for what she's doing. She's really saving me. Whatever she brings, I know it will be delicious."

"Listen, you can just tell everyone Jessa baked and fried the organic out of her food. You don't have much choice. There must be two hundred and fifty people here. How many did you plan on?"

I sighed. "Maybe one hundred? I thought I was being outrageous to make that much food for that many people."

My father shuffled back over on his walker. I expected him to have gone into the farmhouse and putter with his collection of historical Michigan artifacts. It was typically how he escaped anything he found unpleasant.

"Hi, Mr. Bellamy," Kristy said with a bright grin.

He nodded at my friend. "It's nice to see you, Kristy. Congratulations on the girls. They are very cute."

Kristy blinked. "Why thank you, Mr. Bellamy."

I knew she was surprised. My father wasn't one to use the word "cute" for anything or anyone.

Dad turned to me. "You said more food is coming. Where is it? Chesney is about to be mauled for that last piece of pumpkin pie."

"What a terrible way to go," Kristy said.

I shot her a look and said, "Jessa will be here soon. She's the reinforcements."

"You're having Jessa's Place cater?" Dad said. "No one in this crowd is going to go for your hippie granola when they have a fried Twinkie staring them in the face."

"Dad, did you even look at what I made for today? There's no granola at all."

"I didn't have to look to know it was a bunch of hippie stuff you brought back from California with you. Organic." He snorted and shuffled away again.

Part of me really hoped he would hide in the collection room for the rest of the festival.

"I'm sure your dad is proud of you," Kristy said as she watched him go.

I gave her a look and then bit my lip. "Maybe I expected too much out of him and myself to host an event this soon after moving back to the farm. We weren't nearly as ready as I wanted to be. The fact that we ran out of food is all the proof we need of that."

"This soon? Shiloh, you've been back since July. You have to do something if the farm has any chance of success. Also, everyone who is eating your baked goods has raved about them. I think you should apply for a booth at the farmers market to sell them. I can get you an in." She winked at me.

"Really?" I asked. "I never expected to have a slot in the market this year. You said that all the spots are full."

Her face clouded over. "We have a vacancy."

I wanted to ask her what she meant by that when a shrill voice called, "Kristy Brown, I want a word with you!"

Kristy cringed.

From the pasture, Minnie Devani pushed her way through the line waiting to sign up for the corn maze. "Kristy Brown, you had better speak to me!"

Kristy sighed and turned around. Huckleberry galloped in the direction of the barn. I knew he was going to sit this one out with the barn cats. I can't say I blamed him.

Minnie was a squat woman in her sixties. She had gray hair that fell just above her ears and wore a plaid green coat over her olive-green pantsuit. The coat was a surprising fashion choice. Most of the time Minnie was precisely color coordinated.

Minnie wagged her finger at Kristy. "You had better take your lies back or I'll sue you!"

Kristy's cheeks flushed, and she stepped in front of the stroller. "I don't think you're the one who should be calling someone else a liar. Watch yourself, Minnie. If you want to revisit the conversation we had earlier today, I'd be happy to do that, but I don't think that's something you want to do in front of an audience."

"You can't tell me what to do." Minnie jabbed a polished pink fingernail into Kristy's chest.

Kristy clenched her jaw. I grabbed the handles of the stroller and pulled the girls away from the fray. By the look on Kristy's face, there was about to be some fireworks. I had seen the same look on my friend's face so many times. It never ended well for the person on the receiving end of that glare.

"Don't touch me," Kristy said through clenched teeth.

I pulled the stroller back even farther. You could never be too careful. It's not that I thought the two women would come to blows, but I wanted the twins out of the way just in case.

"I will do whatever I please after the way I have been treated," Minnie said. "You have ruined me, and you did it out of spite. You're a spiteful woman."

"After the way you've been treated? I have been nothing but kind and lenient with you. Do you want to tell all these people here that you are six months late on your booth rent for the farmers market? Do you want me to tell them that to help you pay off the debt, I let you work at the market while I was on maternity leave?" Kristy took a step closer to Minnie, so that she was just inches from her face. "Do you want me to tell them that when I got back from maternity leave, I discovered that you stole over six thousand dollars from the market and *still* didn't pay your rent?" She took another step closer to Minnie now. "Is that what you want me to tell them?"

Minnie opened and closed her mouth. Everyone in line for food, the hayride, and the corn maze stared at us. The festival grew deathly quiet.

I hurried forward and patted Kristy's arm. "Kristy," I hissed.

My friend looked at me, and there was fury in her eyes. I jumped back. In all my life, I had never seen Kristy this angry.

Minnie covered her face with her hands. The rings on her fingers sparkled in the late afternoon sunlight coming up over the barn.

"I think the two of you need to talk about this another time," I said in a low voice.

Kristy's face cleared, and her fury was immediately replaced with abject horror as she realized the scene she'd made. "I'm sorry, Shi. This is your event. I shouldn't have let her rile me up so much."

"It's fine." I turned to Minnie. "Minnie, I think you and Kristy should talk about this later, in private."

She glared at me. "You shouldn't be here at all, Shiloh Bellamy. No one wants to know what you think."

I put my hands on my hips. "That may be so, but this is my farm and I'm asking you to leave."

"I was leaving anyway. The only reason I came here was to talk to Kristy. I knew she would be at your little festival." She made a dismissive gesture with her hand. "It's a poor excuse for one, if you ask me. My dear friend Doreen Killian told me all about you, and I can very well see why she doesn't want her granddaughter around such a bad influence."

My face grew hot.

Before I could fire back, she pointed at Kristy again. "I will make you sorry, Kristy Brown. Remember this day. I will make sure you never forget what you did to me!" She spun around and stomped back in the direction of the pasture that served as our makeshift parking lot.

Utter silence fell over Fall Daze.

I waved at the crowd. "Welcome to Fall Daze, everyone! We have more baked goods on the way and fried Twinkies! Who doesn't love a fried Twinkie?"

I don't think anyone was thinking of fried Twinkies at the moment. They were thinking that if anyone could make good on a promise to make another person's life miserable, it was Minnie Devani.

Chapter Two

After the crowd went back to enjoying themselves, I walked over to Kristy, who was speaking with her husband, Kent. Kent had his hands on the stroller, and he rolled it back and forth in place as if it rock the girls to sleep. From their alert expressions, it didn't appear to be working.

Kent was a high school teacher, and his eyes drooped in concern as he listened to his wife speak. I imagined he had the same look of concern on his face any time one of his students came to him with a problem. Mr. Brown was one of the most popular teachers at Cherry Glen High School.

"Kristy, are you okay?" I asked.

She turned to me. "I'm fine. Shi, I'm so sorry that had to happen here. This certainly wasn't the place I wanted to have that confrontation."

"I'm going to take the girls to the pumpkin patch," Kent said. "I can't think of anything cuter than seeing a couple of baby twins on pumpkins."

I couldn't either, and Kristy and Kent's girls were extra adorable. They had Kristy's light-brown skin and dark hair and Kent's blue eyes. As far as I was concerned, they'd hit the genetic jackpot.

Kent gestured at us with his hand. "I'll let the two of you talk."

She smiled at Kent. "Thanks, honey."

As Kent walked away, pushing the stroller, she shook her head. "I don't know what I would do without him. He's been my rock, especially since the twins were born, and with everything happening at the farmers market…"

"What's going on at the market? What was that about six thousand dollars and Minnie calling you a liar?"

She frowned. "When I came back from maternity leave, my computer accounting program seemed to be off. Line items were missing that I knew should be there. I looked into it further and noticed that was the case for the entire time I was away from the market. Minnie had been in charge all that time, so I asked her about it. She accused me of accusing *her* of stealing. Honestly, that hadn't even entered my mind. I thought it was a clerical error because she wasn't as comfortable with the accounting program as I thought she was before I left." She shook her head. "She immediately jumped into defense mode, which, of course, made me even more suspicious of her. If she was innocent of any wrongdoing, why be so defensive?"

"I knew that Minnie was taking care of the business side of the market while you were on maternity leave, but this was the first I heard she hadn't paid her booth fees."

Kristy flipped her long black ponytail over her shoulder. "I was trying to be nice to let her have the booth space so she could earn the money to make the fees, but it wasn't enough. I thought that if she worked at the market for free while I was gone, we could call it even. It seemed like the kindest thing to do and a win-win for us both."

My hands felt cold, and I shoved them into the pockets of my denim jacket. "Did you have a contract with her?"

"A contract? Shi, this is Cherry Glen, not LA. A lot of business here is still done with a verbal agreement and a handshake. Maybe even a hug. Not much is recorded on paper."

I frowned, knowing she was right. However, it was difficult to sue someone on a verbal agreement or a handshake and even harder to win a lawsuit without those things.

"Did she say why she took the money?" I asked.

She shook her head. "She didn't say. Minnie is the last person that I would think to take anything. She is the most self-righteous woman I have ever met. Once I saw her yell at a man in Jessa's Place for asking for extra rolls and then pocketing them just when he was about to leave. She made him sit at the counter and she watched until he finished every last roll. Who does that?"

I raised my brow. That did sound like something Minnie would do.

Kristy twisted the end of her colorful scarf around her hand. "I don't know who else it could have been. She was the only one who had access to the money and the office. With so many merchants at the farmers market, I'm very careful about who has access to the office. Minnie was it."

"Unless she let someone else in."

Kristy frowned. "I never thought of that. But who? As far as I know, she doesn't have that many friends outside of her book club."

I nodded. The book club in question was the one run by Doreen Killian, who happened to hate my guts for something I didn't do fifteen years ago. If someone could hold a grudge for that long, I knew I was dealing with a formidable opponent. Normally, it wouldn't have bothered me. I'd worked in Hollywood long enough to know that not everyone liked me, and some people disliked me for no reason at all. However, in the case of Doreen, it was more complicated because her son, Quinn, and his eleven-year-old daughter, Hazel, were my closest neighbors. They were also my friends. Doreen despised our friendship and hated that Quinn allowed Hazel to visit me at Bellamy Farm as often as he did.

"Have you talked to the police about it? Are you going to press charges?" My questions came fast.

She cocked her head. "What good would that do me other than make things ten times harder? Minnie is Doreen Killian's closest friend, and Doreen is married to the police chief. Don't think for a minute that Chief Randy would give my case fair consideration if it upsets his wife too much. The poor man has to live with the woman. He should win a trophy or something for that. Or our pity."

"She's not that bad," I said.

She gave me a look. "No comment."

"Why would Minnie need the money?" I shook my head. "I mean, if she hasn't been paying her booth fee, she has been having money trouble for a while. What caused this? I wonder if she's in some kind of trouble. Maybe she's sick and has medical bills we don't know about."

Kristy dropped her scarf and folded her arms. "I tried to

help her, but she betrayed me. It sounds to me you're making excuses for her."

I shook my head. "I'm not. I promise. Stealing is never okay, but I'm just wondering what the root of the problem is. If you find that, maybe you will better understand why she did this."

Kristy made a face.

"Again, I'm not saying it's okay, but maybe it will help you to understand her position. Maybe the two of you can sort it out?"

"I've been more than understanding. This entire time, I wanted to settle things privately. I wouldn't make a fuss about any of it if she would just give me the money back. She refuses. Instead, she dug in her heels, saying that I'm the one in the wrong."

I nodded. "I'm sorry, Kristy."

She shook her head. "It's not your fault. Since Kent has the girls, I'm going to take a walk and calm down. I really hope this didn't hurt Fall Daze. You've worked too hard on this place to let something like this ruin it." She looked around. "The farm is like night and day from when you arrived, Shi. You should be proud."

I knew that Kristy was referring to the mended and painted fence, the working barn door, the mowed pasture, and the tilled-up fields that were waiting for winter cover crop, but I couldn't see those accomplishments in the same way. What I saw was the barn's peeling paint, the dead trees in the cherry orchards, the loose shutters on the farm-house, and the hundreds of other projects around the farm that needed my attention—and there wasn't much time left to give it to them. We were already in October, which meant that winter could come any day now to northwestern Michigan. Snow was not out of the question this time of year. When the farm was buried in, many of these projects would come to a complete halt.

When I was in California, my pricey therapist had made an observation about me. "Shiloh, you don't believe you ever make progress, but you have. You're unable to recognize the progress you've made no matter how big." Ever since then, I had tried to be more aware of what I *had* accomplished, as opposed to what I hadn't. But I didn't always succeed.

I forced a smile for Kristy. "Thanks, and don't worry about Fall Daze. Guests didn't know they were getting a show with admission. You and Minnie provided that. It will be the talk of the town for at least a week."

"Don't I know it." She made a face. "I hope Jessa hurries up getting here with those fried Twinkies. I really need one badly. Maybe two."

"There's nothing a fried Twinkie can't fix," I said.

"Make sure Kent puts that on my tombstone." Kristy flipped her scarf over her shoulder and marched away.

"Shi!" a high-pitched voice called out.

I spun around and saw Hazel running through the parked cars in the pasture. She was tall for her age, and she seemed to have grown a good five inches since the summer. Her hair was cut in a bob that bounced around her ears as she ran. She waved her arms widely. Behind her, her father followed at a much slower pace.

Quinn was a firefighter, and he was built like one. He

was tall with a broad chest, and the dark hair that fell over his forehead was in desperate need of trimming, though he brushed it out of his eyes with a calloused hand every few minutes. He was handsome. I could state that as a fact with the same authority that I could say the sky was blue. In the same breath, I could say he was off limits. He had been Logan's best friend. Logan Graham had been my fiancé, and he died in a car accident when we were all in our early twenties. Logan was the reason Quinn was my friend today and the reason Quinn was untouchable.

"Where's Esmeralda?" Hazel wanted to know.

I wasn't the least bit surprised this was her first question. Esmeralda was a Siamese cat that Hazel and I had rescued during the summer. She was sugar and spice and had the loudest meow I had ever heard. Hazel wanted to adopt her, but her grandmother Doreen didn't want to take in the cat. Since Quinn worked long, overnight shifts at the fire station, Hazel stayed with her grandparents several nights a week. Now Esmeralda lived with Huckleberry, Dad, and me on Bellamy Farm.

Hazel loved Bellamy Farm, but I knew that the biggest attraction to the farm was Esmeralda. She adored that cat.

"I think she's in the barn with Huckleberry. They're staying out of the way of all of the commotion."

Hazel looked at her dad.

He laughed. "Sure, you can go see the cat."

She pumped her fist in the air and took off. After Hazel disappeared into the barn, Quinn smiled at me. "I'm looking forward to tasting one of your organic treats."

"Umm." I grimaced. "That might be a problem. We need more food. It sold so quickly."

"Did someone say they were in need of food?" a cheerful voice asked.

Jessa Yates, the owner and lone waitress of Jessa's Place, came out of the rows of cars pulling a blue, foldable wagon full of plastic boxes of pies and pastries. Her white hair was dyed orange and black at the tips in preparation for Halloween. A jack-o'-lantern- patterned ribbon held her hair back in a ponytail. She wore jeans, sneakers, and a sweatshirt with her diner's logo in the middle of it. "I'm here to save the day! I have three kinds of pie. Pumpkin, apple, and pecan. And apple dumplings, banana bread, oatmeal cookies, and pumpkin muffins. Most of it is still in my van. I can only tow so much at a time in this little wagon."

"I heard something about fried Twinkies," I said.

"I would never forget those. I have fried Oreos too. I'm not messing around."

Quinn raised his hand. "Sign me up for both of those."

She winked at him. "You know I always save you extra." She turned back to me. "Now, I know you are probably all worried because I'm not serving organic food, but this was the best I could do on short notice."

I nodded. "Thank you for doing this, Jessa. I don't know what I would have done without you pitching in. How much do I owe you for the food?"

"You don't owe me a dime."

"At the very least, you should keep the money from the food you sell," I argued.

She shook her finger at me. "I think not. I won't take anyone's money today. This is a fun event that you're doing for the community. Just think of it as a donation to bring back Bellamy Farm. The whole town wants you to save this place. Old family farms have been the way of life in western Michigan for as long as anyone can remember. If I have a chance to help save one of those farms, I'm going to take it."

Tears came to my eyes. "Thank you."

She shook her head, reached into her wagon, and came up with a fried Twinkie. "You need this more than anyone else here. It will make your day better. You have a long day ahead of you yet. When the festival is over, you will have plenty of mess to clean up. You need the energy. Trust me on that."

"Are Twinkies known for giving energy?" Quinn asked with a laugh.

I accepted the plastic food box from Jessa's hand. What I didn't know was what a big mess the day would become.

Chapter Three

By five thirty the festival had been over for a half hour, and guests were still making their way to their cars in the pasture. No one seemed to be in a great hurry to leave Bellamy Farm. I heard children laughing and adults chatting. My heart was full. Despite the argument between Minnie and Kristy and the baked goods shortage, Fall Daze had been a success. Everyone was talking about Jessa's fried Twinkies. It was only the first day too. I got to do it all over again tomorrow after a long night of baking. I would have to make double of everything. Maybe even triple.

Jessa patted me on the shoulder. "You did it. You should be proud of yourself. Sully should be proud of you too."

I gave her a half smile. "I think Dad is just happy people are leaving. He can't wait until this weekend is over and Bellamy Farm is quiet again."

She nodded. "Your father is not a people person, unlike me. If I go just one day without speaking to someone, I'm at a complete loss. There's nothing I love more than talking to people. Being alone is just boring if you ask me."

"Then I would say you were in the right business running a diner."

She grinned. "Why do you think I decided to learn to cook? Now, I know that you still want to serve your organic fare tomorrow, but I am going home to bake up a few things and maybe fry a few more Twinkies just in case. You never know, a whole busload could roll in from Traverse City."

"That is so—"

My words were cut off by a high-pitched scream.

Jessa looked around for the source. "What was that? You don't have a haunted house, do you?"

"No." The scream rang in my ears. I was shaken by it. By the pallor on Jessa's face, I could tell that she was too.

Quinn came running from around the back of the barn. "What was that? Is someone hurt?"

"That didn't sound like a hurt scream to me," Jessa said. "That was a terrified scream."

"It came from the pasture," I said. There were only a few cars left in the makeshift parking lot, one of which was Jessa's van. She'd parked the white van way in the back along the tree line that separated my property from what used to be the second half of Bellamy Farm.

Quinn's jaw tightened. "It definitely came from that direction." He ran toward the white van situated the length of a football field away from where we stood.

"I don't think—" I called after him, but my words were cut off by another blood-curdling scream. A shiver ran down my spine.

I picked up Huckleberry and handed him to Jessa. "I have to go see what's going on. Will you hold on to him or put him in the farmhouse? I don't want him to follow me."

She nodded. "Go!"

Before I turned away, I felt a hand lightly tap on my shoulder. The feeling barely registered. I was too focused on what was happening.

I ran after Quinn, well aware I wasn't in the same shape he was. I was halfway to the white van and already felt winded. In LA, I had done countless classes in the gym to stay fit. In Michigan, I counted on the farmwork to keep me in good shape. Perhaps that technique wasn't as effective as I had hoped.

Quinn stood in front of Jessa's van with a teenage girl who was crying so hard she gasped for breath. Her dark eyeliner and mascara ran down her face in black rivulets, and her hair tie was falling down her ponytail. To my surprise, it was Chesney's twenty-year-old sister, Whit. I hadn't even known she came to Fall Daze. As Chesney had once said, Whit was more of an "indoor cat." Chesney's words, not mine.

"Tell me again what you saw," Quinn said in a soothing tone that he must have perfected during his many years as an EMT and firefighter.

Whit wrapped her thin arms around her body. Her long black hair that was dyed bright yellow at the tips flew in every direction as her whole body shuddered at the memory. "She's dead. I saw her lying there dead. I've never seen a dead person before, not even at a funeral. When my great-aunt died, I refused to look into the casket. I didn't want to remember what she looked like dead. Now, I will never forget what this woman looked like. It was so much worse." The tears started up again.

"Okay," Quinn said. "Take a breath. Tell me how you found this person."

She looked up at him and bit her lip. "I was just walking around, waiting for Chesney so we could leave." Her gaze dropped.

I frowned. Something wasn't right with Whit's story. Why would she be so timid about telling us that she was waiting for Chesney? With most of the eye makeup running off her face, she looked no more than twelve.

"Where did you walk?" Quinn asked.

"Just to the tree line. I didn't go any farther than that because I could see the scarecrow, and scarecrows freak me out. They're like clowns. Super freaky."

I, for one, agreed about the clowns. But Whit's mention of a dead body was what really chilled my blood.

Quinn nodded, as if to encourage her to go on.

"I was turning around to walk back when I saw her at the scarecrow's feet. I thought maybe at first it was another scarecrow that had fallen down, but when I got closer, I could see it wasn't a scarecrow, but a person, and she was really dead. Her face was blue."

The bite of fried Twinkie that Jessa had convinced me to take felt like a brick in the pit of my stomach.

"Can you show me where you saw her?" Quinn asked.

"Whit!" Chesney ran from the direction of the barn. "Are you okay?"

"Ches." Whit fell into her sister's arms.

Quinn pointed at me. "Call 911. My father should be on call. I'm going to find this scarecrow." He started to leave.

"Wait! I'm coming with you." I went after him with my cell phone in my hand. "The scarecrow is just beyond that ridge. Hazel and I put him up."

The color drained from his face.

"Quinn, Hazel is fine. She's in the barn playing with Esmeralda and the barn cats."

He nodded, looking as if that was the best that he could do because he was unable to speak.

"Follow me," I said and began to run in the direction of the scarecrow.

The scarecrow stood proudly above the small pumpkin patch. A large crow rested on one of its outstretched wooden arms and stared down at the ground. The bird unfolded its wings and took off, flapping them twice before disappearing in the trees.

"That's not a very effective scarecrow," Quinn said.

I didn't respond because now I was close enough to see what Whit had seen at the scarecrow's feet.

Minnie Devani lay on the cold ground with her right cheek pressed into the dry grass, eyes wide and glassy, Kristy's beloved scarf wrapped tightly around her throat.

Chapter Four

Quinn knelt by the body and pulled the edge of the scarf away from Minnie's throat to check for a pulse.

"Is she dead?" I asked. I knew that it was a stupid question. If she had any chance of life, Quinn would be trying to give her CPR or something. It was what he was trained to do. But he simply shook his head.

There was a rumble behind us. I spun around and saw Quinn's father riding toward us across the pasture on his motorcycle. I winced. There were a good number of groundhog holes in the field. If his front tire caught the edge of one, he could flip over the handlebars.

He made it to us safely and removed his helmet. Tufts of gray hair stuck up in all directions on his mostly bald head. "What on earth is going on? I was just headed home from the station so I could sit down to your mother's famous roast and watch some football when I got the call from Jessa that someone showed up dead at the Bellamy place. As luck would have it, I was just driving by." He leaned over Minnie's body. "Dang, that's Minnie Devani." He said this with a bit of awe. If anyone knew how important Minnie was to his wife Doreen, it was Chief Randy.

He looked at me. "What do you know about this?"

I stepped back. "Nothing. The festival ended and we were just about to clean up everything when we heard a scream."

"A scream?" he asked. "From Minnie?"

I shook my head. "A young woman, Whit Stevens. Her older sister Chesney works for me. Whit saw Minnie first. We left the sisters by Jessa's van."

"There wasn't anyone standing by Jessa's van when I got here."

"Then how did you know where to find us?" I asked.

"Well, Jessa said that you ran this way. When I didn't see you, I just kept going and here you are." He chewed on his black mustache. "My wife is going to be torn up about this. Why would anyone want to kill Minnie?"

Quinn and I shared a look. I thought it was because we could both think of a number of people who would want to silence Minnie. She was not a well-liked person in Cherry Glen. The only one who seemed to care for her at all was the chief's wife, Doreen.

The chief sucked on his teeth. "It looks like murder to me. Doc will have to make the actual determination. I don't want to take that away from him. He does like being the first to note the cause of death." He leaned over the body. "But from the looks of it, homicide by strangulation with that scarf right there. Now, I have never seen a murder in this manner with my own eyes, but I have seen my fair share of suicides by asphyxiation, and Minnie looks a lot like those incidents." He shook his head. "My poor wife. At times I thought she liked Minnie a whole lot more than me. This will be a tough pill to swallow."

Quinn's face turned red at his father's words. "Dad, shouldn't you call the coroner?"

Chief Randy looked up at his son. "Dispatch already did when I called in about the body. He's going to be fit to be tied to come all the way out here on Friday evening."

Quinn cleared his throat. "What about other officers?"

"They are on the way too."

As if he had summoned them, I saw two police officers walk across the field in our direction. There was one male and one female officer, and that was the extent of the small police department. I had met the younger officer, Officer Fenke, before, but the female officer I had never formally met. She was new to the department.

"Good, the two of you are here," the chief said. "Fenke, we need to mark off the area as a crime scene. I'll canvass whoever still might be here and find out if any of them saw Minnie come this way. If we know when she walked over here, we might get a precise timeline." He leaned over the body again.

"Sure thing, Chief," Officer Fenke said. "I just got a text that Doc is five minutes away."

"Good, good." He turned to the second officer. "Barker, I want you to help Fenke with the questioning. There must be a dozen or so people still around. Also ask them who else they knew was here. We might have to talk to the folks who left earlier too."

She nodded without a word and glanced at me.

I gave her a small smile, and she scowled back. Having never said one word to Officer Barker before, I didn't know what I had done to make her not like me, but it was clear she was no fan of mine.

"Now," the chief said, turning back to Quinn and me. "I heard that Minnie had a row earlier tonight with Kristy Brown." He eyed me. "What do you know about that?"

The brick was back in my stomach. "Kristy left a while ago. The twins were getting fussy."

"I didn't ask you where she was. Although I do find it interesting that your first instinct is to give her some sort of alibi. That's telling."

The brick grew larger.

"I only wanted to know about her argument with Minnie. What do you know?"

Quinn stood beside me in silence, and I was grateful he didn't answer for me. I didn't need someone to speak for me even when the questions asked made my skin crawl. "You will have to ask Kristy," I said.

"I plan to."

The chief's cell phone rang, and he removed it from the pocket of his jacket. "Hey, Doc. Yeah, we're on the other side of the pasture to the left of the barn." He nodded at Officer Barker. "Barker is on his way over to show you the way."

Officer Barker headed back in the direction of the barn without a word.

"Quinn, I would like you to stay as EMT," Chief Randy said. "Doc might need some help with the body, and you're best suited for that." He nodded at me. "Why don't you go wait back at the farmhouse? You don't want to see the part when the doc pokes and prods the body."

I swallowed. He was right. I didn't want to see that part, but I was hesitant to leave. I felt like I needed to stand guard for Kristy's sake. I didn't know what Minnie's death meant for Kristy, but it was nothing good. I was sure of that.

Quinn must have sensed my hesitation. "I'll be right back, Dad. I just want to make sure Barker found Doc."

His father nodded as he stared at the body. His forehead creased in worry. Was he more concerned about the murder of Minnie or how the murder of Minnie would impact his wife?

Quinn nodded to me.

As if against my own will, I took one final look at the body. My eyes fell on the scarf, not Minnie's face or her cold hands, but the scarf I'd last seen around Kristy's neck.

"Shi?" Quinn asked in a hushed voice.

I turned and followed him.

When we were back at the van, Quinn said, "Oh, there's Barker coming with the coroner. Hopefully, it won't take him too much time to make an initial determination about what happened, and then the body can be taken to his office."

I nodded mutely. "I didn't like Minnie, and of course, I knew she didn't like me, but I would never wish that on her."

He looked down at me. "No one would ever think that you would."

I wasn't so sure about that. I bit my lip to stop myself from saying that his mother just might think that about me when she learned of her friend's death on my farm. It would be another reason to keep Hazel and Quinn away from my farm and away from me. But how could I worry about what Doreen thought of me when a woman was dead? Another thought occurred to me, and it chilled me to the core. *I* had seen Minnie today before she died. She hadn't appeared ill. Not that I thought she dropped dead from a sudden illness with that colorful scarf wrapped so tightly around her neck. The method of how she died didn't seem to be in question at all.

"Hey, you there? Are you okay?" Quinn asked. He stepped in front of me and looked deep into my eyes.

My thoughts were somewhere else. I stepped back as if I needed physical distance from his gaze, which seemed a little too personal for the friendship we had. "I'm fine. I'm worried about Kristy."

"Don't worry. Kristy might have gotten into an argument with Minnie, but who in this town hasn't? She wasn't here tonight. That's the important thing. She has an alibi, and her husband can back her up."

I nodded, but doubt crept into my mind. I didn't know why. I had no reason to doubt that Kristy went home with Kent and the girls.

"Quinn," Officer Barker said. "The chief wants you at the scene."

Quinn nodded and glanced at me. He looked like he wanted to ask me a second time if I was all right but thought better of it. I was grateful for that. If he asked me again, I just might burst into tears. This was not how I had wanted Fall Daze at Bellamy Farm to go.

Quinn turned. "Can you check on Hazel to make sure she's okay?"

"Of course." I watched the coroner, Quinn, and Officer Barker make their way to the scarecrow before I turned in the direction of the house. I cringed at the thought of telling my father what had happened.

The farm was eerily quiet as dusk approached. There was something about evenings in October that felt different from an evening during any other month of the year. It was the mixture of magic and spook settling in with the evening fog and mist.

I was preoccupied with that feeling when I walked by the barn, hoping Hazel was still inside and didn't know anything about Minnie's death. I was almost to the spot where Jessa, Officer Fenke, and a handful of volunteers stood when someone grabbed me by the arm, yanked me behind the barn, and slapped a hand over my mouth.

Chapter Five

I grabbed the familiar hand and tore it away from my mouth. "For crying out loud, Kristy, you almost made me wet my pants."

"If you had ever had a kid, you would have. Trust me, after childbirth your bladder is never the same."

I grimaced and brushed her hand off my arm. "What are you doing here? I thought you went home with Kent and the girls."

She looked around with the frantic expression of a criminal on the run. "I did, but I came back and learned someone killed Minnie Devani. Is that true?" Her voice jumped an octave.

"Yes, it's true." I grimaced. "I saw the body."

"Oh Lord, Shi, are you okay?"

I nodded, but in my head, I was thinking that Kristy might be the one who was "not okay" and that scared me.

In the fading light, all the color drained from her face. "I can't believe she's dead. She just yelled at me. She was fine. Yelling is normal for Minnie. This is terrible."

"Kristy, are you all right?"

She wrapped her arms around herself. "I think so. Yes,

yes, I'm fine. Why wouldn't I be? I'm not the one who's dead."

I bit the inside of my lip. "What are you doing back here? Why'd you come back?"

"I came back for my scarf. When I got home I realized I wasn't wearing it. You know how important that scarf is to me. It was handwoven by my late tia. I have to find it. Have you seen it?"

I suspected this time my face was the one that went pale, but now it was too dark for Kristy to see it. "I saw it."

"Well, where is it? I want to grab it and go home to Kent and the girls. I just want to comfort myself by looking at those sweet, sleeping baby faces."

"It was with Minnie." My voice was low.

"What do you mean it was with Minnie?" she snapped.

I didn't take offense at her tone. "It was around her neck. Minnie was strangled to death. Your scarf was the murder weapon."

"What?" she cried. I could still hear her shouting as she turned and disappeared around the side of the building. "Who did it? Who killed Minnie Devani with my scarf? How dare they! I want to know right now."

I hurried after her to find Jessa, Chesney, Whit, Hazel, and the animals staring at her. I was relieved to see Hazel since I hadn't had a chance to check the barn before Kristy accosted me.

Chesney wrapped her arm protectively around her younger sister's shoulders. Whit nervously tugged on her uniquely dyed hair. I wanted to comfort the young woman.

I had seen the body. It was a gruesome sight, but I felt I was much more prepared to take it in than she had been. I knew the image would be with her forever.

"How dare someone use my tia's scarf to kill someone?" Kristy cried.

I stepped in front of Kristy. "You will have to excuse Kristy. I just told her the news, and she is…ummm…upset."

"I'm more than upset. I'm furious. Also, who would kill another person at all? Sure, Minnie was difficult, but she didn't deserve to die. Is there no decency left in this world?"

I placed a hand on her arm. "Kristy," I said under my breath. "You should probably take a breath."

She spun around and faced me. "A breath? Someone stole my scarf, Shi, and killed a woman with it!"

"I'd love to hear about your scarf, Kristy," Chief Randy said as he joined the small group.

I stared at him. How did he get here so fast? I thought he was by the scarecrow with the coroner. That's where he was supposed to be.

Hazel stared wide-eyed at Kristy and her grandfather. Jessa wrapped her arm around Hazel's shoulder. "Chesney, why don't you, Whit, and Hazel come help me clean up the food station for the night?" She guided Hazel away from the chief, and Esmeralda and Huckleberry followed them.

Chesney opened and closed her mouth as if she wanted to protest, but then nodded and trailed behind the three of them and the animals.

"Can you tell me how your scarf got around Minnie

Devani's neck?" the chief asked in a tone that feigned disinterest.

"I don't like the tone you're taking, Chief," Kristy said and shook her finger at him. "I have no idea, and I have no idea who would want to kill her, either, before you ask."

I wanted to grab her hand and push it down. This was no way to speak to a police officer when you're a murder suspect. I knew this from personal experience.

Chief Randy hooked his thumbs through the loops in his utility belt. "There is always a motive for murder. In my experience the motives aren't as difficult to find as the people willing to act on a motive. A name or two comes to mind that would have a motive to kill Minnie. Poor woman."

"And what names are those?" I asked, challenging him.

He glanced at Kristy as if that was answer enough. Maybe it was. Then the police chief rocked back on his heels. "I'm just here to serve and protect the community. I don't abide by killers in my town, even if they're locals. It's bad for tourism."

I grimaced. Chief Randy might play the part of a bumbling small-town cop, but I knew he would do whatever it took to restore peace and quiet. His goal was always to keep Cherry Glen the picturesque western Michigan tourist town it had become after decades of rusting away in obscurity. Now it had emerged in the new millennium as a quaint, rural destination for the arts and farm-to-table cooking. I knew the town would not want to go back to its poorer roots.

Jessa came back. I guessed that she left Hazel, Whit, and Chesney to clean up what was left of the food because she couldn't resist hearing what the chief had to say to Kristy.

"It wasn't me," Kristy said folding her arms. "I know you are not so subtly pointing the finger at me, but I didn't do it."

"No one would think you would hurt a fly, Kristy," Jessa chimed in. "Isn't that right, Randy?"

Chief Randy narrowed his eyes. "I don't know what to think about all this. A prominent citizen in town is dead. Jessa and Shiloh, would you mind giving us a minute? I need to speak to Kristy alone."

Jessa made a face. I knew she didn't like the idea of missing out on their conversation, but she would hear it all in great detail soon enough. It seemed that every bit of news in Cherry Glen went through Jessa's Place first, to the point that sometimes the people it was happening to found out about it at the diner.

Kristy grabbed my arm before I could leave. "Shiloh stays."

Chief Randy frowned but instead of arguing said, "Kristy, we are all tired and want to call it a night. Let's have a candid conversation and be done with it."

My friend folded her arms. "I thought we *were* having a candid conversation. I'm telling you I had nothing to do with whatever may have happened to Minnie and know nothing about it."

The chief reached into his coat and pulled out a clear plastic bag. Inside the bag was Kristy's scarf. "This is yours." It wasn't a question.

Kristy reached for it as if she planned to snatch it away from him. "That's my scarf. I've had it forever. I would appreciate it if you returned it to me."

He tucked it back inside of his coat. "I can't do that. It's critical evidence in the investigation now."

Kristy paled in the glow of the twinkle lights that Hazel and I had hung around the barn door for the festival.

"Now, tell me about the last time you saw Minnie Devani," the chief said.

"I saw her three or so hours ago. We had a conversation and said that we'd discuss the topic later in private. That was it."

"I heard it was closer to a fight than a conversation. Rumors were already spreading through Cherry Glen about your *conversation* with Minnie before I arrived."

Kristy put her hands on her hips. "We had a disagreement, but it wasn't a fight."

"And what was the disagreement about?" he asked.

"I'd rather not say."

The police chief scowled at this answer, and I thought that he would press for Kristy to tell him exactly what she and Minnie had been arguing about. Instead, he surprised me by asking, "What happened after your argument?"

"I stayed for an hour or so," Kristy said. "Took pictures of my daughters with the scarecrow and in the pumpkin patch. We went on a hayride, drank apple cider, and went home. It was a very typical fall afternoon."

"You went home." He arched his brow. "Then what are you doing back here?"

Kristy frowned. "I realized I must have dropped my scarf at some point because I couldn't find it when I got home, so I came back to find it. It's very important to me."

"If it's so precious to you, it seems odd to me that you didn't notice it was missing earlier."

"Have you ever been a mother of newborn twins? I'm lucky if I put my shirt on the right way in the morning. My brain is full every waking and sleeping moment with how to keep them safe and happy. It's no wonder I didn't notice that the scarf fell off."

Chief Randy tapped a finger on his cheek as if he were deep in thought.

"Chief," Officer Fenke said as he and Quinn approached us. "The coroner is all loaded up and ready to leave. He wanted to speak with you."

Chief Randy nodded. "Kristy, don't get any ideas in your head about leaving Cherry Glen anytime soon, okay? I don't even want you going to Traverse City. You hear me?"

Kristy looked like she wanted to punch him, but I was relieved when she had the good sense not to respond.

The chief pointed at me. "That scarecrow is an active crime scene. I don't want you or your dog going over there and sniffing about."

"What about Fall Daze?" I asked. "I have another day of the festival tomorrow."

He scowled. "We will tape the crime scene off, but I'm going to count on you to keep everyone away from it. If I hear about anyone messing with it, I'm holding you responsible."

I swallowed.

He looked at me to Kristy and back again. "You girls do what I say and everything will be just fine."

Kristy and I watched Chief Randy and Officer Fenke walk away. Quinn stayed behind with us.

Kristy folded her arms. "*You girls?* Quinn, I know he's your father, but could he be more condescending?"

Quinn grimaced.

"The coroner doesn't need you anymore?" I asked Quinn.

He shook his head. "I don't think he ever needed me. He prefers to do everything himself and found me more of a nuisance than a help."

"I'm in trouble." Kristy's shoulders slumped forward. The fire went out of her eyes. "So much trouble."

I didn't think there was any reason to sugarcoat it. It wouldn't do her any good if I did. "You are, Kristy. You're in a lot of trouble." Unfortunately, I knew what it was like to be a murder suspect. When I first moved back to Michigan, I had been tangled up in the murder of a local developer. He and I had a contract that would potentially save Bellamy Farm, so I had been a prime suspect when he turned up dead. Thankfully, my name was eventually cleared and his heir let me out of the contract. Now saving the farm was up to me.

Quinn ran his hand through his hair. "You were with Kent most of the night, though, right? You just came back here a few minutes ago to look for your scarf. If you had an alibi, there's nothing to worry about."

Kristy made a face.

"Please tell me you were with Kent," I said.

"When we left your farm, I went home with Kent and the girls, yes, but after I fed the babies I went to the farmers market."

"Why?" I asked. My question came out close to a whine.

She threw up her hands. "I was just so upset over my argument with Minnie. I wanted to go back to the office and make sure my numbers added up. I worked there for an hour, maybe an hour and a half, and then realized that my scarf was missing. I came here to look for it."

"You said you realized your scarf was missing after you got home," I said.

She frowned at me. "It was *technically* after I had been home that I noticed the missing scarf."

I rubbed my forehead.

"Was anyone else at the market with you? Did anyone see you at the market?" Quinn asked.

"No," she said. "It's a Friday evening in a small town, and there is a high school football game about to start. Not to mention, there are dozens of fall activities happening. No one was around."

That brick returned to the pit of my stomach. This time it brought friends.

"Dad," Hazel called and came toward us. "Jessa had to leave. When are we going home?" She cradled Esmeralda in her arms. It was a wonder. The cat never tired of Hazel carrying her around. If I had tried that, she'd scratch my arm off.

Quinn looked to his daughter and then back at Kristy and me as if he was unsure what to do.

"Go home, Quinn; there's no more you can do here," Kristy said.

"I hate to leave the two of you in this mess, but I do have to get Hazel home."

"We understand," I said. "And honestly, I don't know if there is anything more any of us can do tonight."

He nodded. "Don't worry, Kristy, my dad will find out who did this, and we can put this all behind us soon enough. It will be like it never happened."

What about Minnie? I wondered. She couldn't put this behind her. Minnie couldn't put it behind her, because she was dead.

Chapter Six

After Quinn and Hazel left, the police and the coroner left too. Chief Randy didn't give any more ominous warnings to Kristy before he climbed back onto his motorcycle and rode away. He didn't have to—he'd made his opinion clear about her part in the murder already.

Kristy shivered.

"You're cold," I said. "Why don't you come into the farmhouse? I can make a pot of tea, and we can talk this through. It's what Grandma Bellamy always did when there was a problem."

"This is a bigger problem than hot tea can fix, Shi," she said, her voice barely over a whisper.

"Or we can go to my cabin, if you're afraid of my dad overhearing. He's probably asleep in any case. He falls asleep in his collection room all the time. He tells me he's just resting his eyes."

Kristy shook her head. "No, Shi, I just want to go home to Kent and my girls. Just thinking of them, of leaving them, terrifies me." She grabbed my hand and squeezed it so tightly that my knuckles cracked. "Shi, you have to help me. I can't go to prison. I'm a mom now. Kent is a wonderful father, but he can't raise the twins alone. They need me!"

"Whoa, that's not going to happen. You're not going anywhere." I gently removed my hand from her viselike grasp. "Kent and the girls will be fine. You have no reason to worry about them because nothing is going to happen to you."

"How can you say that? Shiloh, you're not a mother. You can't know the constant state of fear that grips me. Everything I do is going to affect those two girls. If I go to prison, they're sure to end up with all sorts of emotional problems. I've seen the talk shows about it!"

I bit the inside of my lip. I knew Kristy was upset, so I told myself not to take the comment about me not being a mother to heart. I never had the goal of being a parent, but I was getting to an age that it was more and more on my mind, as it was becoming apparent to me at thirty-eight years old being a mother was close to a now-or-never possibility.

"Tell the chief what you know, and everything will be fine. You were surprised when he questioned you tonight. The next time you talk to him, be calm and concise. The more emotion you show him, the more he will ask. He is a good cop. He knows how to push buttons."

"How can you say he's a good cop? Chief Randy is out of his depth when it comes to murder. He was all set on arresting you and your father when the last dead body showed up in Cherry Glen. You were the one who found that killer. I don't trust him. He just wants this investigation to go away so he can go back to watching golf all afternoon."

"I didn't know Chief Randy watched golf."

She waved her hand at me. "That's not the point. The point is he wants to find the simplest answer to this mess to make it go away. It doesn't take a genius to know the simplest answer is me."

I nodded. "That may be true, but he won't arrest you. You're innocent. He wouldn't want to put an innocent person in jail."

She looked at me as if she couldn't believe that I would be that naïve.

"Kristy, trust me. Everything will be okay. If Chief Randy doesn't want to look elsewhere for a murder suspect, I will. I'm not going to let you go to prison. I promise you that."

Tears sprang to her eyes. "Thank you, Shi. You coming back to Cherry Glen was the best thing I could imagine. I mean, even though I've been framed for murder on your farm, I'm still glad you came home."

"Thanks, I think."

The next morning, I thought it was all a dream. In my secluded cabin tucked far away from the road and out of the view of the farmhouse and barn, it was easy to believe that nothing out of the ordinary had happened on this beautiful land. I felt protected under my down comforter, cozy and hidden from everyone and everything. Nothing bad could touch me.

Sadly, that wasn't true. It wasn't a dream, and slowly, I remembered the events of the day before: Fall Daze, Kristy's argument with Minnie, and the murder.

I groaned and flopped over onto my stomach. A soft hiss

of protest came from Esmeralda, who was curled up in a ball at my feet. The fluffy Siamese didn't like to be jostled about when she was trying to get her beauty rest. She was a beauty by any measure and that took at least sixteen hours of sleep a day.

Even so, I couldn't remain still. My brain reeled from the events of the day before, and I wondered what I should do about Fall Daze that afternoon. Should I cancel out of respect to Minnie?

I rolled over again. It didn't matter how I moved, I couldn't find a comfortable position. My body ached from long hours working on the farm to prepare for Fall Daze, and then I had been up very late baking for Fall Daze that afternoon. I didn't exactly remember what time I stumbled from the farmhouse to the cabin, but I'd had to carry Huckleberry because the pug had been fast asleep. At least the chief was letting Fall Daze go on. I couldn't cancel. I had spent too much time and money to pull out now.

Esmeralda stood up on the bed and hissed at me for all she was worth. She was over my restlessness.

I sighed. "I know, I know. I just have a lot on my mind."

She hissed again as if to say, "Tell it to a cat who cares."

It was still dark outside when my phone beeped with a text message. I scooted across the bed to grab it off the nightstand. In my previous life as a Hollywood producer, I would receive calls and texts at all hours of the day and night. Not so much in Cherry Glen, so I was on high alert.

I squinted at the screen and found a text from Kristy. "Meet at the farmers market at seven. We need to talk."

I bit my lip and texted her back that I would be there. The time on the phone read five a.m. I had plenty of time to get ready and to worry about what she wanted to tell me so badly. I would be kidding myself if I didn't believe it was about the murder.

On the floor, Huckleberry whined. I couldn't see him, but he was at the foot of the double bed. "Come up here, Huck. We have to feed the chickens, check on the farm, and get to town all in two hours."

He made a huffing sound as he tried to jump onto the bed. The bed shook as he bounced off the side of it and flopped back onto the floor.

I sat up and peered down at the pug. "You okay, buddy?"

He looked up at me with his round brown eyes as if pleading for me to pick him up.

"Use your steps. That's what they are there for."

He gave me the saddest expression in the world, which was saying a lot, as pugs were pros at looking downtrodden.

"The steps."

He sighed as if I were killing him. I knew he just wanted me to lift him onto the bed, but if I did that, he would never use his steps. He waddled over to my makeshift pet steps at the end of the bed.

Huckleberry was a stocky dog and not the best jumper in the world, so I had pushed my grandmother's cedar chest to the end of the bed, and then I added a large pillow in front of that. The pug hopped from the pillow to the cedar chest to the bed.

Esmeralda stretched. All the commotion had finally

gotten to her. She sailed over the cedar chest and pillow and pranced out of the room with her tail high.

Huckleberry watched her go with his sad pug face.

"She's a diva," I said. "Just let her be."

The dog waddled across the bed to reach me. He licked one side of my face and then the other.

"Oh! You slobbered me!" But I hugged the pug all the same. He knew I needed to be spurred into action. The temptation to hide under the covers and pretend yesterday never happened was strong.

Huckleberry licked me again.

"Okay, okay," I said and grabbed a tissue from the box on my nightstand. "No more licking! I get the point." I threw back the comforter and swung my feet to the floor. The wood floor was icy cold, and my toes recoiled. It wasn't the first time I was reminded to pick up a rug the next time I went into Traverse City to shop. I supposed I could buy one online, but I wanted a rug that would go with the unique character of the cabin, and in person was the best way to make that determination.

I was still very much in the process of making the cabin my own, but at the same time, I didn't want to erase my grandmother's memory completely from it.

When I'd moved back to Michigan, the cabin had been unoccupied for over sixteen years. When my grandmother died, my father had closed and locked the door. He never went inside the cabin again. I was studying filmmaking in college at the time, on the verge of pursuing a career that would lead me far away from the life I'd known on Bellamy Farm.

When I returned, I found Grandma Bellamy's cabin exactly as it had been when she was alive. It was as if she had just stepped out for an afternoon. Her morning teacup still sat in the kitchen sink. The only indication that any time had passed were the layers of dust on every surface and the terrifyingly large cobwebs in every corner.

Even more surprising than the fact that my father locked the door and never looked back was the discovery of a note from Grandma Bellamy to me tucked into the corner of her bedroom mirror. It was a blessing over my life and a charge to take care of the farm. How she knew I would be the one who would want to save the farm, I would never know. I had never hoped to be a farmer when I was young. Also, the letter included a safety net. She claimed there was a treasure hidden somewhere on the farm. I had to only look in the "heart of the farm" to find it.

Over the last few months living on the farm and transforming the cabin into my home, I'd wondered what she meant when she'd said "treasure." Was it literal? Had my grandmother really hidden treasure, money even, somewhere on the farm? And if she did, where was the heart of the farm? What was it? Or was it a riddle for some sort of lesson I was to learn? Grandma Bellamy was the wisest woman I had ever known and would probably ever know, but she wasn't one to come right out and say what a person needed to hear. She liked to point people in the right direction and then let them figure it out in their own time. It was frustrating that she kept up with this habit even beyond the grave.

I can't say I always lived up to her standard of finding

the right answer to one of her riddles, so it didn't bode well for me to find the "heart of the farm" or the mysterious and maybe not real treasure. That didn't change the fact that a windfall of cash at the moment would be a godsend. I had been able to scrape enough money together to get Fall Daze off the ground, but we were barely covering our monthly expenses at this point. I wondered if I would have to get another job to support the farm until it was viable—though I couldn't see many job openings in Cherry Glen, Michigan, for a former television and film producer.

I left my grandmother's letter tucked in the mirror over her dresser. Even though I had cleaned out the small cabin and replaced much of the décor with my own things, there were items I'd kept, including my grandmother's white and gold bedroom furniture. I remembered pulling trinkets and bobbles out of the many drawers and cubbies in the old dresser and chest of drawers my grandfather had made for her. I never met my grandfather. He died before I was born, but I felt like I was connected to both him and Grandma Bellamy when I used the dresser. It was nothing like the sleek and streamlined furniture that I had back in LA, and I was fine with that. My life there didn't fit in Cherry Glen and certainly not in my grandmother's cabin.

Huckleberry followed me into the kitchen, which looked the most like it had when I was a child. I had decided to keep her vintage appliances. I remembered when my grandmother found the old-fashioned blue appliances at a salvage yard when I was a child. She had been beside herself with excitement and said she had to have them. The cost of the appliances was little more than the cost to have them delivered to the farm, but to get them back in working order was a pretty penny. Despite my father's grumbling about the cost of repairs, she'd been determined.

She'd told my father: "Just because something is old and forgotten doesn't mean it's lost its value. I'm giving them a new life and you can't stop me, Sullivan Matthew Bellamy."

Dad had no chance of winning an argument when his mother broke out his full name. And no one could talk Grandma Bellamy out of a plan once she set it in motion. She had a local repair shop fix and repaint the appliances to their original color. Even if I had the money, which I didn't, I wouldn't have the heart to replace a single appliance. Plus, a sleek stainless steel set of appliances would be out of place and far too big in the rustic cabin.

I made coffee and added almond milk to it. I stuck to my old LA eating habits as much as possible to stay in shape. It wasn't much a challenge when I was in my cabin. But when I went to Jessa's Place and she slid a piece of warm cherry pie in front of me, it was near impossible.

I sipped my coffee with the cat and dog looking on. Both Esmeralda and Huckleberry stood at my feet and looked at me with expressions that were a mixture of pleading and judgment.

"Sorry guys." I fed the animals and got ready for the day. I still had almost an hour before I had to leave for the market to meet Kristy. That should give me just enough time to feed the chickens and check out the crime scene. You know, standard farm chores.

The animals and I went out the door. There was a tiny garden in front of the cabin. It was long overgrown, and it was on my project list to pull out the weeds and see if any of my grandmother's perennials could be saved. When I was a child, it had been teeming with black-eyed Susans, Shasta daisies, hostas, and lemon balm. As of yet, all I saw evidence of was the lemon balm. Only a nuclear blast could take that plant out, and even then, it was no guarantee. To the back of the cabin was a narrow stretch of woods. Beyond the woods was the beginning of the other half of what was Bellamy Farm until my cousin Stacey sold it. For the last few months, there had been no news or developments coming from the other side of the woods. I knew it was only a matter of time before the development company turned it into something profitable or unloaded it.

To my left was an overgrown dirt road that led to the farmhouse and the cherry orchard near the front of the farm. Relentless weeds sprung up along its length, and there were decades' old ruts from the wagons and tractors that had traveled it.

When I first came home, the road had been nothing more than tall grass and weeds, but I cut those down with a brush mower, making it much easier for me and Huckleberry to walk back and forth between the cabin and farmhouse. Someday, I would have gravel put down, but that day would be a long time coming.

Esmeralda and Huckleberry ran ahead along the road and in the direction of the farmhouse. They were creatures of habit. Typically, I started each day checking on my father.

By this time, he would be on his second cup of coffee and pouring over one of his artifacts in his historical collection. My father collected all things related to Michigan history. He was fanatical about it. He scoured the antique shops in the area and searched on the Internet. He had spent a fortune on his collection. My guess was it wasn't worth nearly as much as he put into it. Sometimes when I saw the withered cherry orchard or the loose boards on the barn, I grew angry he had spent so much money on a collection that was rarely seen. However, I had to remind myself I had known about the collection before coming back to Michigan and agreeing to work to save the farm. Talking to my father about selling some of his artifacts to help out was a nonstarter. It always had been and always would be.

I would check in with him before leaving for the farmers market, but there was something I needed to do first. "Huckleberry! Esmeralda!" I called.

The pug pulled up short and looked over his shoulder. As expected, Esmeralda continued on to the house.

I turned and headed to the pasture where Minnie had been found. It wasn't only criminals who went back to the scene of the crime.

The quickest path between my cabin and the pasture was through the narrow stretch of woods behind the cabin. The sun was just coming up, and beneath the trees the light remained dim. However, I knew where I was going. Even though I had been gone fifteen years, there wasn't one inch of Bellamy Farm I didn't know as well as I knew my own name, including those woods. I had spent countless hours playing there as a child while my father did chores or tended his collection and Grandma Bellamy oversaw the farmwork.

As I came out of the trees, the scarecrow appeared. His head drooped to one side as if he didn't have the strength to keep it upright any longer. Crime scene tape crisscrossed in a circle around the scarecrow, beginning six feet from the base.

Crime scene tape on my farm. Chief Randy explicitly said that everyone needed to stay away from the crime scene, myself included, but I had to see it again to prove to myself the events of the day before were real.

I bit my lip. Was it my fault that Minnie was dead? If I had not held the festival would she still be alive?

I shook the dark thoughts from my mind. I couldn't take any part of the blame for the murder. As my friend Briar, a high-powered attorney back in LA, used to say. "If a person chooses to do wrong, they will find a way."

The killer saw an opportunity and took it. It was just extra unfortunate that opportunity was on my farm.

As I stood staring at the crime scene tape, Huckleberry and Esmeralda joined me. Esmeralda meowed as if to remind me I had gone off course.

I looked down at the Siamese. "I know. Just give me a second."

I stared at the scarecrow. The crow was back—the one who had been sitting on the scarecrow when Quinn and I first saw the body. I suppose I couldn't know for sure that it was the same crow, but something told me it was.

Huckleberry saw the large bird too and started barking.

The crow simply flapped its wings and settled more comfortably on the scarecrow's shoulder.

"Huckleberry! Huckleberry!" I said to him. "Hush!"

It was no use, the dog just kept barking.

"Can you quiet that dog?"

I spun around and saw a woman holding a gun on me.

I screamed.

Chapter Seven

❧

S he leveled the gun at me. "Calm down. What are you doing here?" the blond woman holding me at gunpoint asked. She was in her thirties, perhaps a year or two younger than I was. She was built like an elite runner. I could see all the muscles in her hands as she held the gun.

"What do you mean what am I doing here? What are you doing here, and with a gun?"

"That's none of your concern," she said in a deadly even voice.

"Like hell it's none of my concern. You're on my property. This is my farm, and you're pointing a gun at me and my dog and cat!"

By this point, Huckleberry had stopped barking. He knew when I meant business.

She frowned at me. "What's your name?"

"Shiloh Bellamy."

"Do you have ID to prove that?"

"Not on me." I folded my arms. "Excuse me if I don't carry ID around on my own land."

She lowered the gun and put it back in the holster under her jacket, but she didn't adjust her stance. I didn't have any doubt she would reach for the gun again if she was pushed too far. She removed a notepad and pencil from the back pocket of her black jeans.

I breathed a little easier, but just a little.

"It says here that the owner of this property is Sullivan Bellamy." She looked up at me with piercing hazel eyes. It was as if she was daring me to lie to her.

"Sullivan is my father. The farm should be in my name by now, but the transfer was recent."

"Is your father dead? Is that the reason for the change?" she asked.

I bristled. "He's not. He still lives here. However, he's elderly and unwell. It seemed prudent to transfer the farm to my name while he could still make that choice on his own." I added, "I have taken over the financial responsibility of the farm and have been doing that for a long while." I bit my lower lip to stop myself from saying anything more. My father's condition and the financial circumstances of the farm were none of her business.

She nodded at this. It seemed I finally had been able to give her the right answer.

I uncrossed my arms. "Now, I'm going to ask you a few questions. And I expect you to answer them too. Since you are on my farm without permission, I believe you are obligated to tell me who you are."

She shook her head. "No, I'm not."

I scowled and was just about to threaten to call the police when she added, "I'm a federal marshal. I'm here to investigate the death of someone I was investigating for another crime."

I blinked at her. Overhead, the crow flapped its wings again. I wasn't one much for signs, but a giant black bird looming over me while a federal agent questioned me had to be bad news.

"You mean Minnie?" I asked.

She looked down at her notebook. "I suppose I do mean Minnie, although it was an alias. One of several, as far as I can gather."

I opened and closed my mouth like a giant pike in the middle of Lake Michigan. I couldn't be more surprised by this news. Minnie had an alias? Scratch that, Minnie Devani had more than one alias? What alternative universe had I woken up in this morning?

"What's your name?" I asked again.

"I'm Lynn Chuff. I work for the U.S. Marshals Service." She reached into her coat pocket and flashed a badge. I couldn't read the badge, but from what I saw it looked official.

"If Minnie was an alias, what was her real name?" I asked.

She frowned. "I can't tell you that. What can you tell me about the murder?"

"I'm not sure that you should be asking me about it. Shouldn't you give a professional courtesy to Randy Killian? He's the chief of police in Cherry Glen."

She studied me. "What do you know about professional courtesy? Are you a cop too? Or are you married to one?"

I didn't answer, but I had picked up most of my crime lingo as a producer. Many of my projects were true crime, and I'd learned a lot of the language that law enforcement used. At least, I knew enough to *sound* like I knew what I was talking about. However, I didn't say any of that. I doubted my time in film and television would impress Marshal Lynn Chuff. I doubted there was much of anything I could say that would impress her.

"Don't you need a warrant or permission to be walking around private property on a case?" I asked.

She pressed her lips together. "I stopped at the big farm-house at the end of the driveway and knocked on the door. No one answered, and with the house in such disrepair, it seemed deserted to me. I assumed that meant I wouldn't have any interference."

I frowned, knowing that one of two things happened. The first being that she might not have knocked hard enough for my elderly father to hear her, and the second being that Dad did hear her and pretended not to be home. Considering how antisocial my father could be, I was betting on the latter. I bet Marshal Chuff had a very loud and firm knock.

She walked around the crime scene and took photos with her cell phone. All the time the crow never moved. I didn't know if it was stranger that the crow hung around the whole time or that Marshal Chuff never commented on it. After she took the photos she wanted, she made a note on her small notepad, tucked it and the pencil back into her pocket, and turned around and walked back across the pasture.

I followed her. It wasn't until I reached the pasture that I saw her giant black SUV parked in front of the barn. I hurried to catch up with her. "If you don't have a warrant or verbal permission, you have no right to be snooping around on our land."

She scowled. "And you have no right to cross police tape even if it is on your land. This is a crime scene."

"I didn't cross it."

"You were planning to." She looked around. "Looks to me like you should focus more on your farm and less on this crime." She wrinkled her nose and took in her surroundings. "You have a lot of work cut out for you."

I bit my lip to hold back a snide remark or to tell her the hundreds of hours of work I had already done on the farm since only recently returning home. If she thought this was bad, she should have seen it before.

As we drew close to the barn, the chickens came out of their coop in a cloud of feathers and angry clucks. I hadn't fed them yet, and they were not amused with the delay. Huckleberry shuffled over to them to provide some comfort. When we first arrived on the farm, he had been afraid of the chickens, but he'd bonded with them over time. The ten chickens lived in a fine-looking coop that I had built myself. In all honesty, it was the best kept building on the property.

Marshal Chuff walked over to the giant SUV. "I need to get back into town and find the chief, as you so kindly suggested."

"Will you be coming back here?" I asked.

She studied me. "Maybe. I have spent the last three years searching for the woman you call Minnie. Now someone killed her before I could arrest her and hold her accountable for her crimes. I will find out who that is." The muscles in her face tensed like she was clenching her jaw too tightly. I hoped her teeth were in good enough shape to withstand the pressure.

"What are her crimes?" I asked. "Who is she? What did she do?"

She smiled. "You're not in law enforcement, farmer. There is not a single thing that I have to tell you." This time she said "farmer" as if it were a sort of curse.

I glared at her. "The next time you come on my land, you had better have a warrant. I know my rights."

She laughed before she climbed into her SUV, backed up on the lawn, and drove down the long driveway to the county road that led into Cherry Glen.

It seemed like in the last twenty minutes everything I had known about Minnie got turned upside down. Who was she really? I watched the dust the SUV kicked up settle back on the gravel driveway.

It seemed to me that this murder just got a whole lot more interesting.

Chapter Eight

I didn't have much time before I had to leave for the farmers market to meet Kristy, but I had to find out what my father knew about Marshal Chuff. I went inside the old farmhouse with Esmeralda and Huckleberry on my heels. "Dad?"

A grunt came from the direction of the giant walk-in pantry in the kitchen, which had been the original kitchen, back at a time when they did some of the cooking inside and some of the cooking outside. Long before I was born, my father had converted the pantry into his "Michigan History" room. I wasn't sure there was anyone else on the planet who cared as much about Michigan history as my father, not even the college professors who taught it.

When I stepped into the kitchen, I found the pantry door open, a sure sign my father was inside poring over his artifacts. When he wasn't inside of the pantry, the entire collection was locked up tight. Dad used to keep the keys for the pantry on a hook on one of the inside kitchen cupboards, but earlier in the year, someone used that key to steal from his collection. He had since moved the key, and he wouldn't even tell me where it was hidden. I teased him that he had better tell me before he died, to which he said he planned to be buried with his collection.

My morbid thoughts brought me back to Minnie, or whatever her real name might be. I was beginning to doubt Marshal Chuff's story. Could it really be true? Could Minnie really be living in Cherry Glen under an alias? Minnie had told me once that she'd lived here for over ten years. That was a long time to be in hiding, which also made me wonder how Marshal Chuff found her now, right near the time of her death. What had changed to blow Minnie's cover?

But before I got to all that, I asked my standard question. "Did you have breakfast?"

"Yes, I had toast and coffee. Don't you mother me, Shiloh Lee. Your grandmother didn't even mother me, and she *was* my mother."

I knew that to be true. My grandmother had been a loving and caring woman, but tough love had been her method of affection. It had toughened me up enough for the production lots of LA.

"Did you hear a knock on the door earlier this morning?" I asked.

"Sure did." He sipped from a white coffee mug and placed it back on his worktable.

"But you didn't answer the door?"

He scowled at me. "I heard a knock on the door, but I didn't answer it. You never knock, and there is no one I want to talk to. I know Stacey is at play rehearsal, and she wouldn't have knocked either. The only other people I might have wanted to see would be Hazel and Quinn. Quinn is working one of his long shifts at the firehouse now, which means Hazel is over at her grandmother's this morning. Since Doreen Killian can't stand you, I knew it wasn't Hazel. So all that said, it stands to reason that the person at the door was a stranger selling magazines or vacuum cleaners and someone I didn't want to talk to."

"I don't think people go door to door selling magazines or vacuum cleaners anymore. In fact, I don't even know if Girl Scouts go door to door to sell cookies. If they did, they certainly wouldn't have been way out here so early in the morning."

"Maybe not in California, but we still get knocks from vacuum cleaner salesmen from time to time here." He harrumphed.

I wanted to ask my father when the last time was that a vacuum cleaner salesman knocked on the door but realized it wasn't worth the argument.

"Who was it?" he asked. "I'm guessing you tracked the knocker down and asked them a thousand questions. You even got a photo of them, didn't you? Was it the police asking more questions about the murder? That's another reason I didn't answer the door. I don't have anything to say about that, and I certainly have nothing to say to Randy Killian."

I frowned at him. "Not exactly." I told him about being in the pasture and meeting Marshal Chuff and her drawn gun.

"What's a federal agent doing on my farm? Was it the IRS? Those bloodsuckers are always after my money." He shook his fist.

I didn't say it, but there wasn't much money to be found

on Bellamy Farm for the IRS or anyone else to go after. My father had taken out two mortgages to make ends meet, and I had taken a small personal loan just to have cash to feed us and pay for seeds. My goal by the end of this year was to pay back the personal loan and start chipping away at the mortgages, but we weren't exactly liquid with money. If I could find my grandmother's treasure, if such a thing even existed, that would be a great help. If it was worth a few hundred thousand dollars, that would help even more. But I wasn't holding my breath that my grandmother's riddle referred to real money. It was too much to hope for.

"She wasn't from the IRS. She claimed to be investigating Minnie Devani. Minnie committed some sort of crime in the past and has been on the run for over a decade. She lived in Cherry Glen under a false name. Or at least that's what Marshal Chuff said."

Dad stared at me as if I had just said the president of the United States was going to parachute into his living room. I didn't blame him. The idea of Minnie living under an assumed identity sounded even more ridiculous when I said it than when I had heard it from Chuff.

Dad adjusted his glasses with a wrinkled hand. "Well, that's a new one. Minnie Devani was a bunch of things, and not a lot of them were good, but I wouldn't have thought she was a criminal. I mean, perhaps she stole from the convenience store. I could see her making off with a toothbrush or something like that. Minnie was the sort that would think society owed her that toothbrush, but to be an actual criminal that a U.S. Marshal wanted to hunt down?" He whistled.

"That's a new one. This is quite an interesting turn of events, and this is helpful to Kristy too."

"Because there are other suspects for the murder."

He snapped his fingers at me. "Bingo."

"I thought the same thing," I said. "If you are okay here, I need to go talk to Kristy about just that."

He grunted and went back to polishing a brass teapot.

I hoped to be back soon. I had some last minute baking to do before the second and final day of Fall Daze that afternoon. Remembering that reminded me to go to the store for supplies. I had been up late the night before baking, leaving me with five dozen cookies, four pies, and countless muffins in the farmhouse kitchen on cooling racks. I quickly packed them up in bakery bags and boxes. Even with all of these baked goods, I would still have to pick up gallons of hot apple cider. I made a list of everything I needed as quickly as possible.

Before I left, I showed my dad what he would need for the day, including the lunch I'd made him the night before. Maybe he was right and I was babying him, but when I came back to Michigan, he was in such a hard spot and had been nothing more than skin and bones. My goal was to improve his health as much as possible, whether he liked it or not.

With my list in hand, I drove the twenty minutes to town in my red convertible with the top down. Huckleberry rode shotgun and the cold wind ruffled his ears and puggish wrinkles. He braced his front paws on the dashboard and stared into the windshield. He seemed to be as eager as I was to get to the market and speak to Kristy.

I let the wind fly through my long blond hair, even though I knew it would be terribly tangled by the time I reached the market. There weren't that many more days that I could drive with the convertible's top down. In truth, it was a little too cold for it today, I realized, as the chilly air bit at my skin.

The speed limit dropped to twenty-five miles per hour once I hit town. I tapped the brakes, having learned my lesson about speeding through Cherry Glen already. Chief Randy gave me a hefty ticket for speeding when I first returned to Michigan. I couldn't afford another one of those.

The farmers market sat on the west side of the town, but was still within walking distance of Michigan Street, which was the main road in Cherry Glen. The town was so small that when you stood downtown, everything was within walking distance. Cherry Glen was home to farmers and outdoorsmen, and most of the residents lived on the outskirts, like Dad and I did, but recently the small, quaint shopping district had been attracting more people to the Glen, as the locals called it, and there was a housing boom much closer to Michigan Street. There were only about a hundred houses around the town area, but at least ten new ones were under construction. For a town with under a thousand residents, that was noteworthy.

The market was just a giant piece of blacktop that was peppered with booths and white tents. Many of the market booths were put up and torn down for every market day, but there were at least ten that were there year round and had permanent holdings at the Cherry Glen Farmers Market. Minnie had been the owner of one of the permanent booths with her Buzzin' Better Honey. Thinking of the honey booth made me wonder what would become of Minnie's bees now that she was gone.

Aside from the booths, the only other structure on the property was the office trailer where Kristy worked.

Kristy paced back and forth in front of the trailer. When I was a child, the farmers market was a central part of Cherry Glen life, but it had been much smaller and outside the municipal building. In her tenure, Kristy had taken it from being a market you could find in any rural Midwest town to something special.

In fact, it was the market that had led to Cherry Glen's renaissance. The Glen used to be a run-down rural town. Michigan Street had been a mess, and the high school had crumbling walls in some of the classrooms. No one thought much of it. It was the way it always had been.

Today, the downtown was an adorable place to shop and eat, and the reopening of the Michigan Street Theater by my cousin brought entertainment into the mix too.

"Is everything okay with your dad?" Kristy asked as a greeting. "You're usually right on time. Is he not feeling well?"

"I'm sorry I'm a few minutes late. Dad's fine. I got held up because I went to check out the pasture this morning."

Huckleberry waddled behind me, stopping every few seconds to sniff the ground.

She nodded. "Going back to the crime scene? That's not a bad idea. Did you find anything?"

"Sure did. Someone pointing a gun at me."

She blinked. "What?"

I quickly told her an abbreviated version of my morning. She stared at me. "Are you joking, Shiloh Bellamy?"

"I wish I was," I said.

Kristy rubbed her right eye as if she were trying to stave off a twitch. I could relate. I felt like my own eye might start twitching at any second.

"The police can't possibly believe that I would be behind her murder if she was on the run," Kristy said. "I bet she has a whole line of people who wanted to kill her. The money that she stole from the farmers market would be small potatoes compared to that."

It was a chilling thought. "I don't know why the U.S. Marshals are looking for her. She wouldn't tell me what Minnie had done."

She frowned as she considered this.

"Has anyone other than Chief Randy asked you about Minnie?" I asked.

She shook her head. "I was just about to walk over to her honey booth and see if there was anything there that would give me a clue as to why she was killed. I have to do something, Shi. I can't sit back and let Chief Randy railroad me."

"He's not going to do that."

She gave me a look.

I sighed. "I'll come with you." Huckleberry gave me a look but trotted obediently after us as we headed across the parking lot.

It was a couple of hours before the market opened. During the fall harvest, Kristy had decided to add an additional market day to give farmers more time to sell their crops. In September and October, the market was open on Wednesdays and Saturdays all day and Sunday afternoons after the traditional Sunday morning church hours. Even if not everyone in the town attended church, most of them still believed that a person should.

The farmers, crafters, and other vendors were just arriving at their booths and setting up. They angled their squash and pumpkins on their best sides. Sunflowers were attractively displayed in glass vases, and jams and jellies sat in rows in military precision.

The permanent booths cost a pretty penny. I knew, because I had been saving up to get one next season. If I was going to make it as a farmer, I would need to diversify my income stream. I planned to hold events at the farm like Fall Daze, sell my produce wholesale, and hand sell at local stores and markets. It wasn't going to be easy, but I hoped my certification as an organic farm would score me a premium price and a preference with shoppers.

Minnie's booth sat way in the back of the lot, the least expensive location for a permanent booth. It was shaped like a beehive. I shivered when I looked at it. The first time I had stopped by Minnie's booth, I found a dead body. Considering what happened yesterday, I wouldn't be all that surprised if that happened to me again.

We walked around it with Huckleberry trotting behind us. Two cupboard doors were in the back of the booth. They were held in place with a padlock.

I nodded at it. "What do you think she has in there?"

"Well, before all this happened, I would have said signs

for her booth and extra honey. But now, I have no idea at all. It could be anything. Even a den of rattlesnakes."

"Rattlesnakes?" I snorted. "There aren't any rattlesnakes in Michigan."

"So you think. At this point, I'm ready to believe just about anything."

I stopped short of rolling my eyes. I knew that Kristy would not appreciate it. "The only way we can find out what's in there is by opening it up. Do you have the key?"

She shook her head. "What's in the booth is her private property. I don't have a key to it nor would I have asked for one. I have some bolt cutters back at the office. Let me get those, and we can see if I'm right about the rattlesnakes."

I held up my hand. "Let's hold off on the bolt cutters. You don't want to give the police any more reasons to find your behavior suspicious."

"We don't have to tell them it was me who cut through the padlock."

I did roll my eyes at her that time.

"Can I help you?" a deep male voice asked.

Huckleberry hid behind me but not very well. His curly tail was visible to the newcomer.

Kristy and I turned around, and we were both dumbfounded. Before us stood the handsomest man either of us had seen in real life. Or at least that I had seen in real life. And that was saying something, because I had spent most of my adult life in LA, where every person I met was more good-looking than the last.

Kristy opened and closed her mouth, speechless.

Apparently, she was as startled as I was at the handsome man's appearance. He was a few inches above six feet tall, had high cheekbones, and was well-built, judging by the way his clothes fit him. His eyes were amber, and his sandy blond hair was long on the top of his head, while the sides and his face were closely shaved. He could have been an actor or a model. Instead, he wore a burgundy T-shirt that had a pumpkin in the middle of it that read "farmer."

"Can I help you?" he asked again. When we didn't say anything, he went on to say, "This is my booth. Can I ask what you're doing standing around it talking about rattle-snakes and bolt cutters?"

My face flashed red, but for Kristy, his comments were enough to knock her out of her stupor. "Your booth? I don't think so; this booth belonged to Minnie Devani."

"How do you know that?" he asked, wrinkling his brow.

I didn't know how it was possible, but the brow wrinkle made him even more handsome.

Kristy straightened up to her full five-two height. "Because I'm the director of the farmers market."

"Oh!" the man said in a delighted voice. "You must be Kristy Brown! Please forgive me. I went to the office just a little while ago to introduce myself, but I found it empty. I hope nothing I said offended you. I'm so grateful to have one of the coveted booth spots at the farmers market. I know how hard they are to come by, and I know it will be just the thing to get my farm off the ground."

"It is very hard to come by one of these booth spots," Kristy said. "And I'm surprised you claim to have one. I know every vendor in the market and everyone who owns a booth."

"I'm so sorry about the confusion. Minnie said she was going to notify you of the change. It's so strange she didn't. I'm sure I can clear it all up." He had a dazzling smile. "You see, Minnie Devani sold the booth and spot at the market to me. I couldn't believe it was up for sale. I snapped it up, of course. I'm from Traverse City, and I've been hearing about the famed Cherry Glen Farmers Market for years. I couldn't believe I had this opportunity to be a part of it. It's really a dream come true."

"Hold up," Kristy said, raising her hand as if she was in the process of stopping traffic.

I winced because I recognized that tone in her voice from high school. It meant the person on the receiving end was about to get a talking to.

Kristy folded her arms. "She can sell you her booth, of course, but you have to pay for the spot at the market. Minnie has no right to sell her place, and even if she did, she has not paid the rental fee for many months. Since you're taking over, are you taking over her bill?"

He paled. "Minnie didn't say a thing about being behind on her payments."

"I imagine she wouldn't." Kristy dropped her hand. "But I'm afraid until her bill is paid one way or another, Buzzin' Better Honey is closed."

His face turned a burnt red. "I knew it seemed too good to be true. I should have listened to my instincts. Don't worry. I'll talk to Minnie and make sure she pays you. I'll sue her if I have to."

Kristy and I shared a look.

"What?" the man asked.

"What's your name?" I was pretty sure Chief Randy would not want us to tell a possible suspect about the murder. Although I would be very surprised if this man committed the crime, judging by his complete cluelessness as to how the farmers market worked. Then again, he could be the world's best actor as well as the world's most handsome man.

"You can't sue Minnie or make her pay," Kristy said.

"Why not? Anyone can sue anyone for anything in this country."

Kristy and I shared another look. Not if the defendant was dead.

Chapter Nine

"Tell me what's going on," the man said.

"You just can't sue her," Kristy said.

I nudged her. "Kristy."

Kristy pressed her lips together. She wasn't as well versed as I was in being a suspect, so I hoped this would be one time she would rely on my experience, and my experience told me she should keep her mouth shut.

"Why not? I just talked to her yesterday about this. That's when I paid her for the booth."

"You paid her for the booth?" I looked to Kristy. "Isn't she renting space from the farmers market?"

Kristy frowned. "The space, yes, but the booths themselves belong to the merchants. The farmers market has a long-standing tradition that we allow the larger, more intricate booths to stay on- site. So technically, Minnie can sell her booth. Clearly what she didn't share with him is she can't sell her space."

"That's not what Minnie said," the man argued.

"I'm sure it's not," Kristy muttered.

"Do you have a receipt or some sort of proof of sale?" I asked.

He scowled at me, but to my surprise he reached into his pocket and came out with a piece of paper. "Take a look for yourself. She gave me this certificate that says I own the booth. It's right there in black-and-white."

The document did look official, and it was on the Cherry Glen Farmers Market letterhead, which Minnie would have had access to when she covered for Kristy. The certificate was made out to Tanner Birchwood.

"You're Tanner?" I asked.

He nodded.

"Is this real?" I showed it to Kristy.

Kristy studied it. "No. Just because she stole my letterhead doesn't make it real. This document is forged. That's not even my signature." She looked at the man. "Can I keep this? I think I need to give it over to the police."

"Whoa!" Tanner waved his hands. "There's no reason to get the police involved. I didn't do anything wrong. If Minnie tricked me, I wasn't the one breaking the law. She's the one who should be arrested, not me."

"We have to involve the police," I said. "There's a lot more at stake than who is the rightful owner of this booth. Where were you yesterday afternoon?"

He stared at me. "I was at home. Why does that matter to you?"

Kristy put her hands on her hips and gave him her best mom stance. Even though the twins were just a few months old, she had already perfected the stern mom look. In all honesty, she had that expression down in high school. It was a role that she was born to play. "And where is home?"

"I recently bought a farm at a steal."

Kristy and I shared yet another look. It seemed to me that this guy was beautiful, but maybe not the savviest in business. Was the farm he bought at a steal another example of how he was ripped off? Did he have more money than sense? It sounded to me like he just might.

He scowled at us as if he knew what we were thinking. "Yes, Minnie tricked me, but I can assure you that the farm sale was on the up-and-up. There were attorneys, Realtors, mortgage brokers, and titling officers involved. There were too many hands in the pot to be corrupted."

He probably had never been to Washington, DC, I thought.

"Where's your new farm?" Kristy asked.

"It was called Bellamy Farm."

I stared at him. "You bought Stacey's farm."

"Stacey? Who's Stacey? I bought the farm from a corporation that wanted to unload it."

"Stacey is my cousin, and Bellamy Farm is *my* farm."

He turned to me, and his uniquely colored eyes that I thought were amber now faded into green. "Oh! I was told that the original family owned the other half of the farm. I was hoping to come over to introduce myself sometime soon. I have been working nonstop to get the farm into good shape for winter; I just haven't had the time. My goal is to have everything buttoned up by the first snowfall, so I can hit the ground running with the planting in spring."

That was my plan too, but with the lack of money and manpower, it was a herculean task.

"I'd love to talk to you about the land. I'm sure there are some idiosyncrasies about it that you will know much better than I do. It would be helpful to know what fertilizers and chemicals your family had used over the years on the crops and the property. My goal is to have the farm certified as organic, but I know there could still be some residual chemicals in the ground. When I say that my farm is organic, I want to say that with complete honesty. It would be helpful to get some backstory. I'll have the soil tested, of course." He held out his hand to shake mine. "It's nice to meet you, neighbor."

Neighbor. I'm neighbors with an organic farming super-model. Great. This was just what I needed. I shook his hand reluctantly. His grip was firm and dry.

"Now," Tanner said after he dropped my hand. "I would really like to talk to you about clearing up this mess with the booth. Why can't I speak to Minnie? She sold this to me, so I have every reason to want to ask her for answers."

"You can't ask her because she's dead." Chief Randy's voice carried across the parking lot. A couple of other booth workers gasped at the police chief's very loud announcement. I supposed I could have told Tanner this when we first met since the chief seemed to have zero concern about keeping it quiet from suspects or from the general public.

A grayish hue fell across Tanner's face. "Dead? Was there some sort of accident? We just spoke yesterday. She seemed healthy."

"When did you see her last?" Chief Randy wanted to know.

Tanner was clearly shaken. "It was yesterday morning. We

were finalizing the sale of this booth. I handed over my check and she gave me the receipt. She said I could take occupation of the booth this morning. It felt like a dream come true. I was so excited with the prospect of having this spot at the farmers market. Selling my organic produce to grateful customers who care about where their food comes from just as much as I do is what I've always wanted."

She said he could have possession of the booth this morning? Did that mean Minnie knew something was about to happen to keep her from coming back to the booth permanently?

"What happened to her?" Tanner asked.

The chief rocked back on his heels. "That's what I'm trying to find out. I would like to know where you were last evening."

Tanner's face turned an even paler shade of gray. It was fascinating to watch. "Why do you need to know where I was?"

The chief stood up a little straighter. "Well, son, the truth of the matter is she was murdered."

Tanner's face went from gray to white in a blink of an eye. "Did you say murdered? How is that even possible? This is a quiet rural town."

"Crime doesn't worry about the size of the place before striking," the chief said. "It seems to me that you and I need to have a little chat. Why don't we have a seat on that bench over there?"

The two of them walked over to the bench, and I felt like I could breathe again, but every time I thought of Minnie, my breath was taken away. What else was I going to learn about her that I didn't expect?

Huckleberry shuffled around me and sat on my foot. Some backup he was.

Kristy folded her arms over her chest. "I can't believe Minnie would lie to that man like that about the booth. It's terrible."

"What we have learned in the last few hours is she's an accomplished liar. If she lied about who she was for over a decade, making a false sale to a gullible new neighbor wouldn't even faze her."

"I suppose. I wonder who else Minnie lied to. It's very possible one of those lies led to her death."

I nodded. "That list could be a long one."

"Even her closest friends? She kept the truth from them? What about her book club? Are you telling me that no one in her book club suspected anything?"

I stared at her. "I don't know about the rest of the book club, but Doreen Killian couldn't have known. She is the most straitlaced woman on the planet. I'm certain she would not let Minnie into her house, let alone count her as a friend, if she knew the truth."

"I'm not so sure about that. The best way to know for sure is to ask Doreen"

I wrinkled my nose. "Doreen despises me, but I should try to talk to her."

She nodded. "That's true; she doesn't like you. I sure as heck don't want to talk to her. Before this week, I would have told you that I'd much rather deal with Minnie than Doreen.

Doreen is not a happy person. Now that I think about it, I still would much rather deal with Minnie over Doreen. Maybe Quinn would talk to her instead."

"I'm not going to make him do that. His relationship with his mother is difficult enough. I'll talk to her."

"I wonder who else knew Minnie well. There has to be someone in Cherry Glen who knew who Minnie really was. If there wasn't…"

"If there wasn't what?"

She sighed. "If there wasn't, that's incredibly sad. Can you imagine living your whole adult life in a lie? I couldn't live like that. How can you go through life not being known for who you really are?"

I was far less the social butterfly than Kristy was, but I felt the same way. I wouldn't have been able to keep up the lie as well as Minnie had, or I didn't think I could. However, I had never been hunted by federal agents either. Not going to prison would be pretty good motivation to keep my mouth shut. It clearly had been for Minnie.

"At least something good came out of all this," Kristy said.

I looked at her confused. "And what's that?"

"Your new neighbor. Tanner. My, isn't he a sight for sore eyes? I might be interested if I wasn't so happily married, but he's just what you need."

"What are you talking about?" I blinked at her.

"You should date him." She said this in the same matter-of-fact manner that a person would say the sky is blue.

I stared at her. "Have you lost your mind?"

"Did you even see him? He's gorgeous, and he wants

to be an organic farmer just like you do. It's a match made in heaven. You guys can sneak kisses between the rows of organic carrots. It will be just like a Hallmark movie. Big city girl comes back home to save the family farm only to fall in love with the hot farmer next door." She waved her hand across the sky as if she was reading the description off a marquee.

I shook my head. "I think the stress of being a murder suspect has gone and made you crazy. Date him? That is the most ridiculous thing I have ever heard."

"It's not ridiculous; it's genius. Then if you get married, you can merge the farm to its former glory. Bellamy Farm would be back better than ever. It's like a rural fairy tale. You saved the farm and got a handsome farmer in the process. I think he was interested in you. He was very excited when you told him you were a Bellamy."

I scowled at her. "Because he wanted to know the chemicals my family used on his land in the past. There was nothing more to it."

"I beg to differ."

"You can beg to differ all you want." I rolled my eyes. "I think I'm done with this conversation. We have to focus less on this new guy in town and more on the murder. The reason you asked me to come to the farmers market today was to help you clear your name, wasn't it?"

She sighed. "Yes, it was. But don't blame me if I'm a hopeless romantic. I just want you to be happy."

"A man doesn't have to factor into the equation of being happy. In all honesty, a relationship right now would only bring more stress into my life. I have to focus all my energies on saving the farm. I don't have time for a boyfriend. I don't even have time for a casual date."

Kristy pressed her lips together. "Have you looked at yourself in the mirror lately, Shi? You're gorgeous, and I thought you were gorgeous in high school. I always envied your height and blond hair."

"Can we just drop it?" I asked.

"Fine," she said with a shrug, as if it was of no concern to her.

"Thank you. Now, we have to seriously find a way to clear your name." I tried to keep the exasperation out of my voice.

She sighed. "I know you're right. It's just that playing matchmaker is so much more fun."

I didn't even acknowledge her last comment and forged ahead. "The first order of business is talking to the chief and finding out what he knows about Minnie and her secret life. I would hope Marshal Chuff has spoken to him by now. I have a greater chance of learning what her real name was from Chief Randy than I do the tight-lipped federal agent." I glanced around the market. "Where did the chief and Tanner go?"

Kristy's mouth fell open. "They left without telling us. The nerve." She paused. "Do you think Chief Randy arrested Tanner?"

"Arrested him for being yet another person who was tricked by Minnie? I doubt it, but Tanner is certainly a suspect. That's good news for you. The more suspects there are, the less focus the chief will have on you. My guess is the chief went back to the station. I have no idea where Tanner might have gone. I'll go to the station now and see if I can track the chief down and find out what he knows."

She sighed. "I wish I could go with you, but it's a market day at the end of the season. I need to stay here in case something goes wrong. It seems ever since I went on maternity leave the market has been plagued with one problem after another."

"It's better if you stay here. Chief Randy won't be surprised if I stop by the station. Minnie was killed on my land." I shivered at the thought. What would happen to the farm because of this incident? Would we be sued by Minnie's family? Did she have family under her real or fake names?

"Be careful, Shi," Kristy said. "There is a rumor in the town that Chief Randy wasn't pleased when you got involved in the last investigation. He won't like it if you do it again, especially if you're doing it for me."

Chapter Ten

I didn't know how good my odds were of finding Chief Randy before nine in the morning at the police station, but since I had seen him at the farmers market, I knew he was up and working the case.

I did my best not to worry about the chief being upset that I had meddled in an old case. He hadn't given me much choice back then, and for Kristy's sake, I didn't feel like I had much choice right now either.

I left my car parked at the market, and Huckleberry and I walked to the municipal building on Michigan Street. I made sure I had Huckleberry's leash clipped on, even though he hated it. He bit the tough leather and looked up at me as if I had insulted him.

"I know you are a good boy," I said to the pug. "However, we don't know about these tourists, and I can't carry you all the way to the police station."

He made a harrumph sound and shook his head in disgust.

It was early on a Saturday, but there were already a few shoppers meandering up and down the street, peering into shopwindows. At this time of the morning though, most of the people in town made a beeline for breakfast. The tourists went to the brewery and the locals went to Jessa's Place. Occasionally tourists wandered inside the diner, but for the most part, it was a haven for the locals and farmers.

The town's municipal building was in the middle of the block. Being a small town, the building included the city offices and the town hall as well as the police and fire stations. If you needed anything official done in Cherry Glen, this was the place to come. Standing in front of it, I could see from one side of the town all the way to the other. The brewery was inside of an old grain mill across the street to my left, and my cousin's theater was on the same side of the street as the brewery. Between the two were half a dozen specialty shops and boutiques. On my side was the general store, which was the only business that had been in operation when I was a child. Everything else was shiny and new and looked like it was out of central casting for that Hallmark movie Kristy had been talking about.

I smiled at a woman as she strolled by, and she gave me a blissful smile in return, paper coffee cup in hand that smelled strongly of pumpkin spice. Little did she know there had been a murder in this picturesque little town.

I picked up Huckleberry and stepped into the large building. I hadn't expected it to be open on a Saturday morning, but even more than that I didn't expect Connie Baskins to be there, sitting at the reception desk in her long skirt and chunky sweater like it was Tuesday and she had just clocked in. She had a pencil at the ready to jot down appointments. As far as I knew, she had never used a computer, and no one in the municipal building expected her to learn.

"Connie, what are you doing here?" I said. "Shouldn't you get the weekend off?"

The curls piled on the top of her head bounced in place. "Shiloh Bellamy! I should have expected to see you here today. How is that adorable father of yours?"

I suppressed a smile. Connie hadn't been shy in recent months about hinting that she had a massive crush on my father. I didn't have the heart to tell her that she stood no chance with him whatsoever since his only interests for the last two decades had been local history and, more recently, acting small roles in my cousin's theater company.

"Dad is doing fine. He's working on his collection today."

She sighed. "Is working on his collection the only thing that man does? I have been reading up on my Michigan history hoping I might impress him, but I can't seem to strike up a conversation with him. He's such a reserved bloke. Unless he's onstage," she said with a sigh. "He comes alive onstage. Makes me realize what he must have been like as a young man."

"Is the chief in?" I asked. All this talk about my father made me a tad uncomfortable, especially knowing how much he would hate it.

"Is Chief Randy in?" she asked and then repeated the question more loudly. "Is Chief Randy in? Of course. He's working today just like I am. When there is a murder in Cherry Glen, all hands are on deck around here. The chief wants us all to be at the ready in case someone comes to us with questions. Of course, you would have questions on the matter since you were there and the murder was at your farm." She clicked her tongue. "Was Sully terribly upset?"

I didn't believe my father cared one bit that Minnie Devani—or whatever her real name might be—was killed on our farm. "Dad's fine."

She pressed a hand to her chest. "He's so stoic and strong."

I grimaced.

"I'll buzz the chief and let him know you're here." She picked up the phone on her desk. "Shiloh Bellamy to see you, Chief... Okay, I'll send her down in a few minutes."

She looked to me. "If you don't mind waiting. He's in the middle of interviewing a suspect."

"Oh! Who is that?" I asked even though I suspected it was Tanner Birchwood since he and the chief disappeared from the farmers market at the same time.

She waved her hand at me. "You know I can't tell you that." She leaned over her desk. "And hello to you, Huckleberry. Oh, I just love it that you take your little dog everywhere. It's just so Hollywood. I must say everyone in Cherry Glen feels a bit fancier since you came back into town."

I raised my brow. "I'm not sure why. This is my hometown. I'm not any different from anyone else who grew up here."

She laughed. "When you left you were an awkward girl with tangled hair. You came back a woman with golden waves and the body to match it." She shook her finger at me. "Don't think I'm the only one who noticed. I have seen a certain handsome fireman take a second look at you. He's impressed with the changes."

My face felt hot. I knew who she was talking about, but I wasn't going to add fuel to the fire to even acknowledge the comment. Besides, if someone was interested in me just for my outward appearance, I wanted nothing to do with him. I had met more men in LA than I cared to admit who were like that. It's not what I came back to Michigan for, that was for sure.

Connie clasped her hands in front of her chest. "Oh, I can tell I struck a chord with you. Are you blushing? Quinn Killian is a very handsome man and such a hard worker and wonderful father. It always helps to know how a man behaves around children and animals, if you ask me. I have heard that Huckleberry here is quite fond of him. You can't do much better, and since you are getting up in years, you'll have a ready-made family without a pesky ex to deal with, since he's a widower."

I just stared at her. If I clenched my jaw any tighter, I might just grind my molars into dust. "Do you think enough time has passed for me to find the chief?"

She checked the slim gold watch on her wrist. "Oh, I suppose it has. It's so easy to lose track of time when you're talking about boys."

I grimaced.

She leaned across the desk and lowered her voice. "You heard that there is a federal agent here, didn't you? That's why I'm here. It's more than just the murder. The chief called me in to deal with the press."

"The press?" I asked, looking around the large lobby again. It was the same as before. There was no one there but us. Was a reporter hiding someone in the bushes outside of the municipal building? It seemed unlikely, but like Kristy said before, I would believe just about anything now that I knew Minnie lived under a fake identity.

"Well, they aren't here yet. They will be when they hear about Joan the Bandit though. Mark my word about that."

"Joan the Bandit?" I squeaked.

"Oh no!" She clapped a hand over her mouth and said something I couldn't discern.

"I can't understand you with your hand over your mouth like that."

She dropped her hand. "I said, 'I'm afraid I let the cat out of the bag.' You didn't know about Joan the Bandit?"

"Who's Joan the Bandit? She sounds like a 1950s cartoon character."

She ran her fingers across her mouth like she was zipping her lips closed and then threw away the imaginary key.

Connie clearly wasn't going to spill any more beans, but I wasn't quite ready to let it go. "I'll talk to you later, Connie."

She nodded vigorously but didn't say a word. I guessed she couldn't speak because her lips were zipped closed.

I set Huckleberry on the ground. "Okay, Huck and I are going to go see the chief now," I said slowly, as if I were afraid that if I made any sudden movements I might spook her.

She wiggled her fingers at me in return but still didn't speak.

At the stairwell that led down to the police station, I said to Huckleberry, "I do *not* want that woman as my stepmother."

He barked in agreement.

Huckleberry licked my hand.

The chief shook his head. "I should have known you were going to stop by today. As soon as I saw you at the farmers market this morning, I put two and two together that you were going to poke your nose in my official business again."

"I don't poke my nose in anyone's business when it doesn't concern me, but Minnie's death certainly concerns me. Her body was discovered on my farm."

He nodded and stood up. "That's a bad break for you, to be sure." He walked around the desk and leaned back on the front of it. "Just when you're getting on your feet with all the farming. Such a shame." He said this as if he didn't think it was a shame at all.

"How's Doreen doing?" I asked.

His face softened. "It's kind of you to ask after my wife since Minnie was a close friend of hers. She's shocked and sad of course. She couldn't believe what happened. And there have been other developments."

"Like Marshal Chuff?" I asked.

"Oh, you met her then." He puckered his lips as if he had a sour taste in his mouth.

"I'm surprised that she didn't tell you, since she held me at gunpoint on my own farm," I said.

He laughed. "Those feds."

I wasn't laughing.

The chief folded his arms. "Now, we have to be careful with this case. It's my murder case. I can't let some young federal marshal come in here and think she's going to take it over just because she thinks Minnie is…"

Chapter Eleven

The stairs led me into a hallway lined with city offices, but at the end of the hallway was a door I knew went into the police station. It wasn't the first time I had been at the station. My first visit occurred fifteen years ago, when Logan died. There were rumors at the time that I might somehow be responsible for his accident, even though I wasn't in the car or even in Cherry Glen when he got into that fatal accident. They were all lies, but Chief Randy had still asked me to visit him at the station so we could "hash it out."

As soon as I left that meeting with the chief, I'd packed my bags for California with no plans to return to Michigan. Who knew I would be back in the same place so many years later about another untimely death? And not once, but twice now.

I stepped into the station. It was a small place, and half of it was taken up by the jail cell that was thankfully empty at the moment. There were three midcentury metal desks, one each in a different corner of the room, and a metal door across from the jail cell that I knew led into the interrogation room.

Chief Randy sat at the desk closest to the closed door. "Shiloh! Must you take that dog everywhere you go?"

I looked down at the pug in my arms. "Yes."

"She thinks Minnie is what?"

He seemed to consider this. "She believes that Minnie is a bank robber who had been on the run for almost twenty years."

My mouth fell open. "What?"

"I know. It's ludicrous." He shook his head.

"Joan the Bandit," I said softly.

"You heard of her?"

I had, just three minutes ago from Connie. But even though Connie irritated me, I wasn't going to throw her under the bus. "How did she rob banks?"

"It seems that she would come up to people who were at ATMs and steal their money just as they were making a withdrawal. Since bank robbery of any sort is a felony, the feds have to be involved."

"But why a marshal? Shouldn't the FBI be looking for her?" I asked.

"Initially, all those years ago, yes, but she skipped out on the marshals when she was being transferred between prisons. Both were low security prisons, and Joan was a model prisoner, from what I heard. It was easy for her to garner her guard's trust and slip away when he wasn't looking. Since she escaped under a marshal's watch, finding her is that agency's problem."

"Does Marshal Chuff think Minnie's past is the reason that she was murdered?"

He wrinkled his nose. "I don't much care what Chuff thinks about any of it. Those crimes happened decades ago. Do you think someone would hold a grudge for that long?

No." He shook his head. "Take it from me. The murder was the result of something that happened recently in Minnie's life. The killer wanted *Minnie* dead and didn't even know who Joan was."

I wasn't so sure of that. I guessed there were lives that Joan/Minnie had ruined in her past. If those lives were still fixated on it, they might come to Cherry Glen to find her. The question was after all this time, how did Marshal Chuff know she was here? If Marshal Chuff could finally track her down, it stood to reason that someone else had as well.

"Did Marshal Chuff tell you how long she has been in Cherry Glen looking for Minnie?"

He shook his head. "She hardly told me anything at all. She's very tight-lipped. Those marshals don't want to give away their secrets. It costs them."

"Where did Minnie—I mean Joan—commit most of her crimes?"

He folded his arms. "All over the Midwest, from Ohio to Minnesota. She never stayed in one place for long, and back then, without the same computer systems that we have today, it was difficult to piece all the crimes together as interrelated."

"Weren't there cameras? I would assume there were video cameras around ATMs in the 1990s."

"There were, but they weren't what they are like now. Today they might be as small as a pinhead. Back then they were big and bulky, and a criminal could see them easily. She was a real Bonnie and Clyde operation." He paused when he said that.

"Who was her Clyde?"

"Chuff didn't tell me his name."

I blinked at him. Were we really talking about the same Minnie Devani? The prim and proper lady that gave me such a hard time when I first moved back to Cherry Glen? The woman who was a close friend of Doreen Killian, the queen of all things proper?

It made some sense that the day I found my first dead body came to mind. At the time, I had been so shocked I couldn't think straight, but Minnie, who had also been there, didn't seem to be fazed by it. She was more upset that her booth was confiscated for a few days while the police began their investigation. Was seeing a dead man business as usual for her? I shivered. Who was Minnie Devani, really?

"Are you planning to have your festival at the farm this afternoon?"

I frowned at his sudden topic change. "I plan to."

He nodded. "Good. I would like to see who all comes out. I'll be there."

"Don't you think it will scare the killer away if the police are there?"

"I don't mind scaring a crimal, never have," he said.

Huckleberry and I left the municipal building, and I was even more confused by the case than I had been earlier this morning. Minnie Devani was Joan the Bandit? What on the actual earth? I felt like I had landed in the middle of some weird mob movie. If a large man jumped out in front of me with a tommy gun I wouldn't have been surprised.

I stopped in the middle of the sidewalk, as I realized I hadn't thought to ask more about Joan. What was her last name? When exactly was she arrested? How many people did she rob? Did she ever hurt anyone? Kill anyone?

Huckleberry's leash hung around my wrist as I tapped on my phone's screen. I typed "Joan the Bandit" into the search bar and was instantly overwhelmed with results.

Her real name was Joan Marino. She was from Indianapolis and came from a long line of criminals. Thievery, it appeared, was in her blood.

"Are you in the middle of an enthralling Snapchat or whatever the kids are into today?"

I yelped and threw my phone into the air. Quinn caught it in his free hand. In his other hand he held a carrier of four coffees that I recognized came from the general store. It seemed Quinn had again been assigned to make a coffee run for the fire department.

He handed the phone back to me, and I hugged it to my chest. Huckleberry danced at our feet. He had been startled by my outburst too.

Quinn arched his brow at me holding the phone so closely to my chest. "I didn't look at the screen if that's what you're worried about. You can keep chatting with your California beau or whoever it is."

"I don't have a California beau, as you put it, and I was researching."

He cocked his head. "I never thought seed catalogs could

be so engrossing, but maybe I just haven't found the right one."

"I wasn't looking at a seed catalog either."

A couple walked by us, and Quinn and I waited for them to pass.

When they were gone, I said, "I've learned something unexpected about Minnie."

"Other than she was murdered? That was pretty unexpected."

"More unexpected." I held my phone screen out to him. "This."

He looked at it this time. "Joan the Bandit?"

"That's Minnie." I quickly told him what I learned and about Marshal Chuff. "I was just at the police station talking to your father, and he confirmed it."

"Oh wow," was all he could say.

The side door to the building opened, and my high school nemesis Laurel Burger stuck her head out. "Stop flirting and get in here, Quinn. It's time for our morning meeting. The chief is waiting for coffee and is in a foul mood. The longer you take, the worse his mood gets."

"Laurel, it's Shi. I'm not flirting," he said, as if it was the most ridiculous thing that he'd ever heard.

I felt like I had been kicked in the stomach.

Quinn turned back to me, blissfully unaware of how his comment made me feel. Maybe I had been wrong in thinking he'd changed. Maybe he was still the insensitive kid from high school who only talked to me because I was Logan's girlfriend. In any case, if I had needed any proof that Connie

Baskins was way off base with her idea that Quinn was attracted to me, I now had it.

"Shi, let's talk later about this," Quinn said. "I wish I could come to Fall Daze this afternoon and help out again, but I'm on call."

"It's okay, Quinn," I said. "I don't need your help. You just caught me at a bad time, when I was still surprised by the news. I'm sorry if I held you up."

A strange look crossed his face. "You don't have to apologize."

"Huckleberry and I have to hurry to the store to pick up a few things to bake for Fall Daze. I'll see you later." I waved but didn't make eye contact with him again.

"Shiloh?" he called after me, but I pretended not to hear him and didn't turn around.

Chapter Twelve

I went into the small supermarket on the edge of town. Huckleberry waited in my car with all the windows down. Inside the store, I was happy to see there was a small organic baking section. Actually, it was more of a shelf. It had sugar and flour, which were the two ingredients I was most in need of. The ingredients weren't the same ones that I had found in the organic specialty shops in Traverse City, but they would work in a pinch and would let me bake the last few things I wanted to add to the Fall Daze offerings. I could get by with the rest of the items I had in the pantry at home.

It wasn't until I was pulling into the long driveway of my farm that my cheeks flushed red in embarrassment over how I had acted with Quinn. I couldn't even tell him why I'd behaved that way. I'd reverted to a middle school girl in a matter of seconds. Part of me wanted to blame Laurel for that, but I knew it wasn't fair to do so.

I parked my convertible by the barn, and Huckleberry and I got out. I had about four hours before the festival, and I had a lot of baking to do. Thankfully, my mother had been an avid baker and when she and my father married, she made him put in a convection oven. It could be tricky to bake in a convection oven, but it was fast, which was what I was going for. I would have the regular oven going too, for more delicate bakes, like cakes and pies. The convection oven I would reserve for cookies. I had made lots and lots of cookies in it the night before.

I grabbed the groceries out of the back of the convertible and went into the house through the front door. I stopped in surprise as I heard laughter and voices coming from the kitchen. My father never had company. Huckleberry, who was at my feet, stopped too, and he looked up at me as if to ask what we should do.

Holding the bags of groceries close to my body, I stepped into the kitchen. I found my father sitting at the kitchen table sipping coffee with Marshal Lynn Chuff. "What on earth is going on here?"

My question caught them in midlaugh, and they both looked at me like I had stomped in there and ruined their inside joke.

Marshal Chuff stood up. "Shiloh, I was just visiting with your father. He's lived in the town longer than anyone else I can find. He knows the history. It's been fascinating to learn it."

"You stopped by the farmhouse to learn Cherry Glen history?" I asked in disbelief.

She nodded. "And how it's related to Minnie Devani. Your father is a wealth of information and has given me some ideas as to where I should look next."

Dad nodded. "The culprit might return, and she can arrest him on the spot."

"Or her," Marshal Chuff said with a laugh. "Women can break the law too. Your Minnie was a shining example of that."

I blinked at them and wondered if perhaps I had walked into the wrong house. "Don't you mean Joan the Bandit?"

Marshal Chuff's head snapped around in my direction and gave me a level look. "Your father is right; you do have a way of getting information out of people, don't you? How did you learn about Joan?"

"It doesn't matter," I said, not sure why I felt unwilling to tell her the source of the information. "What I want to know is how you knew she was here. If she's been on the run for almost twenty years, what was the break in the case that brought you to our little town?"

She looked at me as if she were considering her answer. "I received an anonymous tip. The informant told me to look for Joan the Bandit in Cherry Glen, and that's where I found her."

"Did you track the tip down?" I asked.

"No. It was a typewritten letter with no signature. The postage stamp was from Traverse City. That's all the information we had."

"So you didn't even verify it was true before you came here?"

"If every law enforcement officer verified every tip before they followed up on it, precious time in cases would be lost." She stood up. "Sully, it was so nice to chat with you, and thank you for the coffee. I need to get back on the case." She eyed me.

My dad sat straighter in his seat. "Of course, it's always nice to have visitors."

I stared at him. Always nice to have visitors? Where was that coming from? My father *hated* visitors with a capital H.

Dad started to get up.

"No, stay there, Sully," Marshal Chuff waved him back into his seat. "I'm sure Shiloh can see me out." She gave me a look that clearly said, "We need to talk."

I set my canvas grocery bags on the counter. "I'll be back in a minute, Dad."

I followed Marshal Chuff into the living room. Huckleberry always wanted to know where I was, so he followed and picked up Esmeralda on the way. The three of us walked Marshal Chuff outside in single file. The absurdity of it wasn't lost on me.

"I know your friend Kristy Garcia Brown is the main suspect for this crime," the marshal said.

"She didn't do it," I said, ready to defend Kristy to the end just like she'd defended me in high school from Laurel the Terror.

The officer held up a hand. "You didn't let me finish."

I wanted to say something but bit my tongue.

Marshal Chuff seemed to be satisfied when I didn't speak and said, "What I was going to say is I don't think that she's the killer either. I suspect it's tied to let's-call-her-Minnie-for-your-sakes' crimes."

"The person who tipped you off that she was here is the one who killed her?"

"Possibly," she said with a nod. "Or perhaps the person tipped someone else off who wanted to do more than just have Minnie arrested…"

"They wanted her dead."

She nodded. "Precisely."

PUT OUT TO PASTURE

"If Minnie is dead, isn't your participation in the case over? I don't believe that U.S. Marshals are involved in homicide cases."

She narrowed her eyes. "You know an awful lot about law enforcement for a farmer."

Again, I didn't tell her that I had produced true crime shows in Hollywood in a former life. I didn't think that would give me much credit where Marshal Lynn Chuff was concerned.

When I didn't say anything, she went on to say, "Minnie had an accomplice all those years ago. I'm looking at his connections too."

"Who is the accomplice?" I asked.

She arched her brow. "I'm shocked you don't already know since you seem to know a lot about the case already."

I shrugged. "I don't know his name," I admitted.

"Hmm, well, that does surprise me. His name was Mack DeMarco. Mack was the person waiting in the getaway car. No one even knew he existed until Minnie's trial."

"How'd they learn of him?" I asked.

"She gave him up." She folded her arms.

"Gave him up?" I asked.

"To get a lesser sentence, she gave the district attorney his name. He was arrested the next day."

"So he's in prison?" I asked.

"He was. He died in prison."

"Would he have anyone who would blame Minnie for his death?"

"That's an interesting question."

That wasn't much of an answer, I thought.

Huckleberry whimpered at my feet, as if he wanted more information too.

I blew out a breath. What if the killer was tied to Mack? This would be good news for Kristy, but I didn't like the idea of someone holding a grudge that long and being in Cherry Glen. A person like that could be very dangerous indeed.

"I'm going to hang around Cherry Glen as long as my supervisor will let me so I can find out." She eyed me. "You know this town better than I do. I would appreciate your help."

"Shouldn't you be asking Chief Randy for help?" I asked.

"Let's just say Randy Killian and I don't see eye to eye on this case. My guess is I only have a few days before he calls my supervisor and asks for me to be removed from his juris-diction. We have to move quickly."

"What do you want me to do?" I asked, still bewildered that a federal officer, who had the authority of the U.S. gov-ernment behind her, would need to ask me for help in an investigation.

"Keep your eyes and your ears open." She looked me square in the eye. "And report back to me."

That last part sounded less like a request and more like an order.

Chapter Thirteen

I spent the next couple of hours baking and preparing for Fall Daze. I was thankful again for my mother's convection oven, which made short work of the last few recipes. I wished I had Chesney or Hazel with me for an extra pair of hands. However, Chesney was working on a paper for class, and Hazel was at her grandmother's house, since Quinn was at the station. I knew there was no way Doreen Killian was going to let her granddaughter come to my farm, especially not after the death of her friend on that same farm the night before.

Chesney arrived when her paper was done and helped me set up around noon, and we had everything in place by one, when the festival was to start.

Nothing happened. No one came. There was no line in the driveway like there had been the day before. There was no backup at the hayride. No one was eating my handcrafted organic pies.

I swallowed and smiled nervously at Chesney, who was sitting at the ready at the baked goods table. "Slow start today. It will get better," I said, not sure if I was trying to reassure her or me. "There are a lot of activities to do in town right now. I'm sure everyone will head this way when they can."

Chesney nodded. "I'm sure that's it." However, she didn't look convinced.

When four o'clock came and went and no one had shown up, I told the volunteers they could each pick whatever baked goods they wanted to eat to pass the time. It was the least I could do after wasting their afternoon.

Finally, I heard an engine coming down the driveway. My excitement faded when I saw it was Chief Randy on his motorcycle. He climbed off the bike and set his helmet on the seat before walking over to me.

The police chief hiked up his pants. "My," he said. "This is like night and day compared to yesterday, isn't it? Yesterday, you could barely feed all the people who came, and now you are going to be left with too many pies."

I frowned. "Chesney," I said. "Can you go see if anyone needs help in the corn maze?"

She gave me a weird look. "There's no one here to need help with the corn maze."

"Just go and check for me."

She sighed and got out of her seat.

After she had gone, I turned to the chief. "Can I interest you in an organic apple pie? What about cherry? That's what Cherry Glen is all about, isn't it?"

He laughed. "I'm never going to turn down a cherry pie."

I stood up and handed the white bakery box to him. "No charge."

"You aren't going to make any money if you give your pies away for free," he said and accepted the box.

I noticed, though, he didn't offer to pay for the pie.

Maybe he simply wanted to make the observation I was losing money. It was an observation I didn't need. I was keenly aware of it. "Is there something else I can help you with, Chief?"

"I heard that Marshal Chuff was here at your farm today." He narrowed his eyes at me as if he was sizing up my answer even before I had a chance to respond.

"Yes, I told you that I had met her this morning by the scarecrow."

"No," he shook his head. "Later. She was back here. I want to know about it."

I frowned. How would he know that? I hadn't told anyone, nor had I been anywhere since Chuff left. I had had too much baking to do. Baking, it appeared, that had all been done in vain. "She's investigating Minnie, or Joan the Bandit, more specifically. I suppose she will go to a lot of places Minnie was seen yesterday to investigate her case."

"Her case? It's my case, and she knows it." He squeezed the corners of the pie box and created an indentation in the white cardboard. If he pressed any harder, he would crush the pie completely.

"Be careful with that pie, Chief, if you plan to eat it."

He looked down at the box as if he were surprised to find it in his hands. "It's a shame there aren't more people here. Murder will do that. In my experience, murder chases everyone away." He held up the pie. "If Chuff comes back here to talk to you again, I want to hear about it, understand?"

He took his free dessert and walked back to his waiting motorcycle.

It seemed the chief and Marshal Chuff both liked to tell me what to do. Too bad I didn't plan to listen to either of them.

A half hour later, I told the volunteers to go home. They each left with a free pie and my thanks. After they left, Chesney did a walk around the farm to check for problems, not that I needed any more of those. No one had come to the second day of Fall Daze. Not a single person. This didn't bode well for the future of Bellamy Farm. Were people staying away because of the murder? Was the farm now cursed in local lore? I felt defeated.

I was folding up the white linen tablecloth on the bakery table when a shiny blue pickup truck with all the bells and whistles came rolling up the driveway. I wasn't the least bit surprised when Tanner got out. Of course he would have the best and flashiest truck in town. It made perfect sense for Mr. Perfect.

"Where is everyone? I thought the event went on until six," he said with his dazzling smile.

"You just missed everyone, I guess." I wasn't about to tell my new neighbor and organic farm competition that no one came to the festival.

"Wow, when I was here yesterday, the place was packed."

I stared at him. "You were here yesterday?"

He nodded. "I just wanted to see how you run an operation like this. It's something I might want to try too when my farm is in better shape."

"So you plan to copy me?" I asked, not even trying to hide the annoyance in my voice.

He shook his head. "Oh no. I would never do that, and certainly if I had an event like this I would coordinate with you so that the two of us weren't in competition. I plan to be a very good neighbor. I just admire what you have done. I didn't grow up on a farm. Everything I know about farming I've learned from books and YouTube. I can tell you that it's been a steep learning curve and your knowledge is invaluable."

"Oh," I said, placated and feeling dumb for getting so upset.

"I think I can be a help to you too. I'm pretty handy. I can see there are some projects that you need to get done around here."

I must have made a face because he raised his hand. "I'm not criticizing you in any way. I just want you to know I'm making myself available to help out. I didn't know until today that you lived here just with your elderly father."

I clenched my teeth. Who was talking to Tanner about me? I knew the people of Cherry Glen liked to gossip, but this was ridiculous.

"It must be difficult having the entire weight of the farm on your shoulders," Tanner said.

It was difficult, and I found myself softening to him. "I'm sorry if I came off as rude earlier. The last twenty-four hours have been some of the strangest of my life. With the murder..."

He nodded. "I know. I just can't believe it. I know there's no chance I'll see that money I gave Minnie. I feel so stupid. If I talked to you first, I might have stopped myself from making a terrible mistake. Seven thousand dollars gone."

"You paid her seven thousand dollars?" I blinked at him. Who on earth had that kind of money to throw around? Who was this guy? A trust fund baby?

He rubbed the back of his neck. "I know, I know. I thought the price was steep too, but I just wanted that spot at the market so bad. I want to make my mark in the agricultural community here."

"Maybe talk to Kristy again about the booth. I'm sure she will understand about Minnie's debt. It's not your fault." Even as I said this, I knew Kristy had hoped to give the booth spot to me, and it would have been great for my organic baked goods if I could get it. However, I had to feel for the guy, losing that much money, even if he had plenty more in the bank.

He smiled. "I might do that, but I looked at the roster today. You don't have a booth at the farmers market. I was surprised. From what I read, Bellamy Farm is one of the oldest in Cherry Glen."

I swallowed. "We had a booth when I was younger, but as my father aged…" I didn't want to say the truth—that my father would much rather spend time with his collection than farm. Dad had been a great farmer once, but truth be told, he physically couldn't do it as well as he used to.

He nodded. "I went to Jessa's Place for coffee, and she gave me the backstory on your family." He looked sheepish. "I know I probably should have come to you directly. I apologize for not doing that."

I shrugged. "I'm actually kind of relieved I don't have to tell you my story." I held up a pie box. "Want a pie? There's no one else here to take it."

He accepted the box. "Is it okay if I taste it now?"

"Sure." I handed him a plastic fork.

Tanner opened the box and stuck the fork into the pie crust. Bright red cherry juice poured out. He took a bite and swallowed. "This is so good. You made this?"

I nodded. "It's organic."

"You're doing organic too?" He looked at me as if he had just won the lottery.

I nodded. "Bellamy Farm is making the transition into an organic farm."

"That's great! I think this is a great opportunity to work together and support each other!"

I mentally chastised myself for my initial reaction to him. When I learned that there was an organic farmer living next to me, I had viewed him as competition. However, Tanner saw me—a neighbor in the same business—as an ally. Had I really lived in Hollywood for so long that I always assumed that people were fighting over the same piece of pie, or this case, over the same piece of organic pie?

"I'd like that. I could really use all the help I can get. You're right. It could be a great opportunity for us both."

"Hey, the way I see it, Shiloh, we're in this together. Together we will do great things to bring organic goods to the public. We're going to change lives!" He said this with the same amount of gusto as a televangelist on pledge Sunday.

I handed him another pie. "Take one for the road."

He grinned. "You bet I will."

Chapter Fourteen

Chesney walked up to me with pad and pen. I arched my brow. "What do you have there?"

"I added a few things to our to-do list for the farm. It's all good things, Shi. Bellamy Farm has so much potential. Yes, it's overgrown and neglected, but it's still rich Michigan farmland. That's hard to come by."

Usually, I would share her optimism about the farm, but it had been a rough twenty-four hours. "I'll look at your list tomorrow, Ches. I think I just need a break from tasks at the moment."

"No problem," she said as cheerful as ever.

Then, I foisted as much pie and muffins as I could on her before she headed home.

"I can't take all this," she argued.

"Yes, you can. You're in grad school. Everyone in grad school is on the edge of starvation. Plus your sister will want it."

"You're right. Whit and I don't eat much that doesn't come out of a box. This will beat cereal for the next few nights, that's for sure." She balanced the bakery boxes in her arms. "Do you need me tomorrow?"

I shook my head. "I think I'm just going to work on my cabin and regroup."

She nodded. "That works for me. I have another big paper due Wednesday, and I'm not even done with the research. I think I'll drive to the university library and lock myself in one of their study rooms after I drop all this off at home. Whit will be at play practice anyway. It will be a nice snack for her when she gets home."

"Play practice?"

"Yeah, I thought you knew. She auditioned for the newest performance at your cousin's theater. She's completely geeking out that a real Broadway actress is the director."

I smiled. "I'm sure Stacey is happy to have her. Enthusiasm is something she wants to see most in her actors."

"Are you sure you don't need me tomorrow?"

"I don't," I promised.

"Great. I could really use the extra time."

I nodded. "We'll get back to work saving the farm on Monday."

"Sounds good to me." Chesney climbed into her old beater of a compact car and drove away.

Huckleberry was at my feet and looked at me as if to ask, "What's next?"

"Your guess is as good as mine, Huck." I told the pug.

The next morning, I was up at five. I fed the chickens and the barn cats before dawn, so I could return to my cabin and get straight to work. Giving Chesney the day off gave me an opportunity to make my new home a little bit more mine. I needed a break from the stress of saving the farm and solving the murder, and cleaning was just the ticket. Or at least that's what Grandma Bellamy would do. If she saw the state of her cabin as it was today, she would have been horrified. Grandma Bellamy liked everything neat and tidy. "When your space is in order, your thoughts will be clear," she'd always say. In fact, it had been her favorite saying when I was a teenager who hated cleaning her room and dropped her shoes and schoolbooks all over the farmhouse. She said it was no wonder I had trouble doing homework in my room since it was always a mess.

Now, I was never quite as neat as my grandmother had been, but again, I had come to appreciate her wise sayings. It was true that when there was more order in my space, I could think more clearly about the things that were bothering me.

And I had a long list of things bothering me.

Esmeralda and Huckleberry looked on while I tied an old scarf around my hair just like Grandma Bellamy did when she was cleaning or working on the farm. Honestly, the only time I ever saw her hair was when she went into town or to church on Sundays, because any time she was on the farm, she was working. She did everything. There was no job too big or small for her. She could fix the engine on the combine and bake fluffy biscuits in the same day. She did it all on her own after my grandfather died, and here I was struggling to get things done with Chesney to help me.

When I moved into the cabin, I had cleaned out the bedroom where I would sleep and the bathroom. Today, I would work on the kitchen. When I first moved into the cabin, I cleaned off the kitchen table, the counters, and the refrigerator, but that was it. Preparing the fields and getting the farm ready for Fall Daze was more important than the cabin's kitchen. As of yet, I hadn't looked inside the cupboards. Instead, I used a few dishes that I brought from the farmhouse over and over again. It was time to see what was in those cupboards. I was afraid at what I might find.

I had a stack of empty boxes ready to be filled with items to sell or donate to charity. I was giddy at the prospect of making the kitchen my own. Maybe when I did, I could at least do some of my organic baking in the cabin instead of at the farmhouse. That would be a great help if I got an urge to bake in the middle of the night. I wondered if my father would be open to me moving my mother's convection oven out here.

I opened the first cabinet, and a dead mouse fell out, bounced off the Formica counter, and landed on the olive-green linoleum floor. I screamed and ran from the room. Huckleberry ran after me. He wasn't the type of pooch to hold his ground. I shot straight for my bedroom, which was the only room in the small building that remotely resembled my taste, and bent over and caught my breath. "Get a grip, Bellamy," I told myself. "You grew up on a farm. You can't let all those years in LA turn you into a sissy." The pep talk had no effect, since I knew I still had to pick that mouse up from the floor and dispose of it somehow. From the brief glance I had, it appeared to have been dead a very long time. I didn't know if that made picking it up better or worse.

"Get it together," I told myself, and with a deep breath, I straightened up and went back into the kitchen.

When I got back into the kitchen, the dead mouse was

gone. I stared at the spot where it had landed. "Oh no, now I'm having hallucinations."

"Meow," came the reply.

I turned around and saw Esmeralda standing perfectly straight in the doorway to the kitchen. Her fluffy tail wrapped around her small paw and the end of the tail flicked gently. There was a small smile on her lips.

"Esmeralda, what did you do with the mouse?"

Her smile grew wider.

I shook my finger at the small cat. "I swear if I find a dead mouse anywhere in this house, I'm going to send you to the barn to sleep with the barn cats for the night."

She unwrapped her tail from around her feet and walked away.

I sighed. The dead mouse was going to be in the middle of my pillow when I went to bed that night, I just knew it.

I took a breath and tried to put thoughts about the mouse and where it might be behind me. Huckleberry hopped onto the seat of the one of the kitchen chairs and barked.

I reached into a doggie treat bag and gave him a treat. "Here, since I know you didn't take the mouse. You would have been too afraid of it."

The cupboard door I had last touched remained open. I peered inside. I didn't see any other dead creatures. There was a stack of dusty ceramic plates and bowls. I realized everything in the kitchen would have to be washed before I used it, and since I didn't have a dishwasher it would be quite an undertaking.

When my grandmother died, it was my senior year of college and I was half-heartedly trying to plan my wedding to

Logan. We had been engaged since we were nineteen, but it never seemed like we could settle on the right time to marry. Actually, that wasn't true. I could never settle on the right time to marry. Logan was settled and ready to farm. He had our whole lives planned out. I was the one who couldn't sign on the dotted line to agree to his plan, no matter how much I wanted to—and I did want to most of the time. It was that tiny percentage of me that wasn't ready that held me back.

Well, a bit like the mouse and dust covering this place, thoughts of my engagement to Logan were another relic of the past. I turned my attention back to the present.

Thankfully, I had a massive shop vacuum to help me with the job. I removed the dishes from the cupboard and turned the machine on it. I sucked everything I could from every nook and cranny. I would have to go back with disinfectant a few times, considering the dead mouse and all.

As I cleaned, I scoured every surface of the kitchen for any sign of the treasure that might or might not be there just in case Grandma Bellamy considered her cabin kitchen the heart of the farm. I found lots of cobwebs, empty oatmeal containers, and orphaned spoons, but not a single clue about the treasure.

I glanced back at my boxes of fancy dishes from LA. Those would have to wait in the boxes a little longer. I would need to sanitize the kitchen. It was possible that a blowtorch would have to be involved too.

I grabbed a bottle of water from the refrigerator. One thing my father had done was empty the fridge and throw all the food away when Grandma died, so I supposed things could have been a lot worse.

Two hours later, all the kitchen cupboards and drawers were empty, and dishes and kitchen utensils I didn't want to keep were packed into boxes for donation. I tossed another garbage bag out the front door. I moved so fast, I didn't even look out when I tossed it. I heard a grunt, followed shortly by a swear word.

Staring out the door, I found Chief Randy holding my bag of trash just as the sun was rising. He dropped it on the ground.

"Even though it does seem at times that I do everything in this town, I'm not the trash collector," he joked.

"Chief Randy, I didn't know you were there." I wiped my hands on a rag and hurried outside.

"I would hope you didn't see me. I would be greatly hurt if you threw that bag at me on purpose. What do you have in there, anyway? Bricks? A dead body?"

I flushed and dusted off my hands. "Expired canned goods. I'm cleaning out the kitchen."

He grimaced. I didn't know if it was over the idea of cleaning or because of the expired food.

"How did you find me here?" I asked. As far as I knew, it wasn't common knowledge that I had moved to the cabin.

"Your father was nice enough to point me in the right direction. I wasn't aware you weren't living in the farmhouse." He eyed me.

I frowned. "I didn't know it was something that I was supposed to tell the police chief, and I still live at the same address."

He put his thumbs through the belt loops of his jeans. He was out of uniform today, wearing a flannel shirt, jeans, and a Michigan State trucker hat, but he was still on duty. I knew that because his badge and gun still hung from his belt. "I assumed my granddaughter Hazel would have told me. She talks about you constantly. She admires you."

I was sure his wife loved that.

"Hazel is a good kid." I removed the scarf from my hair. I felt silly with it on while talking to the police chief. "She's helped me out a lot around the farm. She seems to enjoy being outdoors and working with animals."

"Hazel will do anything to be outside. She loves it." He rocked back on his heels. "That's why she and my wife have so many difficulties. Doreen wishes Hazel would stay in all the time. She worries. Being a cop's wife is not easy. She's more aware of all the dangers out there than other grand-mothers are, especially for young girls."

I had never thought of Doreen's strictness in that way, but it made sense. I realized I probably should give her a bit more grace, even if she wasn't doing the same for me. Cherry Glen wasn't a big city, but it still had problems. No commu-nity was immune to trouble. Being the wife of the chief of police, she likely knew about every last problem in town. I told myself to remember how scared she must be for Hazel the next time Doreen reprimanded me about something.

"Are you here about Hazel?" I asked.

"No, I wanted to talk to you about Minnie."

I should have known.

"I need to speak to you about Chuff as well."

"What about her?"

He rocked back on his heels. "I still don't buy Chuff's story that our Minnie was her Joan. It just doesn't fit Minnie at all. She wouldn't rob a person at an ATM." He said this like such an idea was beneath Minnie somehow.

"Marshal Chuff appears to be convinced."

He grunted. "She's just a federal agent poking her nose where it doesn't belong. It's not the first time. I don't want you speaking to her."

"So if a federal agent comes to me and asks me questions, I'm supposed to say, 'Sorry, I'm not allowed to speak to you'?"

"Exactly," he said with a satisfied nod.

"I'm not going to get in trouble with the federal government because you're having a turf war."

He scowled.

"Even if Minnie isn't Joan, she's not completely innocent. She stole money from the farmers market."

"That's what Kristy Brown says, but there is no evidence that Minnie was the one who took that money. For all we know, Kristy stole the money herself and framed Minnie."

I gritted my teeth. If he thought his argument that Kristy stole that money from the farmers market was going to convince me not to speak to Marshal Chuff about the case, he was wrong.

Chief Randy must have read the expression on my face because he said, "I'm not saying that's what happened. I'm saying we may never know. What we do know is the evidence against Kristy is damning. She had motive, and Minnie was strangled with her scarf. They had a fight not long before Minnie died. Do I have to spell it out for you?"

I swallowed. I knew what he said was true, but I knew my friend too. It was impossible for me to believe what he was proposing. "I know Kristy, and I know that she didn't do this. She was trying to help Minnie, who was having financial problems. Minnie betrayed her by taking that money. Kristy wanted the money back. So why would she kill her?"

"She just had twins. She's not sleeping. There are post-partum hormones flowing through her body. She snapped. It wouldn't be the first time."

I closed my eyes for a moment and told myself hitting a police officer wasn't going to do me any favors. "I'm just going to assume you don't realize how offensive your statement would be to any mother, and any woman for that matter."

He held up his hands. "I wasn't trying to pick a fight about feminism."

Too late.

"Let me ask you this, Shiloh. Were you in contact with Kristy during the entirety of the festival that afternoon?"

"Of course I wasn't. I was the host of the event. There were a thousand things I had to run around and do, but you already knew that before you asked the question."

He smiled. "I'm just asking you. Can you really know what your friend, a friend that until recently you had not seen for over a decade by the way, was doing when you weren't there?" With that, he turned and walked up the weed-ridden path that led to the big house.

He left me standing in front of the cabin, having success-fully planted a dark seed of doubt in a corner of my mind.

Chapter Fifteen

I went back inside the cabin fuming. How dare Chief Randy suggest that I didn't know Kristy? Sure, when I left Cherry Glen after Logan died, I walked away from everything from my youth, including my best friend, but she was still the same person. When I came back to town, she welcomed me with open arms. There were no hard feelings or snide remarks that I had to deal with from her. She let the past be where it belonged, in the past. I couldn't say that's what everyone in the town did.

After I left Cherry Glen, I fell out of contact with everyone. In fact, other than my father, I broke all ties to Cherry Glen when I went to LA. There was social media and other ways I could have kept in touch, but I made a conscious decision not to. I was too wounded over Logan's death and the accusations that were hurled at me. I wanted to start over, completely over, where no one knew me and where no one knew Logan.

What I realized now was that wasn't completely fair to friends who had supported me through it all, like Kristy. I was lucky she took me back as her friend when I returned to town. She could have easily snubbed me like I had snubbed her. She and I just picked up from where we left off. Friends. That was the beginning and ending of that.

Even though I had been away, I still knew who she was at her core. She could be hotheaded at times, I would give the chief that, but she would not kill anyone for any reason. I suspected the sooner he closed this case, the sooner Marshal Chuff would leave the county, which is exactly what the chief wanted.

Now that the chief had ruined my day, my motivation to clean out the kitchen faded away. I was only halfway done. Dishes, boxes, and bags were scattered all over the floor. I took one look at them and left the room. Instead, I went into my bedroom and plucked the last letter from my grandmother out of its corner in the dresser mirror.

I read the note for what must have been the thousandth time since I'd found it. As always, I was stuck on one word. *Treasure.* What was the treasure? Was it real? Was this a legit Blackbeard the pirate thing? I would be lying if I didn't say I wished for a silver bullet to save the farm.

The note said the treasure was in the "heart of the farm." Where was that? I had been playing with this riddle over the last several months. I didn't know if she had been speaking metaphorically. I had to think my grandmother would have told me about it or hinted to it at some point in my life, but whenever I searched my memory, I came up with nothing. I wanted to ask my father and cousin about it, but something told me this was a secret Grandma Bellamy wanted me to discover for myself.

Was the heart of the farm her cabin? If it was, I was certain to find the treasure eventually. I was in the process of turning the cabin upside down, and it wasn't very big. It only had one bedroom, a small bathroom with a stand-up shower, a small sitting room, and the eat-in kitchen. The kitchen was the largest room in the cabin, larger even than the sitting room. It showed the importance of the kitchen to my grandmother, who was an amazing cook and baker. She had said once, "Shiloh, it's not very often that one person can both cook and bake at the same level. There is always one strength above the other. As you learn to do both, concentrate on the baking. Bakers are always loved for what they do. Cooks are taken for granted, especially by their children."

So I had concentrated on baking. I would never say I was as talented as Grandma Bellamy had been in the art of baking, but I could hold my own. It was when I was in California and I fell in love with organic herbs and produce that my interest in baking had really taken off and I started thinking about the farm again. I suddenly felt a pull to turn Bellamy Farm into an organic farm with a café if I could swing it.

I sat on the edge of my bed. I had saved so much money to keep that dream alive, not realizing all that money would go to cover my father's debt and pay back taxes he had ignored for almost a decade. Now the substantial life savings I'd earned during my career in California were all gone, and even that had not been enough to cover all the debt. What was left was consolidated into a payment plan that would take me twenty years to pay off at the current rate I was going.

To say I could use my grandmother's mythical treasure would be the world's largest understatement. I daydreamed that it would be enough to cover the remainder of the farm's debt and make all the improvements I wanted to do. It was a pipe dream, and I knew it.

One thing about being a farmer was there was always plenty to do to keep the hands busy when the mind was full. I tucked my grandmother's note back into the corner of the mirror and got to work.

By midmorning, I needed a break from farmwork. I had mucked out the barn, cleaned the chicken coop—much to the annoyance of the chickens—and plowed the south field to sow winter rye. I enjoyed having Chesney work with me, but it was nice to have a day of solitude and be alone with my thoughts. I went to check on my father midday, but by then, his pickup truck was gone. He left a note that he went to the theater to try out for my cousin's new play.

Even though I could be jealous of Stacey at times because she had a closer relationship with my father than I did, I was grateful she had sparked his newfound interest in theater. Anything that got him out of the house and away from his collection was welcome.

Since I didn't have to worry about Dad at the moment, I decided it was time I got back on the case to find Minnie's killer. I still couldn't wrap my mind around calling her Joan, much less Joan the Bandit. There was something about the moniker that was just too cartoonish and far-fetched.

Huckleberry, who had joined me in my chores, joined me again as I walked around the crime scene, the scarecrow keeping a button-eyed watch on us. The yellow police tape was still there, although some of it had come loose and flapped in the cool wind that came off the lake a couple of miles away. I didn't find anything new, not even a federal agent holding me at gunpoint.

I headed back across the field to the farmhouse with Huckleberry toddling behind me. If there was no evidence at the crime scene of what might have happened to Minnie, then I would have to go to the place where there was most evidence of Minnie—her home. I thought I remembered that Minnie lived on Erie Street in town, but since I wasn't sure, I texted Kristy, who would know where Minnie lived because of the farmers market. She immediately shot me back the address.

With the address in hand, I looked down at Huckleberry. "Want to go for a drive?"

He barked his enthusiasm.

In the convertible, Huckleberry braced his forepaws on the car's dash and stared out the windshield. Despite the cold bite in the air, I left the top of the convertible down for another day. With winter closing in, Huckleberry and I wouldn't enjoy the wind on our faces as we drove through Cherry Glen much longer.

Minnie's home was just a few blocks from the Michigan Street Theater. To my surprise, there was a "for lease" sign in Minnie's front yard. That was fast. It appeared the landlord wasn't wasting any time finding a new tenant.

I got out of the car, let Huckleberry out as well, and walked to the front door. I knocked, but there was no answer. I hadn't expected one. Minnie certainly wasn't going to come to the door.

I glanced around the quiet street but didn't see anyone outside.

I peered through the front window, but only for a moment. The last thing I needed was to be reported to Chief Randy for peeping into people's windows, but at the same time, I was dying to see what was inside of Minnie's home. How did a bank robber live, anyway? From what I could tell from the outside, this particular bank robber lived nothing more than a normal middle-class American life.

It didn't do me any good to try to peek inside in any case. I couldn't see a thing. The blackout curtains were tightly closed on every single window. It must have been as dark as the inside of a coffin in that house.

It was intentional. Minnie didn't want anyone seeing inside. I made a mental note to ask Doreen Killian if she had ever been in Minnie's house. If they were good friends, I would have expected them to have been in each other's homes. That was assuming that Doreen would speak to me about her friend. If I had enough courage, I would have gone over to the Killian home right then and there, but I wasn't that brave.

I heard the hum of bees as I came around the side of the house. There were seven beehives at the back of the property. Bees lazily floated in the wilting flower garden and collected nectar for the hive.

The bees. What would happen to the bees now?

"If you are hoping to rent that place, you shouldn't hold your breath," a scratchy voice said behind me.

Huckleberry yipped, and I yelped and spun around. No one was there. I scanned the backyard. The long lawn was peppered with leaves that had fallen from a large oak tree in the corner. A few potted mums sat in large urns on the back patio, but there was no one there.

"Hello? Is someone there?" I asked.

"Down here," the scratchy voice said to my left. "If you want to talk to me, you will have to come closer. Now that I'm down on the ground, I plan to stay here until I get the job done. I can't get up and down like a blasted jack-in-the-box!"

I followed the voice around a large hedge that separated Minnie's yard from the next-door neighbor's. The neighbor's home was a mirror image of Minnie's, all the way down to the matching oak tree and small patio in the back. The biggest difference between the two homes was that there was a small elderly man on all fours in the grass yanking vines from his lawn.

The man straightened up and sat back on his heels. "If you are hoping to rent that place, you're out of luck. The owner went and got herself killed. Not that she didn't deserve it. She was the most wretched woman you could meet." He shook the vine in his hand at me.

I looked back at Minnie's house. "She owned the house? She wasn't renting it herself?"

"Of course she was the owner. How else do you think she could get away with having all those blasted beehives in the back? Who's going to take care of those now, I ask you?"

The man might as well have held up a sign that said "suspect" over his head. Despite his size, which honestly made me question how he could strangle anyone, he had enough anger to do the job.

Chapter Sixteen

Y ou live here?" I nodded at the house behind him.

He scowled at me, and his eyes receded into his wrinkles, completely disappearing. If I had to guess I would place his age on the other side of eighty.

"What do you think? That's the stupidest question I have ever heard. Do you think I would be on my hands and knees de-ivying someone else's yard? I don't have time for that. I'm eighty-four years old. I'm not going to spend the last few years of my life doing other people's work. I know that's what you young folks expect though. You want someone else to do everything for you."

Before I could respond to that, he went on to say, "I shouldn't even be doing this, but Minnie made me do it."

"She made you weed?" I asked, realizing how ridiculous my question sounded.

"She caused it! She planted this." He shook the vines at me.

"Is that English ivy?"

"Yes, that's exactly what it is. I thought I had gotten them all, but they keep coming back." He shook the dead vines in the air as if he couldn't believe the state of the world.

They were all over the yard. No part was spared. Whoever

planted them had done a thorough job. Since it was October, most of the vines were withered and curled like piles of snake skins all over the lawn.

He glared at me. "She planted this all over my yard. It looks pretty, but it's invasive. It's killing off my grass. It took me decades to have the perfect lawn, and she ruined it in one summer." He yanked another vine from the ground.

I wanted to ask him if removing the ivy was worth hurting his back, but I held my tongue.

I stepped around the hedge. "How did you hear about Minnie's death?"

He looked up at me again. He definitely had a Mr. Magoo, who my grandmother used to watch on reruns, thing going on. "Well, Randy Killian knocking on my door asking me if I knew anything about her murder was my first clue."

"The police chief thinks you're a suspect?"

He scowled and grabbed his cane from the grass. "I can't get any work done on this blasted ivy with you squawking at me." He dug the end of the cane into the ground and laboriously pushed himself up. I wanted to jump forward and give him a hand.

I stepped in his direction.

"If you come any closer, I will wallop you with my cane. I don't need any help, especially not from a friend of Minnie's."

"Minnie wasn't my friend," I said. "She hated me."

He was still straightening up, moving so slowly I almost could hear every click of his spine as it unraveled inch by inch. When he was finally upright, he said, "Did she ever rage-plant ivy in your yard?"

I shook my head. "No."

"Then she didn't hate you enough. Even so, I'll shake your hand as another compatriot in the fight again Minnie Devani." He held out his hand, and I shook it. I took care not to hurt his bent fingers. I guessed the poor man suffered from arthritis. It was a miracle he was able to get off the ground without assistance.

"I have been fighting this infestation since summer. She got perverse pleasure seeing me crawl around on the ground yanking vines from the earth."

I cocked my head. "She rage-planted ivy? Is that what you called it?"

"You don't know the kind of woman she was. She might have acted all prim and proper on the outside, but she was an absolute horror to live next to."

I bit the inside of my lip to fight a laugh. What Minnie had done was awful, but she was a genius in getting back at her neighbor. Rage planting wasn't something you heard about every day.

"The name is Gordon Elmer. Who are you?"

"Shiloh Bellamy," I said.

He shuffled back and took a look at me. "Shiloh. You're Sully's girl then. I've heard of you. It's brave of you to return after you killed Logan Graham."

His words sucked the air out of me. I had believed, apparently falsely, that all of the old rumors of me being somehow involved in Logan's fatal car accident had disappeared. Gordon corrected me on that. I was still held accountable for the local high school football star, who was dead at the age of twenty-three. It had kept me away from Cherry Glen for many years. Now that I was back, it was an opinion that reared its ugly head on a regular basis. All I could do was stand up straight and know my own truth in the matter.

"I had nothing to do with Logan's accident. I wasn't in the car when he died."

"Huh, that's not what I heard. I heard you were the driver." He squinted a little harder at me as if to gauge if I was lying.

My stomach fell. "I wasn't." I left it at that, realizing it would do me no good at all to fight with an eighty-four-year-old man about what happened fifteen years ago, even if I was in the right.

"Your father is a good man, which was why it was shocking to me that his daughter would do such a thing. But no matter who you are, you don't know how your children will turn out. That's why I never had any. The risk was too high. Sully is a prime example of why a man shouldn't get saddled with a woman and a family. Look what it did to him. His wife up and died and he was stuck raising you on his own. It's no wonder he spent most of his time reading and learning about history. He wanted to go to a different time."

Okay, now I was getting to the point I hoped this man was the killer and that he would get thrown in prison, no matter his age. Maybe it wasn't the kindest thought about someone old enough to be my grandfather.

"Were you at Fall Daze at Bellamy Farm on Friday afternoon?" I asked.

He squinted at me, and I couldn't see his eyes behind his squint. "Fall Daze? Never heard of it. Is that some kind of hippie thing?"

I bit the inside of my lip to keep myself from saying something I might regret. No matter how much this man might deserve it and how much I wanted to say something back, I still had to find out what he knew about Minnie's death. I needed information. I doubted he would tell me anything if I corrected him. Gordon Elmer seemed like a man who believed he was always right. I could see why he and Minnie butted heads as neighbors. I had a little bit more respect for Minnie for the rage planting. It was clear she had to stand her ground.

"Fall Daze is a fall festival that my father and I hosted at Bellamy Farm. Minnie's body was discovered in one of our fields."

"You don't say." He shook his head. "It's not the way I would have expected her to go."

"The police chief didn't tell you how she died?"

"He only told me that she was strangled. At which I laughed." He held up the one skinny arm, cane clutched in his gnarled fist. "I asked him how I could strangle anyone with these spaghetti arms. I'm just withering away and waiting to die like these vines."

His arms were thin, I would give him that, but he was angry too.

"And you weren't at Fall Daze?" I realized I was asking the same question again, but I wanted to be perfectly clear.

"I don't go to places. Too many people make me angry, but if someone killed Minnie there, I would like to shake his hand. He sure did me a favor." He scowled at the ground. "But it will never totally get rid of the gift she left me. The hateful woman."

Minnie hadn't exactly been the kindest woman on the planet and she was a thief, but she wasn't as unkind as Gordon. I approved of her ivy attack.

"Are you sure Minnie planted all the ivy? It's all over the yard."

"She denied it, but I know it was her. She came like a thief in the night."

"Did you see Minnie plant it?"

He glared at me. "How am I supposed to see anything when I'm asleep? And I take my hearing aids out at night just like everyone else does."

"But you didn't notice the vines right away?"

"Not until it was too late and they had overtaken my yard. I have a lot going on. I can't stand there and stare at my grass all day. You know what she did when I confronted her about it?"

I shook my head, not knowing if he wanted me to answer or if it was a rhetorical question.

"She laughed at me and said that someone must have really hated me to plant that much ivy. She also said I should be grateful it wasn't poison ivy."

"Yikes." It was the best I could come up with.

Gordon threw the vine in his hand on the pile at his feet. "They just keep coming. Minnie made sure I would never be rid of them. The horrible cow. She was a terrible neighbor."

"Have you lived next to her a long time?"

"Long enough. I was never going to stop being the thorn in her side." A dark smile came over his face. "She knew that."

Oh-kay, so I was sensing Gordon had some anger management issues.

"When was the last time you saw Minnie?" I asked.

"It was just a few days ago when I went over to her house with a court order. I believe it was Thursday morning."

I raised my brow. "What was the court order for?"

"I can show you. I have it right here." He patted the breast pocket of his button-down shirt. "I like to keep it close to my heart, as it was proof to me that she might have won a few battles, but I would win the war." He removed a piece of paper from his pocket and held it out to me.

I took it with the same enthusiasm as I would picking up a snake. The paper had been folded in quarters. I unfolded it and read the verdict. Minnie had to remove all her beehives from her yard by the end of the month. If she did not, she would incur a massive fine. I stared at the piece of paper. "But this was how Minnie made her money. She was a beekeeper."

He laughed. "Exactly. If you're going to take someone down, hit them in the wallet; that's what my father taught me."

"The beehives are still there." I glanced over my shoulder at Minnie's yard but couldn't see the hives, as they were on the other side of the large hedge dividing the two properties.

"Not for long," he said. "They will have to be hauled away."

"How did you get this court order? I thought that beehives were allowed in town."

"Not if you live next to a person who is allergic to bee stings."

"Are you allergic?"

"I'm eighty-four years old. I probably am. If I got stung by one of her bees, I could drop dead."

I shook my head. "But you've lived by her and her bee-hives and not had any issues."

He shrugged as if this was of no real concern. "Allergies grow worse when you age. In any case, my doctor finally wrote a letter to the town on my behalf saying I was likely allergic. As soon as he did that, Minnie's bees were doomed."

I frowned. I wondered if the doctor wrote this letter just to make Gordon go away. Goodness knew, I would have been tempted to if I were in the doctor's position.

"Bees are valuable to so many farmers. What will happen to them now?"

He shrugged. "I don't care; it's not my problem."

I had a feeling Gordon didn't care much for anything that wasn't his problem.

I looked around for my dog and spotted him in the corner of Gordon's yard, digging. I groaned. That was just what I needed to happen with this guy.

"Huck!"

He ran toward me with a piece of ivy in his month.

Gordon pointed at him. "Did you dig that up?"

Huckleberry opened his mouth, and the ivy fell at Gordon's feet.

"Good dog. Maybe I will hire you to dig up the rest of my yard."

I chuckled, and Gordon's eyes narrowed at me. Apparently, his approval of my dog did not extend to me.

"Now," Gordon said. "Leave me be and don't come back unless you plan to do something about those bees."

I was dismissed.

Chapter Seventeen

I gathered up Huckleberry and left Gordon in his backyard with the ivy and walked around the hedge into Minnie's backyard. I stood ten feet from the hives, and my heart sank. It was clear that Minnie took good care of her bees. They happily buzzed around the hives, coming and going. She had a large garden with cone flower, goldenrod, and cosmos. The bees swirled around the last of the blossoms.

"You should adopt the bees."

I spun around and found Chesney smiling at me over a waist-high wooden fence that separated Minnie's yard from the house on the opposite side.

"What are you doing here?" I asked. "How did you find me?"

"I wasn't looking for you, and I live here. I rent this house." She pointed at the tiny bungalow behind her. "It isn't much, but the rent is low. Most importantly, it has a great yard that's close to an acre. That's about as big as you can get in town. Being outside is always more important to me than being inside."

Now that she said this, I vaguely remembered she listed her address on Erie Street, but I would never for a moment have thought she would be Minnie's next-door neighbor.

She went through her gate into Minnie's yard. "You should adopt the bees. I planned to tell you that when I saw you again."

I set Huckleberry on the ground next to me but kept him on the leash. "You've lived next to Minnie all this time and never said anything?"

She wrinkled her nose, which made her glasses slip down her face. She pushed them back up with her right hand in a practiced move. "I guess it never occurred to me to say anything. I've lived here the last two years. Whit and I moved here when I was accepted to grad school in Traverse City. I never wanted to live in the city, and Whit had heard about Michigan Street Theater. She was dying to get in on the ground floor there. Cherry Glen made the most sense for us. I have even been able to convince Whit to take a few classes at the university where I'm getting my master's. Does it matter that I live next to Minnie?" she asked.

Maybe, I thought, but didn't say it aloud.

I frowned. Yesterday, Fall Daze didn't have a single customer aside from Tanner. There would have been plenty of time for Chesney to make that suggestion about the bees or to tell me she was Minnie's next-door neighbor. I pushed this worry to the back of my mind.

"You should take the bees," Chesney said, getting back to her original point. "I could move them to my yard, but Bellamy Farm is the best place for them and they would do wonders for the plants!" she said excitedly.

"I can't just take the bees," I said. "They belong to Minnie's estate."

"I know that, but you should talk to someone about buying them or something. Bees would add so much to the farm. You can sell the honey, and they'll pollinate the cherry grove and the fields. You said you want to bring the cherry grove back to its former glory. If we position the bees nearby, this will be a great start." She took a breath. "Sorry! I just get super geeky about this stuff, especially bees. Saving them is so important for the livelihood of agriculture and frankly all plants. Sometimes I get a little carried away."

I smiled. "I can understand that, and you've made a lot of good points."

Saving the overgrown and dying cherry grove was a major mission of mine over the next year. I hoped to spend the late fall and winter removing the dead trees and making lists of which trees were suffering the most. I trimmed as many as I could in the late summer. Typically trees were trimmed in late fall and early winter when the tree was dormant. However, cherry trees are unique in many ways, which included the best time for pruning, which was in summer since they were prone to bacteria. They were finicky trees that required care, but they were also the lifeblood of western Michigan. To have a farm with a dying cherry orchard almost felt like a sin when living in Cherry Glen.

"I do want to bring the grove back. If we could yield cherries next year, that would be a godsend for sure."

"The bees would be a great help. I'll do whatever I can to help you too. I would love to see those trees blossom again."

I smiled and then glanced over my shoulder. I half

expected to see Gordon peeking around the hedge trying to hear our conversation. He wasn't there.

"It's a good idea," I agreed. "I don't even know where to start to find out where the bees are going to go. Do you know who's trying to rent her house?"

She shrugged. "That sign's been there for a week. I was very surprised to see it. She told me once that she planned to never leave her house. If you met Gordon, you know he and Minnie were in an epic battle. Did he show you the ivy?"

I nodded.

"It's a genius way to take revenge on a person."

"Do you think she planted the ivy like Gordon claimed?"

"If I based it solely on how much the two of them fight, the answer is yes. They are constantly arguing, sometimes even yelling at each other."

"What started the dispute?"

She wrinkled her nose. "That part was never clear. I asked them both individually, and it seemed that neither one of them could remember what made them hate each other so much."

"That's a shame." I stared at the bees buzzing to and fro. "I'll see what I can do about getting them. You're right— having beehives by the cherry orchard might be a game changer in bringing it back." I studied the hives. They were each three-foot-tall squares that were two-by-two feet and made of wood. Moving them would be a challenge, not just because of their size, but because of the bees themselves. Sometimes when hives are moved, the bees become confused and abandon the hive, and if something happened to the queen bee, the entire hive would be lost.

Huckleberry watched a bee fly over his head. The pug ducked down low to avoid it.

"Did you know that Gordon got a court order to have the beehives removed?" I asked.

"Wow, I had no idea their feud had gone so far. The ivy must have sent him over the edge." She cocked her head and her bob hit her shoulder. "I'm surprised the court would side with him on that. Everyone in town knew that Minnie had the hives. It was her livelihood."

"Gordon claimed he was allergic, which was why the order was granted."

"That's weird, because I have seen him at the hives before. He walked right up to them. I think he would have done something to them if I hadn't said something to him."

"What did you say?"

"No more than hello, but I spooked him for sure. If he hadn't had his cane with him, he would have fallen over."

"Did he say anything to you when you spoke to him?" I glanced back at Gordon's yard. There was still no sign of him, but that didn't mean he wasn't back on the ground pulling ivy where I couldn't see him.

"He swore at me, but that wasn't unusual." She adjusted her glasses. "I was super curious what he was doing there. If Minnie had been home, she would have chased him away with a broom or worse. I did note that he went to check out the hives when Minnie had book club. Everyone knew when Minnie had book club."

"Did the book club ever come to her house?"

She shrugged. "Not that I ever saw. I think it was always

held at Doreen Killian's home. That was the impression I always got anyway."

"Did anyone else come around? Did she have any other friends? Family?"

She shrugged. "She never mentioned any family, but I can't say we shared secrets. She said little more than hello all the time we were neighbors."

I sighed. "I know she wasn't the nicest person, but now that Minnie is gone, I wished I had known her better. Maybe if I had given her a chance, we would have gotten along."

Chesney raised one eyebrow. "I hate to burst your bubble, but I seriously doubt that. There weren't many people that Minnie liked. The only people she talked about were her book club ladies. From the way she spoke of them, they were the closest people to family that she had."

That could only mean one thing: I would have to speak to Minnie's book club and its ringleader, Doreen Killian, who hated me. Great.

Chapter Eighteen

M onday morning, I didn't wake up with my usual peppiness. I had been tormented all night long with dreams of Kristy going to prison and Kent having to raise the girls alone. Because I promised Kristy I would not let that happen, I felt immense guilt in my dream to the point I woke up and felt off as I shuffled into the kitchen to make coffee and feed the animals.

I turned the light on in the kitchen and squealed when I saw the dead mouse in the middle of the kitchen floor.

"Esmeralda!" I cried.

She purred and rubbed her lithe body against my leg. Clearly, she thought her "gift" would cheer me up.

I disposed of the mouse, finished the morning chores, and checked to make sure Dad was settled for the day. Then I drove into town. A fog had rolled in over Lake Michigan overnight, so I drove my convertible with the top up and the headlights on. In the passenger seat, Huckleberry made a snuffling sound. He never liked it when the top was up, but it was something he was going to get used to through the long Michigan winter. My California pup was in for a rude awakening.

I glanced over at the dog. "Huckleberry, you just have to adjust to some things now that we live in the Midwest."

He snuffled.

I was about to say something more when an eight-point buck jumped out of the mist and into the middle of the road. I slammed on my breaks just in the nick of time. I threw out my right arm to catch the pug from falling off the seat. "Huck, you okay?"

He lifted his head from where he had hidden it in his paws.

I scratched his head and then gripped the steering wheel in both hands until my knuckles turned white. My heart thundered in my chest. The deer stared at me, and I stared back.

Slowly, two does came out of the mist and quietly walked across the road. The buck waited until they had crossed safely, and then strutted off the road after them.

All of the air whooshed out of my body. I didn't know I had been holding my breath. I could have sat there an hour to recover from the near accident, but then it dawned on me— just like I had almost not seen the deer in time to stop—that someone coming up the road behind me might not see my car cloaked by the fog until it was too late.

With a deep breath, I drove on. Between the dead mouse and now the deer, it had already been a doozy of a morning.

The sun rose higher in the sky, and just as I rode into Cherry Glen, the sunlight had burned off the remainder of the fog. It helped calm me down, and my fingers lost their death grip on the steering wheel.

I pulled into the gravel lot of Jessa's Place and hopped out of my car, holding the door open for Huckleberry to follow. The lot that sat to the west of the small diner was full of work vans, pickup trucks, and old sedans that had stopped being in production two decades ago. It was a typical day at Jessa's Place, with all the regular characters attending. The one anomaly in the gravel lot was my car, an expensive sports car that would be as practical in a Michigan winter as a snow-blower was in LA.

Huckleberry and I walked into Jessa's. The diner was packed as usual. I couldn't remember a time when I didn't come into Jessa's for breakfast to full tables. Locals came to Jessa's Place for the great food and great gossip. Both were the main ingredients to make a small town work. If you wanted information about anyone or anything in Cherry Glen, the diner was the place to get it.

Jessa took one look at me and pointed at the one empty stool at the counter. "That's yours. Fix yourself a cup of coffee. It looks like you need it." She glided by with a pot of coffee in both hands. As she moved, her orange and black streaked white hair and the bright orange bandana that was tied around her ponytail flew behind her.

Huckleberry tucked himself into his usual spot when we were in the diner, which was behind the revolving pie display by the cash register. He knew there he had the best chance of being admired as people came and went from the diner.

Three older gentlemen were at the counter tearing into plates of hash browns, breakfast sausage, and eggs. It smelled like heaven. One of the older men poured hot sauce on his eggs, and I think I might have drooled at the sight of it. I touched the corner of my mouth to check and was happy to know it was just my imagination. I would love a breakfast like that, but it did not fit into my diet.

I went around the counter for the coffee. I did treat myself to real cream. I was in the middle of a murder investigation, after all. I needed something to lift my spirits. I refrained from sugar, but boy, I wanted it. With my coffee mug in hand, I walked around to the public side of the counter and took my stool.

The man next to me cleared his throat. It was obvious he wanted to speak to me but was waiting until I was settled. I took a big gulp of coffee. I had a feeling I would need the boost of caffeine for this conversation.

"I heard you were over snooping on Erie Street yesterday. Are you sure you should be causing trouble like that?"

I sipped my coffee. "Where did you hear that?"

"From Gordon Elmer. He came into the hardware store early this morning looking for some weed killer."

"That's because Minnie Devani planted ivy all over his lawn," a man at a neighboring stool said.

The first man shook his head. "She was quite a woman," he said with a bit of awe in his voice.

I turned in my stool so I could face him. "Did you know Minnie well?"

He wiped his mouth with a paper napkin. "Not as well as I would have liked. She never gave me the time of day."

His friend slapped him on the back. "Russ had a mighty crush on Minnie. Now, he learns that she was a bank robber who was living a lie."

I stared at him. "How do you know that?"

Russ picked up the rolled newspaper that sat between him and his friend on the counter and handed it to me.

It was the *Record-Eagle*, the Traverse City paper. On page one, the very first headline read: "A Decade in Hiding: Notorious Criminal Joan the Bandit Lives and Dies in Cherry Glen." Accompanying the article, which recapped several of Minnie's robberies in the 1990s, was a photo of Minnie in her honey booth at the farmers market. Below the photo, the caption read, "After a life of crime, she sold honey."

Connie had said that Chief Randy worried about reporters when it came to this case. The article mentioned that Minnie had been strangled at a fall celebration at a local farm. I let out a breath of relief that the name and location of the farm were not mentioned. It ended with the sentence "Authorities are determining if Joan the Bandit was killed due to her past crimes or something more recent. U.S. Marshal Lynn Chuff, who has been searching for Joan for the last three years, abstained from comment on the case, but local police chief Randy Killian stated that the case should be wrapped up in a few days and that the culprit was local."

"Whoa," I whispered. It was bad news for Kristy if Chief Randy was confident enough to make such an announcement to the regional newspaper.

"That's what I thought," Russ said. "In a way, it made me feel better though. She couldn't let anyone close to her for fear of revealing the truth. She was a wise woman. I bet she wished that she could have dated me."

His friend shook his head. "She stole from people, and

you're still sweet on her. That's crazy." He lifted his mug of coffee in the air. "More proof that love doesn't make a lick of sense."

Jessa came back then. "What are you two old curmudgeons doing talking Shiloh's ear off here?"

"Russ was just lamenting over his lost chance with Minnie, or should I say Joan the Bandit," Russ's friend said.

Jessa moved around the counter, took four plates from the cook's service window and was back within seconds to top off Russ's coffee. I honestly didn't know how she moved so silently and quickly. If she didn't have the diner, she could have made a name for herself as an international spy.

"Russ." Jessa pointed at him with her empty coffee pot. "I never understood why you set your sights on Minnie in the first place. She was never kind to you. Not once."

Russ blew on his coffee. "She was a strong woman. I like strong women." He smiled at her. "Just like you, Jessa."

She wagged her finger at him. "Don't you be getting any ideas, or you can go find your morning coffee somewhere else. I don't date customers. It's bad for business."

Russ sighed. "How are you going to find love then? Everyone in this town is your customer."

Jessa ignored him.

I read the paper again. "I can't believe the media already got wind of the murder."

"Oh." Jessa slid behind the counter and grabbed two more plates. "I wouldn't be the least bit surprised if Randy Killian didn't call up that reporter himself."

"But Connie Baskins said the chief was worried about

reporters learning of Minnie's real identity. He didn't want the story to come out."

"Connie Baskins has spent her life working in the municipal building. She's never going to say anything that will make any officials look bad." Jessa refilled her coffee pot from the large machine beside the food window.

I nodded, not surprised by Jessa's opinion of Connie. Jessa liked everyone and everyone liked her, but she didn't walk around the town in rose-colored glasses. She knew exactly what was going on all the time.

"Russ," I asked. "When was the last time you saw Minnie?"

I felt Jessa watching me, but I took care not to look at her.

"Welp," Russ said and shifted his seat on the stool. "That would be that last time she was at the farmers market—her booth. So sometime last week? Can't remember the day exactly. When you get to my age, days of the week and dates don't make much difference at all. When you're retired, every day is Saturday." He laughed at his own joke.

"Did you speak to her?"

"Sure did. I took her a new potted purple aster that I'd bought on sale outside the grocery store. I'd read in the paper the week before that purple asters are good fall flowers for bees. I knew that Minnie's bees were her top priority. I wanted to give her the plant to keep them healthy and happy. Maybe the way to a man's heart is through his stomach, but the way to Minnie's heart was through her bees."

"Did she accept the plant?" I asked.

"She did. Usually she puts up more of a fuss, but she just said thank you and took it."

Jessa's mouth fell open. "She said thank you? I don't think I have heard Minnie say thank you in all my days."

"It was notable to me too," Russ said. "I thought I might finally be getting somewhere with her." He sighed. "But I think she was just distracted. She kept looking around like she thought someone might jump out of the bushes and scare her."

"Did she tell you what was wrong?" I held tightly to my coffee mug.

"No." He shook his head sadly. "And I would have been very surprised if she had. I was so much on cloud nine over the fact that she said thank you—even though it might have been a distracted thank you—that I'm not sure I would have remembered what she said if she had told me. But she was jumpy. She fidgeted back and forth on her feet and said something about going home early."

Jessa and I shared a look. What it sounded like to me was that Minnie Devani had been scared. Perhaps even scared for her life.

Chapter Nineteen

After I left Jessa's Place, I headed to the Michigan Street Theater. Even if practice wasn't in session, I knew my cousin Stacey would be there, because she lived there. Literally. In early fall, she had a small one-bedroom apartment put in the old office. She had a private bathroom, a bedroom, and a kitchenette. It was a lot smaller living quarters than she had when she lived in the farmhouse on the other side of Bellamy Farm, but she was happier than I had ever seen her. In fact, she was almost cheerful about life now. Almost.

Huckleberry pranced down the street beside me with the piece of rawhide Jessa had given him when we left the diner. He was quite proud of his gift and lifted his puggish chin as if he wanted to show it off to anyone who happened by.

I glanced down at him. "When we get to the theater, I need you to be on your best behavior. You know Stacey doesn't like you coming inside. If we want you to be able to keep doing that, you need to be good."

He held his rawhide a little bit higher. I wasn't sure if that meant that he had heard me or that he was blowing me off. Knowing how stubborn pugs could be, and especially Huckleberry, I would guess it was the latter.

The Michigan Street Theater was the crown jewel of Cherry Glen's recent revival, and that was all thanks to my cousin, Stacey Bellamy. Stacey was nearly a decade older than me, and other than my father, she was my only living relative. She was a stunning woman in her forties, and when she was in high school, she was voted "most likely to be a star." She tried to live up to that. After high school, she went to New York City with the hopes of making it on Broadway. Except for a few that become megarich, it was hard to make money acting. It was even harder to do it in live theater, but she scraped by until she came back to Cherry Glen when her father died and she inherited the farm.

Last year, she sold her land to a developer in secret. When it came to light, no one was that surprised. She had no interest in farmwork when she was younger, and she always had bigger hopes. What was a surprise was that she used the money to buy the old, dilapidated theater and proceeded to fix it up.

For my entire childhood, the Michigan Street Theater had been an eyesore. It closed down in the late 1970s and fell into disrepair. Every year, the town council talked about tearing it down. The only problem was that the building was so massive the town could not afford to pay the bill to have it razed.

By the time Stacey was ready to make her move, Cherry Glen was in the midst of a revival. The old mill had been turned into a microbrewery, and boutiques were popping up all along Michigan Street. It was a perfect time for my cousin to swoop in and save the theater. It took her over a year and thousands upon thousands of dollars to update the building enough that it would be safe to have people inside, but in the end, she did it. Since opening, Stacey had been able to pull off three consecutive productions of the highest caliber and lowest budget. The *Record-Eagle* had even highlighted the theater in several feature articles, which had brought both tourists and city dwellers to the performances.

My father soon became a fixture at the theater. After playing the soothsayer in the theater's first production of *Julius Caesar*, he had caught the theater bug. I was relieved he finally had a hobby that got him out of the house and around other people.

I went into the massive building through the side door. I knew that was the one the staff and actors used and was likely to be unlocked. I found myself backstage, and I picked up Huckleberry as the door closed with a gentle thump behind us.

We were in the dark, but the murmur of voices floated out to us from the direction of the stage. Huckleberry whimpered.

I scratched the top of his head, and my eyes slowly adjusted to the dim light. "No barking," I whispered to the dog. "You know Stacey hates when you bark in the theater."

He made a muffled snort sound that only a pug could really master. It was a mixture of disdain and a call for sympathy.

"You'll be fine," I said and edged my way toward the voices. I took care as I walked. I had learned the hard way from falling and tripping over things backstage that the way to the curtain was not always clear.

I made it to the right side of the stage. The cast was dressed in prairie garb.

"This is *Oklahoma*," Stacey, who wore jeans and a flannel shirt, said. "You're missing your hope. Put more of yourself into it."

A stuffed crow stood on a hay bale in the middle of the stage. I supposed it was part of the backdrop for the scene. As soon as Huckleberry saw it, he took issue with the crow and growled deep in his throat. Maybe he remembered the crow on the scarecrow that had scared him back at the farm.

"Huck," I whispered. "It's only a prop."

The growl became deeper, and the little dog began to kick his legs like a bull. I hurried to fish his leash out of my pocket so I could set him down and hold him back from the stuffed crow at the same time.

I wasn't fast enough. Huckleberry leaped from my arms and landed on the stage with a thud. The thing about pugs is that they aren't very big, but they are dense. When they land it sounds like the floor is about to give way.

Pugs are fast too when they want to be. It sounded like an elephant invasion was coming for the cast and crew when Huckleberry made a beeline for that crow and pounced. He grabbed it by the throat and shook it with all his might. Black feathers and white stuffing flew into the air.

A member of the cast screamed.

"Shi!" Stacey shouted in her loudest voice. After a decade on Broadway, she had a strong voice and she knew how to project. It sounded like God was calling down from heaven.

I wanted to run away, but I couldn't leave Huckleberry

there on his own. Who knew what Stacey would do with him? She wasn't a pug fan. "I'm so, so sorry." I ran over to Huckleberry and took hold of the crow.

I pulled, but he held fast with his doggie death grip. There was no way I was going to get that crow away from him without a tug of war and a giant mess of feathers and stuffing flying all over the stage.

"Shi!" Stacey cried again. "What on earth is happening?"

I tickled Huckleberry under the chin. I knew that was his ticklish spot. It was enough to make him loosen his hold on the crow. I pulled, the crow's wing came off, and I fell back on my rear end holding the mangled remains.

Stacey marched over to me. I was immediately taken back to so many childhood memories of when Stacey, my older cousin, had loomed over me in judgment when she thought I was doing something stupid, which honestly had been pretty often. It was still a common occurrence for us, even now that I was in my late thirties.

I scrambled to my feet. "I'm sorry about the crow. I'll replace it."

She put her hands on her hips. "You bet you will. It was an important prop for our scene."

My brows knit together. I didn't remember a crow being mentioned in *Oklahoma* any of the times I'd seen the musical.

The three actors on the stage shifted back and forth on their feet.

"Take five," she said to them. "I need to talk to my cousin."

She didn't have to tell them twice. They melted into the

stage wings and disappeared. "Now, tell me what you're doing here. Uncle Sully isn't here."

"I'm not looking for Dad. I wanted to talk to you."

Huckleberry chewed on what was left of the fake crow a few feet away.

"I just have to get that away from Huckleberry first. He could get sick if he swallows any of it." I tried to grab at the crow again, but Huckleberry would not let go of it. "I don't know what's gotten into him."

Huckleberry shook his head, and feathers went flying in all directions.

"Drop it!" Stacey pointed at the pug.

He opened his mouth and the crow fell out. I supposed he knew when there was an alpha present. I didn't know what that said about me. Did Huckleberry not see me as the alpha dog in our relationship?

She snatched the bird from my lap and tossed it back on the hay bale. Huckleberry stared at it. Stacey pointed at him again. "Don't even think about it."

Miraculously, he lay down in the middle of the stage.

Yep, Huckleberry definitely didn't see me as an alpha dog.

"I really am sorry," I said and placed a hand on my sore tailbone. The stage was hard.

Huckleberry lay on the floor with his eyes closed. I wondered if he was playing dead to avoid my cousin's wrath. I wished that was a card that I could play. I would most certainly use it if I could.

"That still doesn't tell me what you're doing here. We don't have a show tonight. I don't need help with ticket sales."

In the past, I had volunteered to run the ticket booth on show nights for my cousin. When I say "volunteered," I really mean I was *ordered* to sell tickets.

"My feet are killing me from standing on them all morning." She walked to the edge of the stage, sat, and let her legs hang over the edge into the orchestra pit.

I did the same a few feet from her. There wasn't much in the pit at the moment, just a handful of music stands and one folding chair. A forgotten piece of sheet music lay on the concrete floor. Before the performance, it would be full with musicians, instruments, stands, chairs, and sheet music. Sometimes it was packed so tightly, I wondered how the musicians could play at all.

Stacey must have noticed me staring down into the pit because she said, "*Oklahoma* is the first musical this theater has done in over fifty years. Musicals are even more popular than plays, and I'm hoping to make a good profit off the production. If we do, we could do more shows and employ more people. We have to be perfect to achieve those goals. Everything must be perfect."

I raised an eyebrow at her. "I'm not sure that theater is that much different from television production in the fact that the one thing a producer could count on was something would always go wrong. In most cases, more than just one thing went wrong. My hope was always that whatever went wrong was fixable. I didn't dare hope everything would go perfectly."

She scowled at me. "Maybe you set your sights too low then."

Before I could respond to that, she said again, "We have to be perfect. There is so much riding on this."

"Then I won't take up much of your time."

She frowned. "That I seriously doubt. Are you here about the guy who bought my old farm?"

"Tanner?" I asked.

"Yes, I think that's his name. I met him briefly at Jessa's Place. Handsome guy. I'd be interested in him if I had time for men right now. I don't. I'm married to this theater."

I bit my tongue to stop myself from saying anything I might regret. Stacey and I had always had a rocky relationship. In many ways she still viewed me as her annoying younger cousin. I decided when dealing with her it was best just to cut to the chase. "I want to talk to you about Minnie, not Tanner."

She eyed me. "You mean Joan the Bandit? Who knew we had such a notorious criminal in our midst?"

"When was the last time you saw her?"

She shrugged. "It was probably when I fired her two weeks ago?"

"You fired her? I thought she volunteered to work the snack booth like I did the ticket booth. Can you fire a volunteer?"

"I can," Stacey said, as if it was the easiest thing in the world.

"Why did you fire her?" I asked.

"I caught her dipping into the till. The theater is barely scrapping by, and she pocketed money from concessions. There was no way I could let her deal with the theater money after that."

"How much did she take?" I asked.

"Forty dollars that night, but it was the only night I caught her. My guess was it was not the first time. I asked her if she had taken money before, and, of course, she said no. I didn't expect her to admit she took more." She paused. "Now that I know she made a fortune robbing banks, it makes more sense. I couldn't understand why she was taking money from the theater when we were so supportive of her."

"Are you sure that money was stolen?" As soon as I asked the question, I regretted it. The way I said it implied I thought my cousin might be lying.

Stacey gritted her teeth. "I saw her take the forty dollars out of the cash register and stick it in her pocket. She didn't know I was there when she did it. I caught her red-handed, and she should have been grateful I didn't call the police. After the show that night and after I had kicked her out of the theater for good and inventoried the snacks we had, the amount of money we made over the last two months didn't match with the number of snacks in storage. With as much food as was gone, we should have had more money. So someone, my guess is Minnie, was either stealing money or merchandise. That was more than enough reason to can her, even if she was a volunteer."

"Couldn't it have been someone else who worked in concessions?" I held my hands up. "I'm sorry. I do not doubt your story, just playing devil's advocate."

"You're not very good at it." She sighed. "I suppose that could be true, but the rest of the concession staff is high school kids volunteering for extra credit in their high school drama class. I have a couple of college-aged kids too, who volunteer because they want to break into the business. Even if those volunteers were the ones to take the money, Minnie, as their supervisor, would be ultimately responsible, and these are nerdy theater kids who are dying to be cast in a production. They wouldn't do anything to put that at risk. I can say that because I was the type too."

I arched my brow. I didn't think anyone in their life would call my knockout cousin nerdy.

"They were terrified of Minnie too," she went on to say. "I can't see a single one of them daring to end up on her bad side for a candy bar or a bag of chips."

"Who's head of the concessions now?"

"Whit. She's one of the students. Great kid and is clamoring to be in one of the productions. She will do any dumb job I give her with a smile on her face. She hopes it will get her closer to a part in a play or musical. It won't hurt her, but the roles always come down to acting and singing talent. If we want to be the top theater in Grand Traverse County, we have to use the best talent we can find. She reminds me a lot of me. I used to hang around theaters in Traverse City and beg for a chance to audition in local groups."

I hadn't known this about my cousin's life, but she was ten years older than me. When she would have been doing that, I would have still been in grade school.

"I know Whit. Her older sister Chesney works for me at the farm." Whit was also someone I wanted to talk to, since she had found Minnie's body first. What had she seen or heard right before she found Minnie? I needed to find out.

"Oh, that's right," she murmured.

"Does Whit know about the stolen money?" I asked.

"She sure does. She was there the night I saw Minnie stealing from the concessions stand. She witnessed me blowing my top."

I had seen Stacey blow her top several times in my life, and it was never pretty.

"So you didn't see Minnie after you kicked her out of the theater?" I asked.

She shook her head.

"Cherry Glen is a small town. It's hard for me to believe that you didn't bump into her somewhere," I said.

She frowned at me. "I didn't." She held her hands aloft. "There are whole days that I never leave this theater. I work here, live here, and sleep here. If I have enough food to get me through, I don't leave, especially not in the middle of a production as important to the sustainability of the Michigan Street Theater as *Oklahoma.* This could be the musical that puts us on the map outside of Michigan and throughout the entire Midwest, if not the country." Her face flushed as she spoke of it. "I'd do anything to get us that kind of publicity."

Even murder?

Chapter Twenty

S tacey said Whit was probably in the concessions area, if I wanted to speak to her before I left the theater. I most certainly did. I would feel much better if Whit could corroborate my cousin's story about Minnie taking money from the theater.

Stacey and her cast returned to rehearsal, and Huckleberry and I left the theater and headed to the building's lobby through a set of double doors. We found ourselves on a wide landing that led to the ornate stairs in the middle of the building. The stairs went from the theater proper to the first floor, where the lobby, ticketing, and concessions were.

On show nights, this was where I would be. I had only seen snippets of my cousin's productions because it was my job—with no pay—to care for the ticket booth. I dreaded those nights. However, I realized I didn't dread it because of the customers or because of the stress or anything like that. I dreaded it because of Minnie. The ticket booth was right next to concessions. Minnie made a point of making me feel unwelcome.

I found Whit in baggy jeans and a hooded sweatshirt sitting cross-legged on the floor behind the concessions window. Her clothes were casual, but her hair was ready for a night on the town—black curls with bright-yellow tips. It was an eye-catching and beautiful look that I guessed would make anyone over thirty look like a clown or worse.

In her lap was a box of corn chips. She counted the bags. "Whit?"

She yelped and the corn chips flew into the air. She scrambled to her feet. "Can I help you?" She more shouted the question than asked it.

"I'm so sorry to have startled you."

She let out a deep breath. "It's okay. I was concentrating hard. Counting is one of my least favorite things to do, but I promised Stacey I would give her an accurate count of everything in the concession booth."

"Can I help you pick up the chips?"

"Sure." She shrugged. "I'm going to count them over again as it is."

I walked to the door to the right of the concession window and went into the booth. We cleaned up the fallen chips quickly.

I set my last bag in the box. "I love your hair. It reminds me of a bee."

"Really? That's what I was going for. Bees are my symbol." She pulled up the sleeve of her sweatshirt and showed me her wrist. There was a black and yellow tattoo etched into her skin.

"Your symbol?"

Huckleberry sat next to Whit, and she scratched his head. "Bees have always been part of my family. My grandfather kept them and so did my parents. They are all gone now, and the tattoo reminds me of them. Chesney and I really want to keep bees, but we never have because we're so busy. They need a lot more care than people think. It was nice living next to Minnie because of the bees. That's the only reason it was nice though." She wrinkled her nose. "I'm sorry she's dead and all, but she wasn't the best neighbor."

"I'm so sorry about your grandfather and parents. Chesney told me a little bit about them in the past."

She nodded and pulled her sleeve back down. "It's just one of those things." She patted her curls. "And thanks for the compliment on my hair. Stacey said if I finish my tasks here in concessions before the end of today's rehearsal, she will let me try out. I want to look my best. That's why I'm so nervous too. I'm freaking out she's giving me a chance. I can't blow it."

I pressed my lips together. In my opinion, my cousin should let Whit try out no matter the status of the concessions. It was Minnie's fault they were in such a mess, not Whit's. I stopped just short of saying that though. I think any criticism of Stacey would only make Whit more nervous about her audition.

"Stacey said that running a theater is more than acting, and if I wanted to break into this industry, I have to start at the bottom."

It seemed that Stacey was making sure Whit was right at the bottom. "She may be right. I learned that the hard way after fifteen years working in film and television in California."

Her eyes lit up. "You worked in film and television? I thought you were a farmer!"

"I was a producer for many years before I came home to take care of the family farm."

She clapped her hands. "There are so many things that you can teach me."

"The first of those is to have a little bit of fun. I'll help you count the snacks that are left, so you can get ready for your audition." I smiled.

Her mouth fell open. "Don't you have something more important to do?"

The truth was I did. I had several more important things to do. I had a farm to save and a murder to solve. However, the girl obviously needed help, and I didn't think Stacey was going to volunteer.

Whit and I got to work counting the snacks, and I got down to business on what I really wanted to know. "You were pretty spooked when you found the body."

She stared at me from her spot on the floor. "Wouldn't you be? It's not that often you find someone who has been strangled."

"You knew she was strangled just from looking at her?" I asked.

"Duh. I mean, she had the scarf wrapped around her neck, and her eyes were bugged out of her head."

I grimaced at the overly accurate description. "What were you doing over by the scarecrow?" I asked.

She blinked at me. "What do you mean?"

"When you found the body, what were you doing over on that side of the farm?"

She looked away, as if suddenly finding the bags of chips

to be oh-so-interesting. "I don't know. It was a festival. I was checking everything out."

I frowned. I was willing to bet my grandmother's mythical treasure on the fact that she was lying to me.

She looked me in the eye. "Where should I have been? I was only there to support my sister. She had been talking about Fall Daze for weeks. After I went through the corn maze and ate a piece of pie, there wasn't much else to do, so I wandered around for a bit. What is the harm in that?"

"Nothing, but the scarecrow is way off the beaten path of the festival on the other side of the parking lot. There was nothing going on over there."

Her face turned red. "Okay, I was rehearsing."

"Rehearsing?" I asked.

Her face turned a little redder. "For my audition with Stacey. I was going to pretend the scarecrow was another actor to play off of. Sometimes it's easier to act if you have a face to look at."

"You were going to act with the scarecrow."

"Don't say it like that," she groaned. "You make me sound like a crazy person."

I held up my hands. "No judgment here. I lived in LA, remember. I met hundreds of actors, and they all have their own methods for getting into character."

She relaxed slightly. "It just makes me feel silly, so I'd rather you not tell Chief Randy. He won't understand. Being part of Michigan Street Theater is *really* important to me. Do you remember what it was like to be my age and want something so bad it almost hurts?"

I did. "I won't mention it to the chief."

Her shoulders sagged. "Thanks."

I changed the subject. "Stacey told me about the money and snacks that went missing."

Whit relaxed and seemed relieved we weren't talking about the murder anymore. "Yeah, I feel so bad about that. I should have kept a better eye on things. If I had, I might have noticed what Minnie was doing sooner. Did you know that she's a convict? It's the weirdest thing I've ever heard."

I nodded. "Everyone at Jessa's Place was talking about it."

She placed a box of gummy bears on the counted stack. "The town's tongues will be wagging about this for months to come. If they don't find the killer, it might be even longer. I heard her death had something to do with the farmers market."

I grimaced at the thought that even college students were hearing about Kristy's possible involvement in the murder. Then again, Cherry Glen was small. Everyone was talking about it.

"I usually run the ticket booth here at the theater on show nights. I'm surprised I've never seen you here before."

"I was here, and I've seen you working. Minnie didn't want anyone up front in the concession stand but herself on show nights."

"Why's that?" I asked.

She shrugged. "Because she was a control freak? I don't know. Minnie was horrible to all of us. You know, the type of woman who hated teenagers and young people. She probably hated them when she was a teenager and young person too. Although I think she was born an adult or made in a lab or something. Like someone wanted to create the ultimate Karen and unleash her on the world."

"That's an interesting theory."

"I read a lot of sci-fi. It's my ultimate goal to appear in a Star Trek movie someday." She eyed me. "Did you work on Star Trek?"

I shook my head. "Nope."

She frowned, and I had a feeling her estimation of me went down a couple of notches. She moved a box of chocolate chip cookies and perked up again. "But you have connections in Hollywood still, right? Do you know any famous directors you can connect me with? If I had an 'in' to the business, I know I could get a lot further. Could you write a letter for me? What about just a text? I promise you won't regret it, and I will thank you in my Oscar acceptance speech."

I held the bags of chips I was counting in my hands and stared at her.

She placed a hand on her smooth cheek. "Sorry, sometimes I get carried away. I just want to act so badly. My drama professor said of all the students he has ever had in class, I had the best shot." She glanced around. "He's like a hundred years old and taught at Cherry Glen High when Stacey was a student there. He thinks I'm better than her." She looked around some more. "Well, better than she was as a teenager. I have seen her onstage and she is incredible. She becomes the characters, you know? I can see why she did so well on Broadway." She folded her arms. "I have to think that if she made a different decision and went to Hollywood, things would have been different. She could have been a star!"

"Stacey preferred live theater," I said. "She wasn't going to find that much in LA. Even sitcoms have moved over to closed sets for the most part. Less liability."

She nodded. "There is nothing like a live audience. I mean, I have only felt it at high school and college productions, but I'm hopeful that Stacey will give me a shot here at the Michigan Street Theater. I love the stage, but I feel like there's more money in television or streaming."

"There can be. But it takes a bit of luck to make any money on either coast. It's a tough business. I'm not saying that to discourage you. I just want to be honest since I can tell you are taking this so seriously."

She tugged on her earring. "I know, but I can do it," she said confidently.

I didn't say anything more that might dampen her mood. She would find out soon enough how difficult acting could be. She would need her self-confidence to go to audition after audition.

"I'm curious if you and Minnie ever talked about bees, since she was a beekeeper."

She began packing up some chocolate bars she had counted earlier. "I asked her once if I could help with the bees. She didn't like that idea. She said no one touched her bees." She wrinkled her nose. "It wasn't like I was going to touch them. I'm not an idiot. I tried another time and told her about my family and beekeeping and I even showed her my tattoo." She shook her head as if it all came to a sad end.

"What happened?" I asked.

She closed the box. "It was the weirdest thing. All of the color drained from her face and she told me to get away from her."

I raised my brow. "Get away from her?"

"I don't know. She almost acted like I was an evil spirit or a ghost."

Could it have been a ghost from her past?

Chapter Twenty-One

I didn't know what to think about Minnie's reaction to Whit's honeybee tattoo. It was just so odd. Minnie had been uninterested in other people to the point of rudeness, but I had never heard of her being scared. But this incident with Whit was now the second time someone had described her that way. How much did that have to do with her recent financial struggles and how much with her past as Joan the Bandit?

Shaking my head, Huckleberry and I went out of the front door of the theater. Just as I stepped outside, a man bumped into me. "Excuse me," he called distractedly as he jogged away.

"What the…" But the question died on my lips when I saw three television crew vans and a group of people gathered outside the municipal building.

I scooped up Huckleberry and held him to my chest, hurrying after the man I assumed was a reporter on the hunt for a good story.

There was such a crowd in front of me I couldn't see what everyone was looking at. It appeared that the entire dining room from Jessa's Place was out in the middle of Michigan Street trying to see what was happening.

Then there was the camera and sound crews holding cameras, booms, and microphones high in the air to contend with too. I couldn't see a thing.

"Thank you all for coming today," a clear, strong voice rang out. To my ears, the voice sounded like that of Marshal Lynn Chuff. "I know you are all eager to hear about our progress in the case."

Holding Huckleberry a little bit closer to keep my elbows close to my body, I murmured excuses and apologies to the people around me as I wiggled through the crowd until I was close enough to see Marshal Chuff standing behind a narrow podium in front of the main doors to the municipal building. Chief Randy stood a few feet behind her, so close to the door that he must have been touching it with his back. He scowled at the marshal and the crowd in turn.

Connie Baskins stood on the other side of the glass doors with her face pressed up against the windowpane. It must have killed her not to be outside with the crowd.

"What we have learned is that Joan Marino was living here in Cherry Glen for the last ten years under the assumed name of Minnie Devani. As Minnie, she was a productive member of the community and made her income selling honey from the bees she kept on her property. She had friends, went to church, and ran her business. She had the typical small-town life, but all this time she was keeping this terrible secret.

"In recent months the U.S. Marshals Service was tipped off that Joan was still alive and living somewhere in the middle of the country. That was all that was known. Joan could have been anywhere. However, just when the agency was going to let the case go, another tip came in and we continued our investigation. It wasn't until after the body was discovered at a local farm that we thought there might be a connection between Joan and Minnie Devani. This case is ever evolving, but the U.S. Marshals Service is dedicated to seeing it through to the end.

"Joan Marino was responsible for more than twenty ATM holdups throughout the Midwest in the 1990s. What she and her accomplice did had a great effect on the people she took the money from. Her actions caused real, lasting damage to human lives, which is why we, as a department, want to know if her death was in any way connected to her life before she was Minnie Devani. That's what we are here to do."

A slim reporter in a gray trench coat with the collar popped up raised her hand, and when Marshal Chuff gave the nod, she said, "Do you have any suspects?"

"We're talking to a lot of people and taking stock of Joan's life as Minnie, but we do not have any formal suspects at this time," she said in a businesslike manner.

I let out a breath, so relieved that she didn't mention Kristy being a suspect.

"You said that the U.S. Marshals Service, your agency, received two tips as to the whereabouts of Joan Marino. Who was your source?" the same reporter asked.

I wondered the same thing. I also wondered why Marshal Chuff told me that she had gotten only one tip as to Joan's whereabouts. Why would she lie about that?

Marshal Chuff made a face. "The U.S. Marshals Service

is very careful to protect our informants. That information is confidential."

I frowned. She told me she didn't know who the informant was. It made me wonder why she didn't say it was an anonymous tip to the reporter.

Another reporter I couldn't see in the crowd spoke up. "What made you suspect that Minnie Devani might in fact be Joan Marino?"

"Joan had a very distinctive honeybee tattoo on her right shoulder, and when the report of Minnie's murder came in with the description of this tattoo, I had a hunch that this might be Joan. Of course, I didn't know until I reached Grand Traverse County that my hunch was right. When looking for missing people who are either abducted or who choose to disappear on their own, you have to follow your hunches."

A honeybee tattoo? Like Whit's? Could that be why Minnie had such a strange reaction to Whit's tattoo? Maybe Whit's tattoo reminded her of her past life?

"Chief Randy, do you have anything to add?" the gray trench coat reporter called out.

Chief Randy stepped up to the podium. Marshal Chuff stepped back, but not before the two of them shared a scowl. It was clear that Marshal Chuff and Chief Randy were not the best of friends.

The chief smoothed his black mustache before speaking. "Now, ladies and gents, I know that it's exciting to have a notorious bandit in our little town—and up and die here of all things, but I can assure you whatever Minnie's alleged past might have been, whoever killed her was from Cherry Glen."

The crowd gasped. Half a dozen camera shutters went off.

Marshal Chuff took a step forward as if she was going to say something, but the chief blocked her with his body. "We have a person of interest in the case, and we're confident that this will all be wrapped up very soon. It will come as no surprise that Minnie was having trouble with the local farmers market. The market had had trouble in recent months…"

I felt sick to my stomach and searched the crowd for any sign of Kristy. She had to know the press conference was happening. It was right in the middle of town. The farmers market was just one block over. I was certain that her phone was blowing up as friends and neighbors wanted to be the first to tell her what was going on.

However, Kristy was petite, and in the crowd of people standing outside of the municipal building, I couldn't see her.

"That seems to imply you think the farmers market is somehow involved," the gray trench coat reporter said. "Can you elaborate on that?"

I stood on my tiptoes to get a better look at the asker's face. Of all the media there, she was the most determined to get answers. She had perfect makeup and hair, so I surmised that she worked for television, not a newspaper. The large cameraman standing behind her was another clue.

Huckleberry blew his doggy breath in my face, but there was no way I was putting him down with so many people around.

"I'd be happy to," Chief Randy said. "It seems that there had been a dispute between Minnie and the director of the farmers market. I believe that is tied to the murder. Not to mention—"

His speech was shortened as Marshal Chuff pushed him away from the podium. Chief Randy gaped at her and stumbled to the other side of the podium.

"What Chief Randy was trying to tell you," Marshal Chuff said, "is that we are not at liberty to talk about the details of an open homicide case. As more information comes to light and when the U.S. Marshals Services deems it is appropriate, we will be more forthcoming."

Behind Marshal Chuff, Chief Randy seethed. I was surprised smoke didn't come out of his ears.

"Thank you all for your time," the marshal said, making it clear the press conference was over.

Reporters shouted out questions, but Marshal Chuff acted like she couldn't hear any of them. The chief and the marshal went back inside of the municipal building, and neither one looked very happy with how the press conference went. Connie's face was no longer pushed up against the glass.

When it became clear they weren't coming back outside, the reporters and camera crews packed up. As they left Michigan Street, I hoped they would go back to Traverse City or wherever they came from and never return. The townsfolk were a little more reluctant to leave. Many of them whispered about what Chief Randy had said. Every time I heard Kristy's name, I winced.

Even if she wasn't there and didn't hear it for herself, it would reach her soon. The entire village knew that Kristy was in the middle of a dispute with Minnie when the beekeeper died.

I pulled my cell phone from my pocket and called my friend. There was no answer, and I knew why. Kristy and her husband stood a few feet away. Kristy waved her hands around when she spoke. She was beside herself. Thankfully, the twins weren't with them. Even though they were too small to know what was happening, they didn't need to see their mother so upset, with her arms flailing in all directions.

I walked over to them but kept my distance so Kristy wouldn't smack me as she waved her arms around as she spoke.

"Kent, this could ruin me. What if the girls learn about this?" There were tears in Kristy's eyes.

"Kristy," Kent said in a gentle voice. "They're three months old and won't remember any of this."

"But having a mother who is arrested for murder, even if I'm found innocent, could come back to haunt them. I don't want that for them."

"And neither do I," he said quietly. "But it won't come to that."

"How do you know?" she hissed. "After what he said, I'm surprised he didn't arrest me in front of the reporters."

"I'm sorry to say that I'm surprised too," I interjected. "Something stopped him. He would have arrested you if he could have. There must not be enough evidence."

Kent nodded. "Shiloh is right."

Kristy threw up her hands. "Could it be because I'm inno-cent and had nothing to do with this?"

"We know that." I glanced over my shoulder to make sure there weren't any reporters lurking about. "However, the chief must have a big reason. Maybe there is another suspect."

"One can only hope." Kristy tugged on the ends of her hair as if the habit comforted her somehow. "Between being a new mom up all night with the twins, the farmers market's missing money, and now, being a murder suspect, I don't know if there is much more I can take."

"Don't worry." I put my hand on her arm. "There has to be another suspect. I'll find out who that person is. I won't let Chief Randy arrest you."

She hugged me. As I hugged her back, I wondered if it was a promise I could keep.

Over her shoulder, I saw the reporter in the gray trench coat watching us like Esmeralda stalking a mouse.

Chapter Twenty-Two

K ent said he needed to return to the high school. Kristy hugged him. "Thanks for sneaking away on your free period. I really needed your support."

He kissed her cheek. "Anytime. You know that."

After Kent left, Kristy squeezed her hands together. "I'm going to go pick up the girls from my in-laws. I can't go back to work at the farmers market office right now. It will be crawling with reporters after what Chief Randy said."

I realized she must be right.

With my friends gone, I should have headed to my farm because Chesney would be there within the hour looking for guidance on what project to tackle next. I shot my assistant a text telling her to use the brush hog, which was just a powerful mower that could cut down weeds and brambles that were several feet high. It hooked onto the back of the tractor. After Chesney finished the mowing, we would tarp the ground with black plastic sheeting to starve the remaining weeds of sunlight. When we removed the tarp in the spring, the weeds and other plants would be dead, decomposed into the earth, making clean, rich soil to plant in. It was a good start, even though I hadn't decided what I wanted to sow in that field just yet. I also told her I was running an errand and would be home as soon as I could.

She texted back and said she would get on it. I let out a sigh of relief, not knowing what I would do without her help. With Chesney and me working our hardest, I knew that Bellamy Farm really had a chance to come back from the brink. I looked forward to next spring and summer, when we would begin to see the fruits of our labor.

I tucked my concerns about the farm into the back of my mind. It was time to do something I had been avoiding since Minnie's body was found: confront Doreen Killian.

The Killians lived on the outskirts of Cherry Glen. The Killian home sat a couple acres back from a county road, two miles from the center of town. As I drove to their house, I thought over what I was going to say to Doreen, but nothing sounded right. "Huckleberry," I said to the pug next to me.

He looked up at me from his post on the passenger seat.

"We are just going to have to wing it."

He covered his face with his paw. It appeared my dog believed this conversation with Doreen was going to be a disaster too.

When I reached Doreen's house, there were three other cars in the driveway. The Killians had company. Maybe that was a good thing. Doreen certainly would be on her best behavior if she knew she had an audience, wouldn't she? One could only hope.

Huckleberry sat up in his seat when I got out of the car. I pointed at the seat. "Stay."

He whimpered.

"I'm sorry, Huck, but Doreen doesn't like animals. I can't upset her from the get-go by bringing you with me. It's a nice cool day." I grabbed his car blanket from the back seat and tucked it around him. I cracked the car windows for some airflow too. "Snuggle in and take a nap. I wish I could join you."

The pug sighed, as if this was another example of the suffering he endured as a pampered pet, but snuggled down into the blanket and closed his eyes.

At the front door, I heard the murmur of voices. I stood there for a few minutes trying to work up the nerve to ring the doorbell.

I lifted my finger just an inch from the button, when the door flew open. I jumped back as a woman with her hair pulled back in a tight coil held on to the doorknob. She wasn't looking at me, but back into the house. "Doreen Killian, I will never forgive you for this. Never."

"That doesn't hurt me in the least," Doreen's sharp voice shot back from somewhere inside.

"Get out of my way!" the woman ordered me as she pushed out of the door.

I tripped over a large potted mum by the front door. A little bit of dirt fell out of the pot onto Doreen's pristine wooden porch. I brushed it away with the toe of my boot.

Doreen stepped into the doorframe. She was a thin, tall woman with an exacting silver bob that fell just below her ears. She wore slim fit khaki pants, a floral blouse, and gold jewelry. On her feet she wore loafers so shiny they looked like they had come straight from the store. She waved at the woman's back. "You're not welcome back into my home,

Clementine, or in my church. If you keep this up, we will have you run right out of Cherry Glen."

Clementine made a rude gesture with her hand before climbing into a blue minivan and driving away.

"What are you doing here?" Doreen glared at me.

Two other women close to Doreen's age poked their heads out of the door. "Doreen," the taller of the two said, "was it really necessary to chase Clementine off like that?"

Doreen glared at the woman who dared question her.

"Can we go back to talking about the book? Isn't that why we are here?" the second woman asked in a breathy voice. She couldn't have been a millimeter over five feet tall and had short, red hair. With her small features, she reminded me of a pixie.

"Is this a book club meeting?" I asked.

"Yes," the pixie woman with the breathy voice said. "Are you a reader?" She glanced at Doreen. "We've recently lost two members. We would love to have another person."

"She's not joining our book club. She shouldn't be here at all. You're not welcome in my home." Doreen put her hands on her hips.

"She's not technically inside your home," the first woman said.

"No one wants to hear your opinion, Ruby," Doreen snapped.

That wasn't true. I would have loved to hear Ruby's opinion. It was quite a change to hear someone correct Doreen.

Ruby stepped through the door, and the smaller woman followed her. "I think we have to call this meeting of the book club a bust. Minnie is dead, and now you have kicked Clementine out of the group. How are we even supposed to have a decent conversation with just three people?"

Doreen scowled. "We can discuss the future of the book club at a later time. We haven't even had Minnie's funeral yet."

"Don't you mean Joan?" Ruby arched her penciled-on eyebrow.

Doreen's face turned bright red. "Don't say that to me. The rumor going around that Minnie was Joan the Bandit is completely and utterly false. I won't hear it."

Ruby looked like she wanted to say something more but thought better of it.

"In fact"—Doreen pointed a manicured red nail at me—"I wouldn't be the least bit surprised if *she* wasn't the one who started that rumor to remove suspicion."

I placed a hand to my chest. "Remove suspicion?"

"Yes, you said something to distract from the fact that Minnie was killed on your farm. What do you know about her death?" Doreen asked.

"Oh, you must be Shiloh Bellamy," Ruby said. "Doreen talks about you all the time."

"And not in a good way," the pixie added.

"I don't think that was called for, Louise," Doreen said.

Louise dropped her head.

"Don't get on Louise's case, Doreen. We can't afford to lose another book club member. Really, if it was just you and me discussing the books, we would never get anywhere. We rarely have the same opinion." Ruby paused. "About anything."

Doreen pressed her lips together. "That doesn't change the fact that Shiloh is a problem." Doreen narrowed her eyes at me. "Randy told me about the federal agent. Are you the one who called her?"

I blinked at her. "No. I had no idea about Minnie's past, so I wouldn't have called anyone about her at all."

She pressed her lips together. "Minnie told me someone was harassing her. I wouldn't be the least bit surprised if it was you."

"Did you tell her about her real identity?" I asked.

She glared at me. "Minnie Devani *was* her real identity. It was the only identity that mattered to me as her friend. This story claiming her real name is Joan Marino is complete trash. I won't listen to it anymore. Clementine insisted on spreading that rumor, and you saw what happened to her."

From what I could tell, what happened to her was that she had been kicked out of the book club. I knew it was a close-knit group, but I'm not sure that punishment would have any lasting impact on Clementine.

"Clementine will be back," Ruby said with confidence. "You two just had a little tiff." She turned to me. "There is not a single person in the group that Doreen hasn't kicked out of her house before. That goes for Minnie too."

I raised my eyebrow. I would have loved to know what led Doreen to kick Minnie out of her house.

"Doreen's never kicked *me* out of her house," Louise said barely above a whisper.

"You're a mouse, Louise. No one ever kicked a church mouse out of anywhere."

"What are you doing here, Shiloh? Hazel is not here. She's in school. If you had children of your own, you would know that."

It seemed to me Doreen chose to ignore Ruby's comment that Clementine would be back. Perhaps Doreen didn't want to reduce their numbers any more than she already had by kicking Ruby out too.

"I'm not here to talk to Hazel. I wanted to give you my condolences about Minnie."

Doreen looked me up and down, and it felt like she was sizing me up for a straitjacket or, worse, a prison uniform. I guessed that Doreen would be happy to see me in either place if it kept me away from her son and granddaughter.

"Your condolences? Minnie has been dead for three days and you are just now coming around to say you're sorry to hear about it? Wouldn't a card have worked just as well to share your sentiments?"

If I had sent Doreen a card of any sort, she probably would have burned it.

She shook her head. "I don't care what false narrative you make up about my friend. I know who she really was. She was my friend." Her voice broke. "And now she's dead."

Louise and Ruby shared a look.

I wanted to reach out and touch her arm to comfort her. I clasped my hands together, physically holding myself back. My gesture would not be welcome. Instead I asked, "Did Minnie ever talk to you about having money trouble?"

"No, Minnie was a talented beekeeper. She wasn't in need of money. She was doing so well for herself."

"How much has your husband told you about the case?" I asked.

"He's told me enough to know that you, Kristy Brown, and this so-called federal marshal are all determined to make Minnie look bad. You won't listen to the facts." She pointed at her chest. "I knew Minnie better than anyone. She was my closest friend. If she was an escaped convict or having money troubles, I would have known about it. Friends don't keep secrets from each other."

Again, Louise and Ruby shared a look, and I was really starting to wonder what that was all about.

"I do care about what happened to Minnie," I said. "There have just been a lot of surprising details, and we are trying to sort it all out."

She took a step toward me. "Why?"

I swallowed. "Why?"

She narrowed her blue eyes. "Why are you trying to sort it all out? You aren't a police officer. It's not your place. My husband is the one who should be doing this."

"I agree; Chief Randy should head up the investigation, and you're right, as a farmer, maybe this is not how I should be spending my time. However, I don't think the police chief is considering all the evidence. I know it must be upsetting to have another murder so soon in Cherry Glen, but he can't jump to conclusions just to put an end to all this more quickly."

Her face flushed beet red, and I realized my mistake. I should have never criticized her husband. Ruby winced and stepped back as if she didn't want to be near in case Doreen spewed fire.

Doreen shook her bejeweled finger at me. "Get off my property, and stay away from my granddaughter. I know the plan that you have for her."

"Plan?" I asked. "What are you talking about?"

She pointed at me with her pink manicured nail. "You think that by getting Hazel to love you, you'll become closer to my son."

"What?" That was *not* what I had expected her to say.

She put her hands on her hips. "Quinn is my only child, and you will not sink your claws into him like you did Logan Graham all those years ago. Logan was killed because of you. You don't get a second chance with his best friend."

Louise and Ruby both gasped. I suppose I might have gasped too if I hadn't stopped breathing. I knew Doreen didn't like me, but I didn't think her hate for me went this far.

My mouth was dry, but I forced my lips to move. "I don't know where you got that idea, but you're wrong. Hazel and Quinn are my neighbors and friends. Hazel enjoys being on the farm. There is nothing more to it than that."

"If that's what you think, then you are lying to yourself as well as everyone else." She went back into the house and slammed the door in all our faces.

Chapter Twenty-Three

"Oh dear," Louise said, wringing her hands. "I left my reading glasses in there."

"Forget about them," Ruby said. "You don't want go back in there right now. She'll cool down by the time we meet for book club next week. She always does."

I wanted to ask these two seemingly normal women why they kept coming back to Doreen's book club if this was the way she behaved, but I held my tongue.

"But what am I supposed to do until then? How am I supposed to read the next book if I can't see it?" Louise whined.

"Buy a new pair at the general store. They have a nice display there. I got a pair with red sparkly frames." She glanced at me. "Are you all right, Shiloh? You look like you're in shock."

Because I was. I was very much in shock. How could Doreen think I was after her son? Yes, people in town (most notably Connie Baskins) had made suggestions that Quinn and I should date, but that did not mean Quinn and I wanted that sort of relationship. Sometimes I thought people put us together in their minds because of our age and our mutual connection to Logan. That wasn't fair to either of us.

I shook my head. "It's my fault. I knew Doreen wasn't my biggest fan. I just didn't know how far her dislike went."

"Well," Ruby said. "I have seen Doreen yell and be rude to just about everyone in this town, but she's never been that vicious before. You must have really ticked her off."

"Not on purpose." I sighed.

"She doesn't want to lose her son to you," Louise murmured. "That's what she's afraid of. She was heartbroken when Quinn ran away to Detroit after Logan died. Even worse, he fell in love, got married, and had Hazel. She was convinced he would never come back."

Ruby nodded. "Sometimes I think that she was happy when Quinn's wife died. It gave her the opportunity to twist his arm to come home. It's difficult to turn down free childcare when you are a single parent."

"That's horrible," I said.

Louise shrugged. "Families are complicated."

I wondered if she had a lung condition like asthma or something else because it sounded like every breath took some effort. Ruby must have noticed it too because she said, "Louise, do you have your inhaler with you?"

The smaller woman nodded. "It's in my car."

"Well, take it. Don't stand around having an asthma attack if you can avoid it."

Louise nodded and went to her car.

Ruby shook her head. "Louise just lets Doreen fluster her so much."

"You don't get flustered by Doreen?"

"Not really, but I was close this time when she was saying all the horrible things about you."

"What she said about Hazel and Quinn isn't true," I said and then immediately regretted it. I didn't need to explain myself to a woman I had just met.

"You don't need to make any excuses to me. If it were true, I wouldn't blame you. Quinn has to be the handsomest unattached young man in the county."

I wondered what Ruby would think when she saw Tanner.

"Hazel just helps me out at the farm when she can." Again, I was explaining myself. It seemed to me I was protesting a bit too much. I changed the subject. "The woman who was here earlier, Clementine, why did Doreen kick her out of the house?"

"For the same reason she asked you to leave. Clementine was saying truths about Minnie that Doreen just isn't open to hearing."

"About Joan the Bandit?" I asked.

"Among others. Clementine, Doreen, and Minnie all were members of the same church, and Clementine, who is in charge of the church's monthly dinners they use as fundraisers for their mission groups, claimed Minnie stole from the coffers. She really got that idea in her head when the news about Joan the Bandit got out. Did you know that there was a press conference in town about it today? I would have gone if I didn't have book club. I knew Doreen would need our support today. I didn't know it would end in a screaming match or you would show up to make an already bad situation worse."

I winced. "You and Louise don't go to the same church?"

"I'm not religious myself. I haven't set foot in a church since my last grandchild was married ten years ago. Even then, I thought God might strike me dead when I crossed the threshold. I didn't know then he let criminals like Minnie run the place. Louise does her own thing when it comes to religion. She does a lot with crystals and that sort of mumbo jumbo. I glaze over when she talks about it. I'm an equal opportunity ignorer of all religion."

I didn't think that believing God would strike you down when you stepped into a church was truly atheist, but I wasn't going to correct her. I had already made enough trouble for these ladies as it was.

"If you want to talk to Clementine, you can find her at First Baptist Church on Huron Street. She will be there. She's always there when we don't have book club."

"Thanks." I paused. "Why are you helping me?"

She fluffed her hair with her fingers. "It's nice to not be the only one who ruffles Doreen's feathers for a change." She dropped her hand to her side. "But I'm sorry about Minnie. Whatever she might have done in her past, she didn't deserve to have her life ended like that."

"Were you and Minnie close?"

"Not as close as Doreen and Minnie, as you must have surmised. Doreen will defend Minnie's reputation to the end, no matter the mounting evidence to the contrary. Minnie and I were both members of this book club the longest, and you get to know people in that time. When you listen to someone discuss books in particular, you learn more about what they think than about the book itself."

I nodded. "Did you know that Minnie had a tattoo?"

She laughed. "Minnie had a tattoo? That's hard for me to believe, but then again, had you told me she was a bank robber I wouldn't have believed that either. Minnie was always too rigid about rules and doing the right thing. Just like Doreen." She glanced back at the house. "I wonder what secrets Doreen has." She shrugged. "Everyone has a secret. Some are just better at keeping them than others."

Louise rejoined us holding an inhaler in one hand and a cell phone in the other. "Ruby, are you ready to go? The funeral director just called me and said he has an opening this afternoon."

"It's always good when the funeral home has an opening," Ruby said with a laugh and then added, "We are making arrangements for Minnie's funeral."

"I'm surprised Doreen doesn't want to do that."

"She says she's too upset to, but she gave us a very detailed list of everything she wants. You had better believe that if we don't do it right, she will let us know. I'll plan it, but I'm sure not paying for it. Funerals are expensive."

"Is Doreen footing the bill?" I asked.

She shrugged. "I believe she thinks her church might help. In any case, I'm going to tell the funeral director to send the bill to her, because it's sure not coming to me."

That wasn't going to end well.

Chapter Twenty-Four

The First Baptist Church was on Huron Street, just like Ruby said. I remembered going to vacation Bible school there as a child. Other than Christmas and Easter, I hadn't attended church much growing up. Both my father and grandmother weren't into formal religion. Grandma Bellamy always said she felt closer to God on the farm than inside a church. Occasionally, when I was a teenager and young adult, I attended the Presbyterian church in town with Logan and his family, but I was never completely comfortable there either. I supposed I had too much of my grandmother in me. It was when I was outdoors that I felt closer to God or whatever my understanding of him was. What I believed was something I was still sorting out at age thirty-eight.

Unlike Logan's Presbyterian church, which had been heavy on brick and mortar and leaded stained-glass windows, the Baptist church was very simple and nondescript. In fact, it didn't even have a cross on the side of the building or on the large sign facing the street. If I didn't know better, I would have thought it was an office building, not a church.

It was a weekday afternoon, but the parking lot was a quarter full. I wondered if I should go in with that many people about. However, the crowd could work to my advantage. If there were a lot of people inside, maybe I would go unnoticed wandering around the church looking for Clementine.

Huckleberry whimpered when I got out of the car, and I peeked back in through the open door to take a look at him. Taking him inside the church was a terrible idea, but I had left him in the car at Doreen's house. He looked so forlorn.

I sighed and stepped back from the door. "Come on."

He yipped happily and jumped out of the driver's side door.

I pointed at the little pug. "You have to be on your very best behavior. This is a house of worship."

He bowed his head like he understood everything I'd said. I knew better. This was going to be a disaster.

Even though he didn't like it, I snapped a leash on his collar. If Doreen ever learned I was taking the dog inside, she would never forgive me.

Huckleberry and I walked up to the glass doors and let ourselves in. Memories flooded back into my mind of those few occasions I had attended church with my mother before she died. More than anything, it was the smell that took me back to that time. There was a heavy yeasty smell in the air that was mingled with roasting meat and candle wax. It was a combination I had never smelled anywhere else.

The hallway was empty. There was a set of double doors in front of me and a sign that said "sanctuary" on the right door.

Since Ruby had told me to look for Clementine in the church kitchen, I knew that wasn't the way to go. Instead, I followed my nose to the right and down a closed set of stairs.

In the stairwell, the scent of roasting meat was almost over-powering, and it was a relief to step out onto the basement level and take a breath.

The kitchen was in front of me, and the door that led into the fellowship hall was to my right. Through the window in the fellowship hall door, I saw volunteers setting the tables with silverware, water glasses, salt and pepper shakers, and napkins. It looked to me that the church was going to have one of their meals tonight.

"Can I help you?" A woman stepped out of the stairwell I had just left. She wore a sweater dress and nude pumps. It was quite a different outfit from the rest of the volunteers, who were dressed in jeans and T-shirts as they worked.

"I was looking for Clementine..." I trailed off because I realized I had not asked the other members of the book club what Clementine's last name was. But then again, how many Clementines could there be that attended this church?

"Oh." Her face cleared, and she studied me with less suspicion. Apparently, Clementine was a secret password of sorts. "Clementine is our kitchen coordinator. She's the best one the church has ever had. We're so grateful for her work. Since she came along, we have increased the number of dinners and fundraiser meals at the church tenfold." Her face clouded over. "Even with the latest disruptions, she hasn't missed a beat." She held out her hands to me. "Claire Elliot. I'm the pastor's wife. As such, I'm here just about every day and know Clementine quite well."

I shook her hand. It was delicate and cool, but strong, like she could crack your fingers with her handshake but refrained from using her ability to do so. I immediately knew from the handshake that Claire Elliot was a woman I didn't want to mess with.

"Are you looking for Clementine to volunteer? That's what most of the people who come to the church looking for her are here to do. She has an amazing ability to attract volunteers to the church for dinners and other meals. Many of the other volunteers you see here today aren't even members of our congregation. You have to give it to Clementine. She can mobilize people." She chuckled. "I think my husband is a bit jealous, since we have more people at Clementine's dinners than we do in the pews on Sunday."

Before I could answer, she went on to say, "Clementine went out to pick up a few more things for tonight's dinner, but I can show you around and put you to work."

"Uh. Okay." What else could I say? Volunteering might be my best chance to get close to Clementine to ask her about Minnie.

"You have an adorable little dog there. I'm a dog person myself, so I love seeing dogs in the church. My husband constantly brings our King Charles spaniel to the church office, and he's even been known to attend Sunday services when he doesn't sleep in too late. He's an old dog and sleeping is his main occupation now." She studied Huckleberry in my arms. "I will have to ask you to leave him in the hallway. We can't have a dog around the kitchen or anywhere anyone will eat. Is he well-behaved? I can't have him piddling on our floor. It's new and the church board would blow a gasket. I'm surprised that they didn't ask for the floor to be blessed after it was installed." She chuckled, but there wasn't much humor in her laugh. I took that to mean the flooring had been a sour spot at some point.

"Huckleberry is very well-behaved," I managed to say with a straight face. "He is very good about piddling." At least that part of my statement was true. I couldn't say it was true for all pugs. As a breed, they were notorious for having accidents in the house. But when Huckleberry was a puppy, I had been close to religious about making sure he could go out whenever he wanted to.

A chair sat against the wall. "I'll leave him here, and he will be fine." I tied the pug's leash to one of the chair legs. Huckleberry gave me a look of betrayal. "Sorry buddy," I whispered, "but this is better than being stuck in the car, right?"

Claire opened the double doors leading into the dining room, where a beehive of people set dozens of tables. "I would say when you come in the future that you leave your dog at home. As much as we would like to see him, it would be easier that way."

"Of course," I agreed.

"And take him home before the dinner tonight if you will be volunteering this evening."

"I certainly will," I said, having no intention of staying for the meal that evening. I still had a farm to take care of, and poor Chesney was brush hogging the field all by herself. I had some guilt about that.

"The meal tonight will be to raise money for Minnie's funeral. No matter what she did, she needs a proper Christian burial."

My brow went up. As soon as she said that, I changed my mind about the dinner. "I will be here tonight."

"Good. We will need the extra set of hands." She lowered her voice. "We expect quite a crowd this evening. Quite a crowd."

"Oh, why is that?" I asked feigning interest.

She looked around. "Sadly, our church member Minnie was murdered at a local farm, and there are some rumors about her that came to light after her death. Some very scandalous rumors, in fact. We expect some reporters to be coming to the dinner to get the scoop."

"Oh," I said.

"Did Clementine tell you the job she wanted you to do?" Claire asked.

"No, she didn't," I said. "I think I was to be instructed when I got here."

"Hmm, that's odd. She usually has very strong opinions about who should be doing what at the dinners. She assesses everyone based on their skill set."

"I think I'm just filling in as needed. More of a floater."

She nodded as if this made perfect sense. "All right, so I will show you a little bit of everything so that you can jump in." She began walking rapidly.

"There's the drink station. Guests get their own drinks if they want anything other than water, iced tea, and coffee. We serve dinner at the tables, so I expect that you will be waiting tables. There is only one menu. The only variations are allowed for those with dietary needs: gluten intolerance and vegetarians. Why anyone would be a vegetarian is beyond me." She shrugged. "We don't get many of those kinds around here." She pointed at a conveyor belt that led into the kitchen. "That's where we drop off the dishes as people are finished with the different courses. It's important to keep the tables moving. Even though we're set up to feed a hundred guests at a time here, we expect twice that under the strange circumstances of Minnie's death."

"You plan to let the gawkers and onlookers in for the meal?"

"Oh, we don't care at all if they come. They have to pay their ten dollars to enter the church for the meal just like everyone else. This is a fundraiser, after all. The more people who come, the more money we will make to cover Minnie's funeral expenses. Furthermore, any extra money raised will go into the church's coffers. I think we will do very well tonight. We have wanted to put on an educational addition to start a church preschool for several years. This will help us toward that goal."

I began to wonder if I should be taking business advice from this pastor's wife. She seemed to have a much better handle on supply and demand than I did. She showed me the rest of the dining area, and we only peeked into the kitchen.

"If you didn't already know, you won't be working in the kitchen," she said. "Clementine is very specific about the training she puts the ladies and a few older men through to work there. You haven't had the training, have you?"

I shook my head.

She nodded. "You didn't look like it to me."

I frowned, not sure what she meant by that. Did I look like I wasn't a great cook? I could hold my own in the kitchen, but maybe not to Clementine's exacting standards. Also, from what I could tell, the crew working in the kitchen never left. They were chained to their pots and pans, knives and spatulas. Being part of the kitchen crew would put a major cramp in my snooping plan, and I very much planned to snoop when I came back to volunteer.

She checked her watch. "I hate to run off on you like this, but I must. My husband should be ready for lunch. He's working on next week's sermon, and I can guarantee you he's forgotten to eat. Honestly, I don't know how unmarried men navigate the world at all. They need a woman's hand, don't they?" She glanced at my left hand. "Oh, you're not married. Divorced?"

I arched my brow. Just because I was a woman over thirty and not married didn't mean I was divorced. "Never married. I'm from California," I said, afraid she might try to match me up with some lonely parishioner.

"Ohhh." She drew out the sound as if that was enough explanation. "I hope my comment about vegetarians didn't offend you. People become upset about the funniest things nowadays."

"I'm not a vegetarian."

"Oh, thank goodness. I really don't know what you would find to eat here."

"What time does the meal start, and when do the volunteers need to be here?" I asked.

"The meal is at six sharp. We have a lot of people moving through, so we will start on time. We can't wait for stragglers. The more people that dine, the more money the church makes."

Making money for the church seemed to be a major priority.

I walked with her back to the double doors.

"It was nice to meet you…" She put a hand to her cheek. "I'm sorry, I can't remember your name."

She couldn't remember it because I never said it. "Shi," I said.

"It's nice to meet you, Shi." She walked back to the stairwell. "Welcome aboard." She went through the door.

"I knew you were here." A deep male voice said behind me.

I spun around and saw Quinn standing by Huckleberry's chair. The pug had his leash wrapped around Quinn's legs and the other three chair legs. Neither of them looked particularly concerned about it.

"Quinn, what are you doing here?"

"This is my church. What's your excuse?" he asked with an arched brow.

Chapter Twenty-Five

U mmm," I said.

"That's what I thought." He bent down and began untangling himself and the pug from the chair legs.

Once the pug was free, Huckleberry ran circles around Quinn and me as if he had been in a cage for forty years and could not believe his good fortune of finally being released.

"So?" Quinn cocked his head.

I cleared my throat. "Would it surprise you to know that I am volunteering at the dinner tonight?"

"Not really. You like helping people."

I blushed at the compliment and felt a smile form on my lips.

"However, I know you are volunteering tonight because you hope to learn something you can use in the search for Minnie's killer more than out of the sheer goodness of your heart."

My smile faded. I hated it that Quinn had me pegged so well. It was super annoying. I didn't find the skill attractive in the least.

"I also know that you went to my mother's house."

"How did you know I went to your parents' home?" I asked.

"Mom called me, and she wasn't too happy about it."

Several people came out of the kitchen and began talking in the hallway.

He glanced at them and said to me in a low voice. "Let's talk outside. There are spies everywhere in this church."

Picking up Huckleberry, I followed him down a hallway to a door that led outside. I buttoned up my denim jacket as we went out; the temperature had dropped at least ten degrees since I entered the church. There were murmurs of an early snow at Jessa's Place that morning. The old farmers who congregated there were better at predicting the weather than any meteorologist sitting behind a desk.

I set the pug on the ground. "What do you mean there are spies everywhere in the church?"

"That's right, you didn't grow up in the church."

"My father isn't religious."

"Sully is religious in his own way," Quinn said. "It's just not conventional. If he had to sit through a sermon every week, I have a feeling he'd start booing from his pew."

Quinn was probably right about that.

"Now, I'm not sure it's wise for you to be here." Quinn shoved his hands into the pockets of his coat. "This is my mother's church. It was my mother's church before I was born, and we both know she's not your number one fan. Anyone who sees us talking will report back to her."

"I'm kind of surprised she's not involved in the dinner tonight. Minnie was her best friend."

"Oh, she's involved."

That sounded ominous.

"Did you go to her house to talk to her about Minnie?" Quinn asked.

I nodded. "I did, and I know it was probably a waste of time. She was never going to answer my questions. I learned from the members of her book club about Clementine working at the church. I wanted to talk to her. It wasn't until I got here that I learned about the dinner and sort of volunteered."

"Sort of volunteered?"

I shrugged. "Well, I met the pastor's wife, and she just assumed I was one of Clementine's volunteers."

"So you plan to volunteer tonight?"

"Sure. It's a good cause and promises to be a good show."

He sighed. "You will see Hazel and me there too. I just got off my twelve-hour shift, so I'm busing tables to help out. Hazel usually refills water glasses."

"You volunteer at the church dinners?" I wasn't sure why this surprised me. It could be that, sometimes, I compared the man that Quinn was today to the careless young man I'd known when we were young, as unfair as that was.

"This is my church."

"I know, but..."

"You think I'm a church member in name only?"

I frowned. "I didn't say that."

"If someone asks how you ended up volunteering, just tell them I asked you to help out. That way you won't get in trouble with Clementine. My mother won't like to hear it, but even she can't begrudge someone who wants to do church work." He paused. "At least I don't think she can."

"She's not happy with me, that's for sure. She got this wild idea in her head that I let Hazel hang out and help me at the farm so that I could spend more time with you."

A strange look crossed his face. "That is a wild idea."

"Completely insane," I said, feeling a pang in my heart. "You're Logan's best friend. We would never..."

"Of course not. I would never do that to Logan."

"Neither would I," I agreed as I realized neither of us were looking the other in the eye. Quinn stared into the parking lot, and my gaze wandered to a flower bed to my right that was overflowing with yellow mums.

"It's time to pick Hazel up from school. We'll be back here at five to help out," Quinn said in a shaky voice.

I snuck a peek at him. He was still looking into the parking lot. A lock of his hair had fallen into his left eye, and I had the urge to brush it aside. Then Logan's smiling face came to mind, and the urge passed.

"Why are you willing to go out on a limb for me with your mom?" I asked.

He finally looked at me. "You've been kind to Hazel. The move here from Detroit hasn't been easy. You're the first person she's shown any sign of being excited to hang out with. It gives me hope."

"Hope for what?" My voice was halted. I was both excited and fearful of what he might say.

"Hope that I didn't make a mistake moving back to Cherry Glen. I thought it would be easier to be close to my parents. They could help me with Hazel, and the job here is cushy compared to working for a fire department in a big city. Every time I got called out in Detroit, I wondered if I was going to come back to my daughter. I couldn't let her lose both her parents, but being a firefighter was my passion." He brushed the lock of hair out of his eyes. "I love what I do, and sure, it's not as exciting here, but I'm helping people. And truthfully, I'm not risking my life every day like I was back in the city." He took a breath. "But I wonder if I was wrong to move us across the state. My mother and daughter are always at odds, and I think sometimes my father questions my place in the town." He shook his head. "You didn't need that long-winded answer."

"A long-winded but honest answer. Rarely in LA were people that candid about the tough choices they'd made in their lives. It's refreshing."

He smiled at me. "I find you refreshing, Shiloh Bellamy."

"I—I—"

"Not the mums!" a woman shouted.

Quinn and I spun around to find Huckleberry digging up one of the large yellow mums in the garden.

An elderly woman wrung her hands not too far away. "They're ruined."

"Huckleberry!" I cried.

The pug stopped digging and looked up at me with his round brown eyes. Dirt covered his forepaws, nose, and mouth, and a yellow blossom hung from his black lips.

Quinn had a murmured conversation with the woman and promised that we would replant the mum right away.

"What do you think you're doing?" I put my hands on my hips and looked down at the pug.

He opened his mouth, and the blossom fell from his lips into the hole he'd dug.

Chapter Twenty-Six

B y the time I returned to the farm, Chesney had finished clearing the field. As I pulled up the driveway, she came from the opposite direction with the tractor. She cut the engine and jumped from the seat. Removing her work gloves, Chesney said, "Field's done. Do you want to tarp it today?"

I walked to the right of the barn for a better view of the field. It was about fifteen acres back from the barn. From where I stood, I could tell the tall overgrown weeds and grass were all mowed down. Just seeing the field cleared gave me hope we could actually bring the farm back to its former glory.

"There were a lot of multiflora roses back in there." She removed one of the plants' nasty thorns from her sleeve. "I think brush hogging it and tarping so it's starved of light is the only way to control it." She bent over and removed another long thorn from her pant leg and tossed it in the grass. "That stuff is nasty. I ran into several patches that caught on my clothes even high on the tractor seat."

"I should have thought to tell you to wear gaiters."

"I don't think gaiters would have been much help against this stuff. Did you want to tarp?"

"I do, but let's leave that until tomorrow. Are you able to come back?"

"I can. I finished my paper and already turned it in. That day off really helped." Her shoulders relaxed. "I have to say I'm grateful you don't want to tarp today. I'm exhausted."

"You worked hard, and you deserve a break. I can put the tractor away."

"Thanks, Shiloh." She wiped her sleeve across her brow.

"I stopped by the theater and saw Whit."

Chesney's tired face broke into a smile. "She's in her element there. It's all she wants to do. I guess I should be happy that she's taking any classes at all at the university, even though they are all in the theater department."

"She showed me her bee tattoo."

The smiled faded from Chesney's face. "She got that in honor of our family of beekeepers."

"I guess I didn't know how far beekeeping went back in your family until she spoke of it."

She picked another thorn from her clothes. "It goes way back. I want to farm because of it. We always knew the importance of bees."

I wanted to ask her more about it. I wanted to know if she ever tried to talk to Minnie about her bees like her sister had, but she said, "I should go. My paper is done, but there is always more schoolwork to do."

I bit my lip to fight back the urge to press her for more information. She had brush hogged fifteen acres all by herself that day. I could give her a break.

"If that's all you need, I'll take off. It's best we aren't

tarping tonight anyway," she said. "The wind is picking up, and I think we'd have a battle on our hands keeping those tarps on the ground while we weighed them down."

As if she had beckoned it, the wind did begin to pick up. Leaves fell from the oak tree in the yard and were carried away in the breeze.

"Tomorrow will be better," I agreed. "But the tarping can wait another day. I would really like to work on the cherry orchard tomorrow and see what trees can be saved."

She nodded. "I've been eager to work in the orchard too. Let's do that. As long as we tarp by the weekend, we should be good."

I smiled. "I'm glad you are here to keep me on track."

She chuckled and rocked back on her heels. "I heard there was some kind of press conference in front of the municipal building this morning."

"How'd you hear about that?"

"A friend texted me. Was it about the murder?"

I nodded. "The police and the U.S. Marshals Service are eager to solve the case."

She nodded. "I can understand that. It's pretty scary that something like that can happen in Cherry Glen, and not just in Cherry Glen, but here on your farm." She shivered.

"Are you uncomfortable working on the farm? I wouldn't want you to keep working here, especially alone, if you don't feel safe."

"No, no one has any reason to want me dead, and I can take care of myself. I've taken at least a dozen self-defense classes. You can never be too careful, even in a small town."

"I'm glad to hear that," I said.

"It's a shame it happened here, but J—Minnie was kind of a terrible person." She shrugged.

I cocked my head. "Did you almost call her Joan?"

Her face flushed red. "It's her real name, isn't it? A friend told me about the whole Joan the Bandit thing. It's unbelievable. I guess I don't know if I should call her by her given name or the name she chose for herself."

"I've just been thinking of her as Minnie," I said. "It's how I knew her."

"Do you think the stories about her being a bank robber are true?" She studied my face with such scrutiny it made me fidget.

"The U.S. Marshal certainly thinks so."

"It kind of boggles the mind that that would be the reason she would be killed," she said softly. "Her crimes were so long ago. Her murder couldn't have been related to what happened all those years ago, could it?"

I shrugged. "Maybe. Maybe not. She had an accomplice," I said, "who drove the getaway car. He died in prison, but there could be other people out there that are holding a grudge against her."

She gasped. "How did you know about the accomplice?"

I studied her, surprised by all the questions. Usually all Chesney wanted to talk about was the farm or her schooling, even when I brought up other subjects. "The marshal who was trying to find her told me."

She nodded. "I guess she would know. My friends and I have been talking about it a lot. None of us can believe something like this happened in Cherry Glen. I've only lived here a couple of years, but I always thought it was such a quiet place. It seems a lot has changed in the last few months."

Doreen Killian would have said a lot had changed because I moved back to Michigan. I knew that wasn't the reason, and it wasn't my fault. However, I couldn't ignore the correlation of murders to my return. Doreen wouldn't have missed that either.

Chesney brushed a lock of black hair that had fallen out of her ponytail behind her ear. "I need a shower. I'll see you tomorrow, Shiloh."

"Tomorrow," I agreed.

I watched her walk to her hatchback parked on the edge of the field. She was a hard worker. Perhaps the hardest worker I knew. I would have given her a bonus for all the extra work she did if I could afford it. Since I couldn't, I would have to settle on baking an organic pie for her.

I checked on Dad and did a few chores around the farm before walking back to my cabin. Huckleberry ran ahead of me. I thought it was because we hadn't seen Esmeralda in the barn. When she wasn't bothering the barn cats, which were a trio of orange tabbies, she could be found taking an afternoon nap in the cabin.

Even though my cabin was out in the middle of nowhere and very few people even knew it existed, I still locked all my doors and windows when I wasn't home. I had lived in LA for too long not to. My father teased me about locking my car when it was in the driveway, but I didn't care. It was a habit I didn't plan to change, and with the rising crime rate in Cherry Glen, it seemed like it was a good decision.

However, since Esmeralda was her own mistress, I'd installed a cat door on the cabin's back door. Originally, I put it in for her and Huckleberry, but it only took one attempt by the dog to realize I hadn't ordered the pug-sized door. Esmeralda loved that she could come and go as she pleased, and Huckleberry was stuck on one side or the other, dependent on me to get him in and out of the cabin.

To my surprise, there was a note taped to my front door when I got there. I swallowed and unfolded it.

Dear Shiloh,

It was so nice to meet you the other day. I love it that an original Bellamy is running Bellamy Farm. I think we can be a big help to each other moving forward. I don't have your number so this note will have to suffice for now to make contact. How arcane it feels to be writing a note with paper and pen in this day and age. If you miss this note, which is possible, I'm sure we will bump into each other soon in town or I will try to catch you again at your cabin.

Sincerely Yours, Tanner Birchwood

I stared at the piece of paper in my hand. Who used the word "arcane" nowadays? I wondered.

I let myself in the cabin and looked around. Nothing

appeared to be out of place, but would I really know? Some of the mess was from my grandmother's day, and some came from the unopened bins from my storage unit in California. My friend Briar had them shipped to me. I told her she could sell the rest and make a commission from me on what she sold.

Briar was a high-powered entertainment attorney and had a newborn baby at home, but she had an obsession with buying and selling things online. She was the perfect person to unload my possessions.

The boxes in question had been at the cabin for three weeks, and I hadn't even opened them yet. I told myself I couldn't deal with my own junk until I dealt with my grandmother's.

Esmeralda sashayed into the sitting room from my bedroom. She straightened her forelegs and bowed deeply in a downward dog move. I supposed in this case it would be called downward cat.

Huckleberry waddled over to her, and she patted his nose with her paw. He obediently sat next to her. I shook my head.

Huckleberry was the only dog she tolerated, but I thought that had more to do with the fact that she was tougher than him and therefore knew she was in control. Control was very important to Esmeralda in all facets of her life.

I waved the note at her. "I'm surprised you didn't scare off the visitor. What kind of guard cat are you?"

She stretched a little more deeply and yawned, showing off her full range of fangs. "I think that you and Hazel get along so well because you are both tough cookies. You respect that in one another."

She perked up at the mention of Hazel. She loved that girl.

"I'm going to see Hazel tonight," I told the cat. "And I will find out when she can come over. I think the two of you need a playdate."

Esmeralda purred and rubbed her body on both of my legs.

"If I knew that was all it would take for you to snuggle up to me, I would have said that a lot more often." I smiled down at the cat, but all the time I considered Tanner's note and the unwritten intentions behind it.

Chapter Twenty-Seven

I had the good sense to leave Huckleberry at home while I was at the church fundraiser. I dropped him and Esmeralda off at the big house to spend the evening with my father. Before I left, they were all snuggled in with game show reruns, a TV dinner for dad, and kibble for the pets.

Huckleberry and Esmeralda split a can of tuna as well. That was to cheer up Huckleberry since I was leaving him behind, as well as Esmeralda since she hadn't seen Hazel for the second day in a row.

I arrived at the church at five o'clock, but it was clear that most of the volunteers had been there much longer. Maybe they had never left, and every one of them knew what to do. I stood in the doorway of the dining room, uncertain what my next move should be.

"Put this on." Quinn held out a white apron.

I thanked him and took the apron.

"Hazel could use some help at the drink table," he said. "From there, you should be able to see the entire dining room."

I wrapped the apron ties around my waist and tied them in front of me, and then I spotted Hazel across the dining room filling glasses of water. "Thanks."

"Happy sleuthing." Quinn winked at me and walked away. I frowned. He knew me too well for my own good.

Hazel's bright, brown eyes lit up when I walked up to her.

"Reporting for duty." I saluted her.

"You really came!" She smiled so big you would have thought she'd won a prize. "Dad said you were coming, but I didn't want to get my hopes up. I have never seen you at church before."

I smiled. "Well, I'm here. Put me to work. I was told I should help you with the drinks."

She nodded. "It's easy. I fill the water and iced tea glasses and take them to the tables. I don't do coffee. Clementine thinks I'm too young to handle coffee because it's so hot." She rolled her eyes. "She's never seen me drive your tractor."

It was true that I had let Hazel drive the tractor a few times, but always under supervision.

I grinned. "You're more than qualified to pour coffee. Honestly, you'd do a much better job at it than I would."

She beamed. "Thank you. I'm working on the water, so you can get started with the iced tea."

"Yes, ma'am." I saluted again.

She chuckled.

We worked for a few minutes, sinking into a deep concentration in order to avoid any mishaps. I had a feeling that mishaps here would be greatly frowned upon.

Across the dining room, I spotted Clementine. I ducked my head. What would she say if she caught me here? I wasn't even sure if she would recognize me. She had been so furious outside of Doreen's house, it was possible she hadn't even seen me.

When I looked up again, I realized the person she was with would certainly know who I was. Doreen. She had her thin arms folded across her chest, and she glared at her former friend. Clementine wasn't nearly as composed. She waved her arms wildly in the air as she spoke. Doreen said something back, but they were too far away for me to eavesdrop.

"Grandma looks really mad," Hazel said in hushed tones.

I glanced at Hazel. I hadn't realized she had been watching the pair too. "How can you tell? She seems calm to me."

"That doesn't mean she's not mad. Trust me, I know. When she is really, really mad, she gets cold. She's like the iceberg that took out the Titanic."

I nodded. It was a pretty astute observation of her grandmother.

I was dying to hear their fight. It had to be about Minnie. I picked up one of the pitchers of iced tea. "I'm going to do a walk around and see if anyone wants refills."

"We aren't supposed to do that," Hazel said. "Clementine said people who want refills have to come to the drink table themselves."

I could hear the anxiety in her voice. It seemed to me that Clementine ran a very tight church dinner.

"It's nothing to worry about," I said and walked off with the pitcher.

As I made my way across the large room, I stopped every so often to ask a table if anyone would like some more iced tea. Almost everyone I asked did. At this point, I would run out of iced tea before I reached Doreen and Clementine.

I stopped offering until I was just one table away and could hear their hushed, angry voices.

"How dare you speak to me like this after everything I have done for you!" Doreen said. "Do you think that you would be in the position you are in this church if it wasn't for me?"

"Would any of you like some more iced tea?" I asked an elderly man at the table.

He nodded, and I poured iced tea into his half-full glass.

"What you've done for me to be in this church?" Clementine asked. "You've done nothing for me. All you and Joan ever did was take credit for everything I did." She pointed at Doreen. "You wanted to take credit for the dinners, even."

Doreen swatted Clementine's finger. "Don't you dare call her Joan. I knew Minnie best. She told me everything. I knew who she really was."

"Don't touch me. If you touch me again, I will have you arrested for assault."

"Arrested by who? My husband?" Doreen laughed at this.

By this point, I was openly staring at Doreen and Clementine, making no attempt to hide my curiosity. I wouldn't be the least bit surprised if they came to blows any second.

"Miss. Miss! Miss!" the older gentleman cried and pushed his chair back from the table.

The iced tea glass overflowed onto the table and the floor. I had been pouring it the entire time.

"Shiloh, what happened?" Hazel asked, appearing at my side.

Several vigilant volunteers ran at me with paper towels. I didn't even have a chance to try to clean up my own mess before I was pushed aside by the other volunteers. Whatever Clementine did to have her volunteers be this dedicated was impressive. There were a lot of nonprofits and government agencies that would benefit from their dedication.

The commotion caught the attention of Doreen and Clementine. Doreen narrowed her eyes. By the looks of it, she bumped me up a few notches on her loathing list. I was right under Clementine.

I had also managed to pour iced tea down the front of my pants, so it looked like I had wet myself. It wasn't a good look. I mumbled excuses and found the ladies restroom out in the hallway. As I came out of the restroom, I bumped into the reporter with the gray trench coat, who I'd seen at the press conference. She held a microphone in my face. "Alexis Zueller, West Michigan TV. Ms. Bellamy, what can you tell us about the murder of Joan the Bandit that occurred at your farm?"

Behind her was the large cameraman I had seen shadowing her at the press conference.

"I…" Much to my horror, I looked down at my damp lap, and the cameraman panned his lens down in that direction.

"Ma'am, what do you have to say about the case? Is it true you have some sort of history with the police chief's wife, who was a good friend of Joan the Bandit while she lived under the assumed name of Minnie Devani?"

"I don't know what you're talking about. I'm here tonight to help with the dinner. That is all."

She held the microphone a little higher. "Is that true? From what we know, you have a history with murders in the county."

Murders in the county? I had been involved in one murder before this. Just one.

I tried to step around her, but the huge cameraman blocked my way. "Please move, I have to get back to the dining room to help."

Alexis gave a slight nod, and the cameraman stepped aside. I hurried to the dining room door.

Just before I stepped through the doorway, the reporter called, "I will be talking to you again, Ms. Bellamy." There was no question that was a threat.

Chapter Twenty-Eight

When I got back to the drinks table, Hazel shook her head. "I don't think they're going to have you back to the dinners, Shiloh. Both Grandma and Clementine were really upset about the iced tea. I'd stay away from them if I were you."

It was sound advice, but not advice I could carry out because Doreen spotted me and made a beeline for the drinks table.

Hazel stepped forward, putting herself in between me and her grandmother. I appreciated the gesture but stepped around her. There was enough tension between the two of them even when I wasn't involved. I didn't want to add to it.

"What are you doing here?" Doreen asked through clenched teeth.

"I'm volunteering. The pastor's wife said the church expected a large crowd for the fundraiser and an extra set of hands was welcome."

"Not your hands. We don't want you at this church. You already made a mess of things."

"Grandma," Hazel said.

Doreen glared at her granddaughter. "Don't you say a word. I told you to stay away from this woman."

"My dad said that I could be friends with Shiloh," Hazel said in a quiet voice.

"I don't care what your father said. When he's at the station, I'm your guardian, and I tell you what you should and shouldn't do. I said you should not be around her, and here you are. You're being disobedient."

"She's not," Quinn said. He stood just behind his mother with a silver cart loaded down with dirty dishes. He held the handle of the cart so tightly his knuckles turned white. "I told Hazel she could work with Shiloh tonight."

His mother glared at him. "I don't know how you can continue to encourage this relationship knowing what she did to Logan."

"She didn't do anything to Logan, Mom. I have told you a thousand times that I was wrong about that, but you refuse to listen to me."

"Just because you have stars in your eyes over this woman doesn't mean I do too."

Stars in his eyes about me? Doreen was delusional.

"I think we are all here today to help raise money for Minnie's funeral," I said. "Whatever personal issues we might have need to be set to the side. Today is about Minnie."

She scowled at me. "It is about Minnie. Don't think for a second that I don't know you are volunteering here because your friend is in trouble." She took a step closer to me. "Kristy Brown killed my friend. I know it. My husband knows it, and I will spend the rest of my life making her pay if the system won't." She spun on her heels and stomped away.

Quinn was pale. "Hazel, you know those accusations your

grandmother said about Kristy were wrong, don't you? You should never spread rumors like that about another person."

She nodded and went back to filling water glasses, even though it was the end of the meal and fewer and fewer people were in need of them. She needed something to do. I could understand that. I had a sudden urge to run back to the farm and clean the chicken coop.

"Shi, I'm so sorry," Quinn began.

"It's not your fault. I'm glad Kristy wasn't here to hear her."

Quinn glanced at his daughter. "Why don't you take those water glasses to the tables?"

"But Clementine said that people are supposed to come to the drinks table for refills."

"It's the end of the dinner. I don't think it matters at this point," her father replied.

She shrugged and loaded up a tray of water glasses.

Quinn looked like he wanted to say something while she piled the glasses on but held his tongue. Hazel shuffled away with the tray.

"I think we might have another spill on our hands in a few minutes," he said.

"Better water than iced tea."

He smiled, but the smile faded from his face. "I'm sorry about earlier."

I shook my head. "I was eavesdropping on your mother's conversation. It's understandable she's upset."

"Still, she shouldn't have said those awful things. Mom has been struggling since Minnie's death. I never realized how close they really were." He held up his hand. "I'm not making excuses for her. What she said is inexcusable."

"What she said about Kristy was unkind, but I'm not worried about her comments about me. It's clear she doesn't plan to change her opinion of me. At this point, I'm not asking her to." I glanced at Hazel, who seemed to be doing fine passing out the water glasses. "I enjoy having Hazel at the farm. However, I can understand if you don't want her to be there to keep peace in your family."

He shook his head. "No. I want Hazel to be around you. She likes you, and you're a positive influence. Also, I don't have to worry about you saying something I don't want my daughter to be exposed to, like my mother's disregard for people's feelings." He glanced over his shoulder. "The meal is ending, and I need to get back to busing the tables. Can Hazel go to your house after school tomorrow? She can get off the bus stop at our house and then walk over to your farm."

"Yes, of course." I bit my lip. "What about your mom?"

"Let me worry about her." He pushed his cart away.

Chatter and laughter floated through the kitchen doors as the men and woman working there appeared to be relieved the event was finally over and had been a success.

I carried pitchers of iced tea and water back to the kitchen, and an elderly volunteer told me to set them on a clear bit of counter.

I thanked her and went back for more pitchers but stopped in the doorway leading into the dining room. Doreen stood there with the pastor's wife.

"We raised almost five thousand dollars for Minnie's

funeral. Pastor Elliot is doing the funeral for free, so this will be enough for a simple burial. I already spoke to the funeral home," Doreen said.

"You and Clementine have done a wonderful job, Doreen," Claire Elliot said. "Your love of Minnie is evident to everyone."

Doreen's body tensed at the mention of Clementine. "*I* cared about Minnie. Clementine is good at organizing these meals. I will give her that."

"I heard a rumor that Clementine was going to give them up."

"She won't," Doreen said, as if that were a great failing on Clementine's part. "She has a stranglehold on the church dinners, and she won't let go."

Claire smiled, completely missing the animosity in Doreen's voice. "The church is so lucky to have such dedicated volunteers."

I stepped back into the kitchen. I wasn't going to be caught by Doreen eavesdropping for a second time that night. I went out another kitchen door and into the hallway, making my way back into the dining room with Doreen none the wiser. When I reached the place where the drinks table had been, I found everything cleared away and the table folded up and leaning against the wall.

Clementine's volunteers meant business. In fact, the dining room was empty. There wasn't as much as a stray fork for me to carry back to the kitchen. I didn't see Quinn or Hazel anywhere. Perhaps they had already gone home? I frowned. I'm not sure why I expected Quinn to tell me when he was leaving.

Shaking my head, I walked out of the dining room and

back into the hall. I was relieved Doreen wasn't around. I hadn't learned much from coming to the dinner other than exactly how much she disliked me.

I found my way out of the church. It was eight thirty at night. In October in Michigan, it felt like midnight. The parking lot was half-full. There was an eeriness in the air and a bite in the wind. I would have to order some winter clothes soon or make a trip to Traverse City to buy some. We had some nice boutiques downtown, but the fancy clothes sold there weren't suited for farmwork. When I moved back to Michigan, I'd traded in my power suits and stylish dresses for overalls and flannel-lined jeans.

"I was wondering when you were going to come out of there," a smooth female voice said.

I spun around, and Marshal Lynn Chuff stepped out of the shadow of the building.

"Have you been here all night?" I asked.

Her hair kept falling into her eyes from the breeze. She tucked it behind her ear. "Most of it. Long enough to see your little conversation with Doreen Killian. She sure doesn't like you."

"I don't know what that has to do with your investigation into Joan the Bandit."

"From what I had gathered, Doreen and Joan were quite close."

"Assuming Joan and Minnie are the same person."

"They are. That's what I wanted to tell you. I guessed Chief Randy wasn't going to be very forthcoming with you, given your history with his wife."

"It's a long story as to why she dislikes me. It goes back a long time."

"To the death of your fiancé Logan Graham?" she asked with an arched brow.

I gasped. "How do you know about that?"

"I do my research when I go into a new investigation, and in a small town like this, there is going to be some deep history between all the people living there. It helps to know that history."

"You can't know all of it."

"No, but enough to know who hates who and who is most likely to speak poorly about someone else. All of that helps in an investigation. If someone doesn't like another person, they are more likely to talk about them. That helps me."

I scowled. "And what do you know that Chief Randy won't tell me?"

"The DNA tests came back. It's a match. There's no shadow of a doubt that Joan and Minnie are the same person."

"Wow." It was the answer I was expecting, but it still hit me as a surprise. Maybe I was hoping Minnie was exactly who she said she was: a late middle-aged beekeeper who didn't really like people. Even if I was one of the people she didn't like, at least it was honest.

"Does Doreen know?" I asked.

"I'm sure she will soon. Both the U.S. Marshals Service and the Cherry Glen Police Department were given copies of the report. Chief Randy knows by now. I can only assume that he will tell his wife."

I shook my head. "This is going to crush Doreen. She's been adamant Minnie was not a bank robber."

"Friends and families of criminals typically have a hard time believing someone they love has the ability to commit such horrible crimes."

"And you are still convinced that Minnie—I'm just going to keep calling her Minnie—was killed because of her past, not something more recent?"

"That's my theory, and it's a good one. I can't find anyone here in Cherry Glen who has a convincing motive to kill her. Yes, she wasn't well-liked, and yes, she got into arguments and spats with almost everyone that she met, but was that a reason to kill her? I don't buy it."

"Do you think it was a victim of one of her robberies?" I asked.

"Possibly. We've been able to track all but one of them down. Of the ones that we did find, two are dead, and five were nowhere near Cherry Glen at the time of the murder."

"And the one you couldn't find?"

She shook her head. "We just don't know. It looks like he fell off the map. People decide to disappear all the time. You'd be surprised. It doesn't mean he's the killer."

"You said she had an accomplice in the robberies, but that person was also dead."

She nodded. "Mack DeMarco. He died in prison. The most interesting thing I learned about Joan was that she went into beekeeping when she moved to Cherry Glen. She got that idea from Mack."

"Why do you say that?"

"Because he was a beekeeper before he and Joan got together."

"They were a couple?" I don't know why it surprised me that Minnie had a romantic history. Maybe it just didn't fit with what I knew about her. I couldn't see her caring about anyone in that way.

She nodded. "Up until Joan turned on him to lessen her sentence. From what I could tell, before Mack hooked up with Joan, he had a very simple life. He lived in Indiana and kept bees. He and his family lived on a farm."

"He was married?"

"He was at the time he met Joan. He had a daughter too. He left his wife and child for Joan. From what people said she swept him off his feet."

"What happened to his farm and the bees after he left?" I asked.

"The whole place went under. His ex-wife—well, she was never technically his ex-wife because they never got divorced—couldn't care for the bees. They all died, and she lost the farm. From what I can tell, she and her daughter lived a nomadic life after that, moving from place to place."

"Are they suspects? I would say they had a good motive for murder since Minnie broke up their family and caused them to lose their livelihood."

"They would be, but they're both dead too. Mack's wife died of cancer when she was in her fifties, so that was before he died in prison. And her daughter, Malina, died of a drug overdose."

"How horrible." I wrapped my arms around myself.

She nodded. "They certainly got in with the wrong crowd after Mack was convicted, or maybe before that. From what

I gathered, Mack leaving destroyed their lives." She held up her hand. "And I know what you're thinking. They would make great suspects. Perhaps the best suspects, but nothing can change the fact that they were all dead before the murder. It's unfortunate."

Unfortunate indeed.

"Did Malina have children?" I asked.

"Three. A son and two daughters. The father or fathers of the children isn't known. She was a drug addict and made poor choices. From what I have learned, the children were in and out of foster care. The son was the oldest." She cocked her head. "He was about your age. They are all out of foster care now. The girls are in their twenties."

An oddball idea began to form in the back of my mind. No, it wasn't possible, was it? I pushed it back.

Marshal Chuff distracted me from my train of thought when she said, "And what is it that you know that you're not telling Chief Randy or me? I have learned that you like to poke your nose into investigations."

I frowned. "I imagine Chief Randy told you that."

"He did on more than one occasion."

"If he told you I was a pain, why did you tell me all that history about Minnie and Mack?"

"Chief Randy has not been forthcoming with me when it comes to the investigation. In fact, he has tried to hamper me at every turn. If I can't get the help I need from him, what better person to get it from than you, since you irritate him so much?"

I wrinkled my brow. "Thank you, I think."

"People find me irritating too. Sometimes that's the price of being a strong and decisive woman. So tell me what you know."

I shivered, partly from the chill in the air and partly from our conversation. "There's not much to tell. In comparison to what you've told me, I haven't learned a thing." Again, the idea tickling the back of my mind came to the forefront, but I wasn't going to share that hunch with Marshal Chuff until I checked it out for myself. "Minnie fought with the members of her book club, and she was in a major feud with her next-door neighbor, Gordon Elmer. It's hard for me to believe that either of those disputes would lead to murder. Gordon is in his eighties and can barely stand up without shaking. He's in no condition to strangle another person, much less someone as sturdy as Minnie."

"You would be surprised. I didn't see Gordon when I was at her house, but I will look into it." She removed a business card from her pocket and handed it to me. "That's my cell number. Contact me day or night if you learn anything, anything at all, about the case. We'll be a couple of women against Chief Randy." She grinned. "I like the sound of that."

"Sure," I said, uncertain I would keep that promise. The last place I wanted to be was in the middle of some turf war between the local police department and federal law enforcement.

Unfortunately, that's exactly where I stood.

Chapter Twenty-Nine

❧

The next morning, I was up early and did my best to work on the farm. As a surprise for Chesney, I tarped as much of the field as I could without her. I wasn't able to do all the acres she brush hogged. It was far too many for one person, but I got at least a third covered. It was a start. Just covering that much took me several hours. By the time I was spent, it was midafternoon. I went home and cleaned up.

I had hoped that the manual labor would have distracted me from the murder case. No such luck. I kept worrying over the questions about the murder in my mind. What if Tanner Birchwood was Mack's grandchild? He was the right age to be the grandson. He had only shown up in the village recently. Mack's grandchild would have more than enough motive to kill Minnie. The family had lost everything when Minnie seduced Mack away from the family. Revenge and hate were powerful motives, and now Minnie was dead.

My head spun. If I was willing to suspect Tanner because of his age and being new to Cherry Glen, wouldn't I have to suspect Chesney and Whit too? They were also the right ages, and they could be the two girls. I had never heard Chesney speak of their parents, but I assumed they had to be out of the picture. And I couldn't forget two important clues. The girls had moved next door to Minnie. Why? Coincidence? Or to be close to the woman who destroyed their family? And there was the bee tattoos too. I couldn't forget Minnie had a bee tattoo and paled when she saw Whit's.

What if all three of them were Mack's grandchildren? Now I was really giving myself a headache. I just couldn't believe that Chesney, after working so closely with me the last few weeks, could do such a thing. It just wasn't possible.

Any of them being Mack's grandchild seeking revenge was a far-fetched idea. Unfortunately, it was a far-fetched idea I couldn't shake even though the logical side of my brain was telling me how ridiculous it was. I had to find out if my wild idea was true and planned to start with Tanner. Of the three, he was the one I was most comfortable suspecting.

Huckleberry sat next to me on the four-wheeler we used to move tools and feed around the farm. I buzzed through the almost-dead cherry grove and tried my best not to be depressed by its condition. I failed horribly at that.

The cherry grove on my side of the old Bellamy Farm was the demarcation between my land and Tanner's. A large black crow flew overhead. I couldn't know for sure that it was the same one that had been sitting on the scarecrow when Minnie's body was found, but I thought there was a good chance it was.

As soon as I came out of the dead grove, my heart sank even lower.

Tanner had only been on the farm a few weeks, and already his land was so much more groomed and polished than mine.

There were rows upon rows of winter wheat sowed into the rich dark earth. Burlap covered what I assumed where herbs and perennials to protect them from frost. The farmhouse in the distance looked like it was straight from the centerfold of *Martha Stewart Living*, unlike my dad's house, which more closely resembled the backdrop for a true crime documentary.

The bushes and trees around the house were neatly trimmed, and colorful mums filled giant planters to the brim. It wasn't just the fields and house that looked good. The old Bellamy Farm was well on its way to being an organic and sustainable farm. Much farther on its way than my farm was.

There were rain barrels at the end of every downspout to collect rainwater. Solar panels lined the house and barn roofs. Cans of paint sat outside the barn door, and the labels read "toxin-free." The air smelled of lemon and vinegar, which led me to believe that Tanner, the organic wizard, was using those to clean and shine every surface inside and outside of his house. It smelled and looked like money.

I cut the four-wheeler's engine. The front door to the house opened, and Tanner came down the steps with a wide smile on his face. He wiped his hands on a tea towel and tossed it over his shoulder like a chef in a five-star kitchen. "You got my note! I'm so glad. I was wondering if I should go back and leave another one or just ask in town for your phone number." He laughed as if that was a hilarious idea. "I suppose I could have done that from the start."

"I got your note," I said in a far less cheerful tone, and then I shook my head. I knew where my attitude was coming from. It was jealousy. Plain and simple. I was jealous of everything Tanner had accomplished here. That wasn't fair to him, even if he did turn out to be a killer.

"You should have called the number I left in the note. That was my cell," Tanner said. "If you had called, I would have had a pie out of the oven and cooling for us to share a slice. It's pecan. All organic of course."

I looked down at Huckleberry. He can bake an organic pecan pie? Why don't I just give up now?

"Huckleberry and I were just surveying our cherry grove and thought we'd stop by."

The pug looked at me. "Liar!" his little face cried.

"Well, I have some oatmeal cookies I made earlier today. They aren't pecan pie, but why don't you come in and try one." He smiled down at Huckleberry too. "You too. I bet you would like a cookie too."

Huckleberry barked. Cookie was his very favorite word.

Huckleberry and I followed Tanner into the house, and I gasped. It was beautiful, like Joanna Gaines had sprinkled fairy dust on the place. It was modern farmhouse gorgeous. There was even shiplap on the walls. Shiplap in Michigan. It was everything I would want my father's farmhouse to be—and wasn't.

"Your home is beautiful." I picked Huckleberry up. Everything was so pretty and clean, I was afraid he would get his dirty paws on the shiny floor.

He blushed. "Thank you. I did it all myself. I take pride in teaching myself just about everything I do here on the farm. You can put your dog down. He can't hurt anything I can't fix."

I wasn't so sure about that. "You did this yourself? With no help?" I set Huckleberry on the floor. He immediately placed his nose to the floorboards and slowly sniffed his way around the room.

He shook his head. "I used to flip houses in a former life. All self-taught too. But the grind of it got old. I did well, made the money I needed to follow my dreams, and got out before it sucked too much of my soul away."

"You got tired of working on houses?" I asked.

"Working on the houses was fine. It was all the Realtor things and paperwork that was required to buy and sell multiple properties all at one time. It was a lot to juggle. One of my clients owned an organic coffee company in Chicago and told me about the challenges of finding organic food from local farms. Something about it captured my imagination, and I was hooked. I made what more I could and started looking for a farm. I love coffee, but you can't grow that in the Midwest. I wanted to stay in this region, where I could use my connections in the housing market to reach more customers. Western Michigan seemed to be the perfect spot. When this property came up for sale, I couldn't believe my luck. It was a time when it was good to have contacts in the Realtor community. I have friends who knew I was looking for a farm in Michigan, and they let me know before it even went on the market."

I nodded. That explained how I didn't know about the sale.

He blushed again. "There I go again, talking away. What about you? I heard through the grapevine that you were some hotshot producer in LA and left it all behind to be a farmer."

I arched my brow. "The grapevine?"

"Well, from Jessa. She really loves you, and I think she was bragging a bit. It was as if she was trying to convince me to like you." He paused. "It didn't take much convincing."

I changed the subject. I came here for information, not to flirt. "What do you plan to grow?"

"The question is more what I don't plan to grow. I have two hundred acres to play with. The possibilities are overwhelming at times. I do know I want to start my own cherry grove." He smiled. "When I was told the cherry grove wasn't on my property, I was disappointed. What's more Michigan than cherries? But there is always a bright side, and I realized I can start from the beginning with my cherries and plant them just how I want."

"Oh," I said. That didn't sound good for me. I thought the one leg up I had on Tanner was the cherry grove. Grand Traverse County was known for cherries. I didn't need to worry that a clearly talented, motivated, and well-to-do farmer who lived right next to me also planned to have an organic cherry grove. That was no reason to panic at all. Besides, cherry trees are fussy. It could be three years before his trees bore fruit.

"Of course, it would have been easier to grow cherries if I already had the start of an orchard, but in the end this was still the perfect farm for me. Spots like this are hard to find. All cherry trees will cost me is money."

Yeah, just money, I thought. It grows on trees just like cherries. Maybe in Tanner's world it did, but not in mine. Unfortunately.

I shook my head. I was being ridiculous. This man was living his dream because he worked hard and was self-made. I shouldn't begrudge him that because I was strapped for cash. There was a time when I had money I'd earned too. I would have been hurt if anyone belittled me for it.

"I'm not sure there is much to be jealous about there. The grove is in terrible shape," I said. "I have a lot of work ahead of me too."

"Maybe that's where we can help each other out," Tanner said. "I know you must be running thin taking care of your farm all by yourself. I am too. We should work together to make it easier on both of us."

I hesitated. I needed help, but I also suspected this man to be a killer, as far-fetched as that seemed.

When I didn't reply, he went on to say, "Your farm looks a little rough around the edges. Your father is a fascinating man, but I got the impression he doesn't care much about farmwork anymore. He's really into his collection. I've never seen anything like it."

I bristled at his comment, even if it was true. "He showed you his collection? When was that?"

"I was there the same day I dropped the note at your cabin. He told me about the cabin. It's charming, and your father sure knows his Michigan history. I think learning about the region will be a great help to me as I improve the farm."

I frowned. This was the second near stranger that my usually reclusive father had shown his collection to. He had done the same thing for Marshal Chuff. What was going on with him?

"Listen," he said, sounding almost desperate. "Let's work together. You have a vision of an organic farm, and so do I. The difference is that I have the money to make it happen. You have the expertise. If we put those two things together, we'd be unstoppable."

It was a tempting idea, especially after visiting his farm and seeing the signs of what money could do. At the same time, I couldn't see his bank accounts. How did I know that he had one red cent in the bank after spending to fix up his farm? He could be digging himself into a giant hole of debt, just like my father had. In any case, this wasn't an idea I was just going to jump into. I had learned my lesson about making rash decisions in my last investment disaster.

"I'd have to think about it," I said. "There is a lot going on right now, and I have a new farm assistant, who's been a great help. We're still getting our footing, but she's been able to help me prioritize what to do."

"Chesney, right?"

I stared at him. How did he know Chesney's name? I found it very odd. "Do you know Chesney?"

"Sure. I met her that night the woman was murdered. I saw you there." He blushed again. "I tried to talk to you once, but you seemed upset and were heading to the pasture. You were with a guy too. Is he a friend of yours?"

"A guy?" I blinked. "Do you mean Quinn?"

"Right. I heard he's your boyfriend."

I pressed my lips together. "I don't have a boyfriend. Quinn is my neighbor. Yours too. His farm is on the opposite side of my farm from yours."

"Good."

What did that mean?

I shook my head and told myself I didn't care to know. On Saturday, after Whit discovered the body, I remembered someone tapping me on the shoulder, but I had been so caught up in what was going on that it barely registered. "What did you want to talk to me about that night?"

"I wanted to talk to you about organizing events here on Cherry Blossom Farm."

Great, more direct competition. As if I didn't have enough of that already. Maybe I should join forces with him just to stay afloat. It sounded like if his plans for his farm went through, he was going to crush Bellamy Farm, and me along with it.

"Cherry Blossom Farm?" I asked.

He nodded. "It's what I decided to name my place. I know it might be premature because there are no cherry trees, but I hope to change that soon. And I'd really love to pitch in and help you with your trees."

"I will have to think about working together," I said again. "There are a lot of details that would have to be worked out. Right now might not be the best time. There is the issue of the murder."

"Oh, yes, the murder. I'm so sorry that happened at your farm, and in such a public way." He shook his head. "It's so sad that a member of this small community was killed, and now the town has to deal with all the rumors about it. It's all that anyone was talking about at Jessa's Place."

I was sure that was true. I abruptly changed topics. "How did Minnie approach you about the sale of her booth?"

He pressed his lips together. "I'm sorry she's dead, but I'm still angry that she lied to me. Even worse, Chief Randy ordered me to go to the station to give a statement. I've only been here a short time, and the last thing I need is a reputation that I'm a troublemaker or a murderer."

"I don't think anyone wants that reputation."

"I'm sure you're right," he said with a smile.

"How did you meet Minnie?" I asked again.

He cleared his throat. "At the farmers market about two months ago. I was just a few days from getting the keys to the farmhouse, and I was living in a hotel in Traverse City. I came to Cherry Glen as often as I could to get to know the town."

I frowned. In all the time he was visiting Cherry Glen, he never once tried to stop by Bellamy Farm to introduce himself. That seemed odd to me, especially since he was so eager to work together. Had he thought my father or I would try to stop the closing on the farm? I supposed back then I might have, had I enough money to buy the land back.

"As soon as I heard about the farmers market and how popular it was," Tanner said, "I knew it was something I wanted to be a part of. I was so excited. I hadn't even known about it when I bought the farm, and to me it seemed like another sign I'd made the right choice to buy the land. I visited the market on a Thursday, I believe it was. I was just going to walk around, get the lay of the land, when I bumped into Minnie."

I realized this must have been during the time when Kristy was on maternity leave.

"Minnie said she worked in the office, and I explained who I was and asked her about the chance of getting a booth this season. She said there weren't any open and they were hard to come by, but that she might be able to help me. She then walked me over to the honey booth and told me that she planned to get out of the honey business."

"Did she say why?" I asked.

"She said she loved her bees, but she would have to sell them because she was moving. Where she was going, she couldn't keep bees."

I wondered if this was the same time that she put her house up for rent. "Where was she going?"

He shrugged. "She didn't say, and I didn't ask. I was just elated at the idea of getting a booth. That's all I cared about. In hindsight, I should have asked more questions, but she was so sure and confident about the sale of the booth. Besides, she worked for the market. I saw her come out of the office trailer. I had no reason to doubt her."

I could have said there was always a reason to doubt in business, but since I had made my own poor business choices when it came to my farm, I held my tongue. "That was the first time you met her."

He frowned. "Yes."

"You never heard of her before that day."

He folded his arms. "No."

"What about the name Joan Marino?"

"I don't know her. Should I know her?"

I frowned. He honestly looked confused, but I had spent most of my adult life in Hollywood. I was accustomed to good actors. I tried another tactic. "How does your family feel about the farm?"

"They're supportive. I grew up in Chicago. Both my parents are doctors, but that's not the way I wanted to go. Luckily, my younger sister, who is in med school, fulfilled that dream for them."

I frowned. It seemed to me I had been way off base. Tanner had a stable childhood with two parents.

There went my theory that Tanner was Mack's vengeful grandson.

Chapter Thirty

I smiled at Tanner. "I should get back to my farm. Chesney will be waiting for me." I looked down at my dog, who stood at my feet. "And it seems Huckleberry has sniffed every inch of your home and is satisfied with his work."

"Please give the idea of helping each other some serious thought."

"I will," I said, and I would, now that I didn't think he was a killer.

"There is another option that might be advantageous to us both," Tanner said in a way that made me think he believed I wasn't taking his suggestion seriously.

I frowned. "What's that?"

"I could buy half of your cherry orchard. It's on the line between our properties as it is. It would just be a matter of moving the property line ten or so feet."

Without taking a second to think about it, I said, "No."

He blinked. "No?"

"No."

"But you need the money. Anyone can see that. The murder and notoriety from that murder can't help. Everyone in town knows no one went to Fall Daze the day after it happened."

"No. I am not giving up another inch of Bellamy Farm."
My decision was final.

He smiled as if it wasn't a huge concern. "Well, just know
the offer stands. If I were you, I would feel better if the
orchard, or at least half of it, was to be nurtured back to life.
The state it's in now is heartbreaking."

It was heartbreaking, but I would save the cherry orchard
myself, on my own terms. If he thought I would work with
him on organic farming now, he was insane. I didn't leave my
life in California to sell Grandma Bellamy's cherry orchard. I
knew what he was up to. He wanted to buy my farm, bit by bit.

"I think the cherry orchard would be a great place to start
a partnership if you're not interested in selling. If we both
care for it, and share the profits, we can really go places."

I ground my teeth. "I'll pass. I could never give up the
cherry orchard. It's the heart…"

What I was about to say was the cherry orchard was the
heart of the farm. My heart stopped. The heart of the farm.
Could it be the place where my grandmother hid her treasure? This was assuming the entire treasure story wasn't a
riddle Grandma Bellamy made up. I wouldn't be surprised if
she did. My grandmother had a mischievous streak.

"I have to go," I said, scooping up Huckleberry and turning to leave.

He frowned. "I understand. I was too forward about
buying part of the cherry orchard, wasn't I? I'm sorry about
that. I should have waited until we knew each other better
and had built up some trust. I just want to help you in your
tough financial situation."

I spun around. "My financial situation isn't as dire as all that. And it, truly, is none of your business."

He gave me a look as if he knew differently, and I wondered who he had been talking to. I didn't need to wonder long.

"Your father seemed open to the idea."

"My father?" I asked.

"I mentioned it to him when I was there to drop off my note."

I closed my eyes for a moment. "That is all well and good, but the farm is now in my name. It's not his decision. If he wanted to sell the farm off piecemeal, he could have done that years ago and saved me the trouble of coming back here to try to salvage what's left."

"He wants you to save the farm, and he's very proud of you for trying. However, I think he's now realizing, after seeing everything you are doing trying to keep it together, that it's a near impossible task."

"Near impossible is not impossible." With that I walked away, still fuming. I didn't know the last time I had been so angry, and here I thought Tanner was actually going to help me. I was angry at myself for thinking any stranger *should* help me. Even more than my inner anger or my anger at Tanner, I was angry at my father. How could he agree to this idea after everything I'd done, after every cent I'd spent?

Tanner followed me down the porch steps. I heard him but didn't look back. Instead, I got Huckleberry settled into the four-wheeler and climbed in myself. I started the engine. The only good news—if I could even call it that—I had learned from coming here was that Tanner had been at my farm the night of the murder. He had opportunity, but did he have a motive? He wasn't Mack's grandson; I would stake my farm on it. Maybe it was time to talk to Marshal Chuff and ask about the DeMarco grandchildren again.

"Shiloh, I think that we can work together. We don't have to be enemies. There doesn't have to be a winner. We can both win," Tanner said. He still was smiling but instead of charming, the smile came off as condensing.

"There can be only one organic farmer in Cherry Glen," I said. "Even if we both make a go at it. Only one of us is going to be successful. That's just the way it is in small towns, and the Bellamy family has been here for four generations. Just keep that in mind when you try to compete with me." I shifted the four-wheeler into gear and roared down the path toward my cherry grove, a cherry grove that would always be in the Bellamy family if I had anything to say about it.

Within the quiet of the orchard, I let out a breath and slowed down. I came to a complete stop in the middle of the trees. Huckleberry whimpered.

I sighed. "I'm sorry, Huckleberry. I handled that all wrong. I should have been kinder to Tanner. He's new to Cherry Glen. I'm not going to sell this orchard to him, but I could have been a little nicer when I said no. I think LA crushed some of the Midwest niceness out of me. Hollywood will do that to you."

He barked as if in agreement.

I stepped out of the four-wheeler and studied the trees. They were all in need of trimming. Some needed to be uprooted, but others had the potential to come back to life. It would be an immense amount of work, but I was up for the challenge. I was going to save this farm, not just to prove I could—although I will admit that was part of my motivation—but also to preserve the memory of my grandmother.

My grandmother, who may or may not have hidden a treasure in this very grove, died almost seventeen years ago now. Wherever she may have buried the treasure would have been overgrown and possibly dug up by an animal that spirited it away. Assuming the treasure was real.

"The treasure is in the heart of the farm." The line played over and over again in my mind. I wished she would have just come out and said where the heart of the farm was and where she had hidden it, while she was at it.

"I don't even know where to start," I said to the pug.

"The trees really aren't that bad, and with the bees in place, it will make a huge difference. They will pollenate them and bring them back to their former glory."

I jumped and spun around and found Chesney standing in the middle of the row with a set of tree clippers. At her feet was a small chainsaw. Both tools I recognized from my barn. "What are you doing here?"

"You said that you wanted to work on the cherry orchard today," Chesney said. "To evaluate the trees and mark which ones need to be replaced, so here I am."

I shook my head. "Yes, that's right. I'm sorry. It's been the craziest few days and I forgot. Not that that is an excuse at all."

"Where were you coming from?" She nodded at the

four-wheeler. Huckleberry sat up straight in the driver's seat and looked like he was ready to take it for a spin.

"I dropped in on my new neighbor, Tanner Birchwood. He bought Stacey's old farm recently. He said he met you at Fall Daze."

She set her clippers next to the chainsaw at the base of a tree. "I met him the first night, when…"

She didn't need to finish that sentence. I knew she meant when the dead body was found.

"He said he didn't know I was the owner of Bellamy Farm until later," I said.

She shrugged. "I guess that didn't come up, or I just assumed he knew. Everyone else in town knows. I didn't know that he was new himself."

"What did you talk about?"

She folded her arms. "He asked if I worked at the farm. I said yes, and then he asked how we did things. I told him what I could, but he kept digging for more and more details and I got uncomfortable. Then Whit came running from the scarecrow, and I didn't see him again after that."

I frowned. My brain was spinning. Tanner wasn't Mack's grandson. At least, I didn't believe he was any longer. Could Chesney be throwing suspicions on him now because she and Whit were Mack's granddaughters? Was I losing my mind?

"I have something that will cheer you up." She smiled.

I blinked. "You do?"

She started down the row. "Leave the cart there, and come with me. You won't be sorry."

I whistled for Huckleberry, and he trundled behind me. I

came out of the grove of trees and saw five beehives standing at the edge of the cherry grove. Bees buzzed around them, clearly agitated with the move.

"Ta da!" Chesney crowed.

I stared in disbelief. "Are those Minnie's hives?"

"Yep," she said proudly.

"How did they get here?" I asked.

"I borrowed Sully's truck. He thought it was a great idea. He said there haven't been bees at Bellamy Farm in decades."

I wasn't the least bit surprised that my father helped Chesney with this heist. He never liked Minnie and would revel in taking her bees. "When did you do all this? It takes a long time to move five hives with one pickup truck," I said.

"Whit and I moved three late last night and two this morning. We both grew up around bees."

I stared at her. Now was the opening I was waiting for to ask her about Mack, but I wasn't sure I wanted to take it. "Whit showed me a bee tattoo."

"We both have one in memory of our parents." She unzipped her coat and lifted her T-shirt underneath. There was a black and yellow bee etched into her side. It was identical to the one I had seen on Whit's wrist.

I winced. The tattoo was tasteful, but I could image that was one of the most painful places to get one, especially for someone as thin as Chesney. It seemed to me the needle wouldn't have much cushion there.

She lowered her shirt and zipped up her coat again. "We put them in places where we can see them but where they could be hidden if need be, you know?"

I nodded. "I've thought of getting a tattoo for my grandmother before, and for a friend." I didn't say Logan's name.
Chesney didn't know about Logan, and I saw no reason to
tell her. "But I always chicken out." I paused. "Minnie had a
tattoo too."

She blinked at me. "Minnie Devani had a tattoo? No way!"

What would be even crazier, I thought, was if their tattoo
matched Minnie's. "Chesney, does the name Mack DeMarco
mean anything to you?"

"Mack DeMarco?" She wrinkled her smooth brow. "No.
Who is he?"

"Turns out he was a beekeeper. Minnie's tattoo is of a bee
too. She and Mack were a couple. He was her accomplice in
the robberies."

She frowned. "A beekeeper turned bank robber? That's a
wild idea. Did he have killer bees?"

"No." I studied her face.

She stared back at me. "What?"

"You don't know Mack?"

"I just said no." She stepped back. "Why are you looking
at me like that?"

"Like what?"

"Like you think I did something." A lock of hair fell over
her eyes, and she brushed it away.

I sighed and told her about Mack DeMarco's family and
the three grandchildren who were out there somewhere.

She held up her hand. "Wait, let me get this straight. You
think Whit and I are Mack's granddaughters?"

I held my hands aloft. "I know, it's outrageous."

"Our parents died in a car crash when I was in college. I have been taking care of Whit ever since. If you don't believe me, look at this." She pulled her phone from her pocket and tapped on the screen.

She held it out to me. The website browser was opened to a double obituary for the girls' parents. I saw their names and stopped reading.

"I'm so sorry, Chesney." My face felt hot. "It was an awful thing to even think."

She twisted her mouth. "I guess it makes sense. The bee tattoos are an odd coincidence."

"Still. I should have known better." I'd inadvertently forced her to relive a terrible memory and felt awful.

"I know you're worried about Kristy," she said, "and that makes you question everyone. Anyone would be lucky to have a friend like you."

"That's kinder than I deserve."

She shrugged. "I think the thing I got most out of my parents' death is cutting people a break. You don't know what they have been through or are going through. Everyone could use a little kindness."

"You are an amazing young woman, Ches."

She blushed. "I need to calm down the bees. They're still a bit overexcited." She slipped on a hat and veil, picked up the smoker, and smoked the hives. "They'll calm down soon. The queens are all intact and seem to be doing well. The workers and drones just need to settle. I think they'll be fine in an hour or two. Plus, as soon as they realize they've been moved from town to a farm, they'll be happy. They have way more opportunity to gather pollen out here."

"Chesney, do you mean to leave the hives here?" I asked.

"Why not? This is a better home for them than Minnie's backyard ever was."

"We can't take Minnie's bees without asking," I said.

"Minnie is dead. She doesn't need them anymore. I couldn't just leave them there. They'd die."

"But they are her property and must go to her heirs or whoever she named in her will, if she even had one. We can't do this. We have to tell Chief Randy that we have the bees."

She frowned. "Why? He was going to let them die, and they would have if they had been left in Minnie's yard. I saw Gordon with a can of insecticide. There's no way I was going to let him kill those bees. Moving them was my only choice. We saved them. It's what you would have done, Shi."

She was right. I would have saved the bees too if I knew they were being threatened.

"Why would he kill the bees now?" I asked. "Minnie is dead. She's not tormenting him by planting ivy in his yard any longer. Is it because he's allergic?"

She rolled her eyes. "He's not allergic. I already told you I saw him by the bees when Minnie wasn't home on more than one occasion." Chesney puffed the hives with the smoke two more times before she came closer to me and removed her hat and veil.

I grimaced. "Then you did the right thing, even if it's only temporary. We can keep the bees here for safety's sake, but I have to tell Chief Randy. If not, he might believe the bees were stolen. If they are discovered here before I tell him that would be much worse."

"The police chief really thinks the bees are related to the crime? Who would kill someone over bees?" Chesney asked.

"I'm sure someone would."

"If you have to tell him, go ahead." She folded her arms. "I don't care, and if I get in trouble for it, I don't care about that either. It was the right thing to do, and that's all that matters."

I wasn't sure Chief Randy would agree with her on that last point. I removed my phone from my pocket. This wasn't a call I relished the idea of making.

To my relief, Chief Randy didn't pick up, and I left a message. "Hi, Chief Randy, this is Shiloh Bellamy. I just wanted to let you know that Minnie's beehives were moved to my farm by—"

Chesney waved her hands wildly. It seemed for all her bravado, she still didn't want me to include her name in the call.

"Umm. The hives were moved to keep them safe. I know that Gordon wanted them out of the neighborhood ASAP. I'm happy to have them delivered to Minnie's rightful heir if need be." I ended the call and cocked my head at Chesney. "I thought you didn't care if he knew."

"I don't care, but I also don't think it needs to be on his voicemail, which can be used in court."

I sighed. "When Doreen gets wind of this, she will blame me."

"Maybe don't bring me into it. It's probably easier if she only has one person to hate."

I frowned at her.

"Shiloh!" a high-pitched voice called.

Huckleberry took off after the sound of Hazel's voice. Chesney and I followed the dog.

We found Hazel, Huckleberry, and Esmeralda on the edge of the orchard.

"How did you know where I was?" I asked.

"Esmeralda showed me." She scooped up the cat and nuzzled her close. "She's a very smart cat. Are you working in the orchard? I'd love to learn how to take care of the trees."

I looked at my watch. It was after three in the afternoon. The day had gone quickly, and I'd spent more time at Tanner's farm than I realized. The bus had already dropped Hazel off for the day. "What time is your dad picking you up?" I asked.

"He's not."

I stared at her. "He's *not*?"

"He's not today." She put her hands on her hips. "Dad told me that he was going to text you to tell you I was staying over today."

I frowned and removed the phone from my pocket. Sure enough, there was a text from Quinn apologizing for the late notice but asking me to watch Hazel this afternoon through tomorrow morning. He said that his mother suddenly had to go out of town. I frowned. That didn't sound like Doreen at all. Could it be related to Minnie's death?

I smiled. "The text must have come in when I was talking to the neighbor. Looks like you will be bunking with Esmeralda, Huckleberry, and me tonight."

She pumped her fist in the air. "Yes! Can we order pizza? Grandma never gets pizza."

I laughed. "Sure."

"Yes! We will farm and eat pizza! This is the best day."

Chesney cocked her head. "You're a strange kid."

"Anything is better than being stuck in my grandmother's house all afternoon and night."

I chuckled. "Before we farm, I have to ask, do you have homework?"

"Sure, but this is way more fun. I can do it later over my pizza dinner." She said it with the confidence only a tween could muster.

"Why do I think your grandmother made you do your homework before you did anything fun?"

She rolled her eyes. "She never let me have any fun, ever. The only good times were when her book club was there, and she didn't have time to tell me what to do. They had the best conversations."

"You eavesdropped on your grandmother's book club?" Chesney asked.

"What else could I do? She takes my phone as soon as I walk in the house and doesn't let me watch TV or go outside. All I had to do was my homework, or I could see what the book club was up to. I used to hide on the landing in her staircase. From there, I could hear every word, but they couldn't see me."

"What was so interesting about their conversations?" I asked, wondering if I really should be pumping an eleven-year-old for information about her grandmother. I'd worry about the ethics of that later.

"Well, it was barely ever about the book. I think sometimes one of them would try to bring the book into the conversation, but it always went back to a gossip session about people in Cherry Glen. They talked about you a lot, Shiloh."

"Me? Why?"

She shrugged. "I don't know. They talked about Dad's friend Logan who died."

"Who's Logan?" Chesney asked.

I shook my head. "It's such a long story, but he was a local star high school athlete. He passed away about fifteen years ago when he was in his twenties. He was Quinn's best friend." I left it at that. I took care not to mention how close Logan and I had actually been.

"They had to have talked about other things. Logan passed so long ago. What else did they say?" I asked.

"Mostly Minnie and Clementine argued. Minnie thought dinners at the church should be handled differently. She wanted Clementine to step down so that someone else could do the job. Clementine said she would over her dead body or something like that."

"Minnie wanted the church job?" I asked.

"Maybe. She never said it. At least I never heard her say it." She wrinkled her nose. "The last book club that she came to, she was so upset that she said she wasn't coming back. Grandma was very upset and tried to talk Minnie into staying. Minnie said that she lost trust in them. She said she should know better than to trust anyone. Then Minnie just left."

"When did this happen?"

Hazel thought for a moment. "Thursday. They have book club on Thursday afternoons."

Thursday was the day before Minnie died. I didn't know if it had any bearing at all on her death or not, but it was a detail no one in the book club thought to share. That fact wasn't lost on me.

Chapter Thirty-One

Chesney, Hazel, and I worked in the orchard for two hours. We numbered the trees and marked the ones that couldn't be saved with a yellow X; they would have to be removed. Overall though, I was relieved to see the orchard was in better shape than I had first thought. The trees were just overgrown, and many of them had dead branches. Tears came to my eyes as I looked at the trees and hope filled my heart.

I was dying to follow my hunch—that this was the heart of the farm I had been looking for. Unfortunately, it would have to wait. Searching for the treasure wasn't something I could do with Chesney and Hazel looking on.

Hazel came out from under the tree. "I'm hungry."

I looked at my watch and saw it was five thirty. The sun was beginning to set. I knew it wasn't long until the time change, and work would have to stop at four thirty. I wasn't looking forward to that. "Pizza time?"

Hazel did a happy dance.

"Ches, you want to stay and get pizza with us?"

She shook her head. "I promised Whit I would bring her something to eat at the theater. She's there more than she is at home these days. She would sleep there if Stacey let her."

I smiled. "I think it's great that you both found your passions."

Chesney grinned. "Me too. Our parents would be proud."

I nodded but felt a twinge of regret for ever suspecting her of murder. I turned to Hazel, who cradled Esmeralda in her arms like a baby doll. "After pizza, it's homework time."

"You sound like a parent," Hazel said.

"Thanks," I said with a grin.

"It wasn't a compliment," she said, but her smile took some of the bite out of her words.

We gathered up the tools, then Hazel and Chesney, the two pets, and I climbed into the four-wheeler. It was a balance, but we all made it back to the barn without anyone falling off.

Hazel held Esmeralda close. It was clear to me the girl and cat really loved each other. Esmeralda was nice enough to me and occasionally she let me pet her, but it was nothing like how close she was to Hazel.

At the farmhouse, Chesney stopped me. "Shi, I know that you are trying to find out what happened to Minnie for Kristy's sake."

I nodded. "I am."

"Talk to Gordon again. I just got the feeling that he knows more. Sometimes when I heard them arguing outside my window, I got the impression they weren't fighting about the condition of their yards, but something much deeper."

"What do you mean?" I asked.

She shook her head. "I can't put my finger on it, but it was like everything had a second meaning."

"You said before they didn't remember why they were feuding."

"That's what they told me, but if Minnie's life and death can teach us anything, it's how easy it is for people to lie."

I frowned. "I can't imagine living next to someone I hated for so long."

Chesney cocked her head and her bob brushed her shoulder. "Gordon and Minnie didn't live next to each other that long. Minnie has been there a long time, but Gordon moved onto the street after I did. His house was for rent too when I was looking. I liked the one I rented better because it had a larger yard."

"I just thought he lived there forever."

She shook her head. "He hasn't." Chesney said goodbye and climbed into her beater car and drove away.

My phone beeped to tell me I had a text message. I removed it from my pocket to find a new one from Quinn.

"Everything good? Sorry to spring Hazel on you for the night. I will only have to work until seven in the morning. I'll be at your farm shortly after to take her to school."

"We are all good. Hazel requested pizza for dinner," I texted back. "And she's been a great help on the farm."

"What is it?" Hazel asked.

I looked up from my phone. "It's just a text from your dad that he only has to work until seven a.m. tomorrow."

Dad, Hazel, and I had a simple dinner of pizza and salad. I wished I had time to make her a home-cooked meal, but it's what she asked for. The pizza was a hit at least. I don't think she touched her salad at all, even though her lettuce was swimming in a lake of ranch dressing.

"After dinner, I'll show you some more of my collection," Dad told Hazel.

"Awesome," Hazel said around a bite of pizza. "I have to do a report for history on something local. It's due next Friday. Can you help me?"

Dad's face lit up like he had just been told a special museum exhibit just opened in Traverse City. "You bet I can. I have everything you need right here. I have a whole library of books on local Michigan history."

They quickly finished their meals. Dad hadn't touched the salad either. While the pair disappeared into his collection room, I tidied up the kitchen. "Hazel, we are only going to stay another hour and then go to the cabin for the night."

"Okay" was her cheery call from the collection room.

I went outside to check on the chickens. Huckleberry, my ever-loyal pup, came with me. Esmeralda stayed with Hazel. She really loved that girl.

I zipped up my coat as soon as I was out the door. It had to be near freezing. Huckleberry shivered at my feet. "I think it's time to order you a dog jacket."

He looked at me like I was bonkers.

The sun had set, but the farm was illuminated by a large harvest moon. Blue-white light fell onto the barn, every fallen leaf, and every blade of grass. But there was much in shadow too.

Watching my dad with Hazel brought a pang into my heart. I wished I could say he had been that way with me. While I was growing up, my father was still in the middle of grappling with my mother's death. He wasn't emotionally able to care for a child as much as I needed. If it hadn't been for my grandmother stepping in and insisting on being the one to care for me, I'm not sure how I would have turned out.

I bit my lip. I was happy Hazel and Dad had a connection and enjoyed each other's company. I only wished I had that with him too.

I shook my head. "I can't go back thirty-some years and change my childhood." I nodded at the pug. "Let's go check on the chickens."

I walked the short distance to the coup. There were no chickens in the chicken run. I had to check to be sure. It wasn't safe for the girls to roam the farm at night; there were too many predators. I lifted the hatch that let me peek into the coop and shone my phone's flashlight into the coop and counted six chickens. There should be seven. I knew who was missing right away.

"Where's Diva?" I asked the hens.

The other chickens huddled down on their nests. They weren't talking. Diva was the tough chick in the flock. They were enjoying a break from her bossy ways.

I closed the hatch. "Huck, Diva is missing."

He made a concerned snuffling sound. They bossed him around, but he loved those chickens.

Somewhere behind me, at the edge of the barnyard, there was a loud snap like something or someone had stepped on a stick. I jumped.

"Diva?"

Another snap came. This one was much louder. A chicken wasn't heavy enough to break a branch like that.

A chicken screamed, and in the moonlight, I saw Diva throw herself from a sapling with her wings out. She gave a mighty battle cry, and a woman came yelling and running out of the tree cover.

I recognized her by her gray trench coat.

Diva landed on the ground with feathers splayed, ready to fight. Huckleberry barked.

"Oh my Lord! Help! Your chicken is going to kill me!" Alexis cried.

"What are you doing here?"

"I'll tell you if you call off the chicken."

I folded my arms. "I don't think so. You're trespassing. Diva knows when we have an intruder."

"Please! I'm afraid of birds. Just pick her up. Please!"

I waited a beat and then relented. Normally, catching Diva was a challenge, but she was so angry at Alexis that she didn't even notice I was behind her until I scooped her up. She pecked and scratched. I ran her to the coop and tucked her inside, latching the door behind her. The commotion coming from the coop as Diva made her dramatic entrance was deafening. I wasn't going to be getting any eggs tomorrow, that was for sure. The girls couldn't lay when they were stressed.

I walked back to Alexis, who was still shaking over her encounter. "What are you doing here?"

"I wanted to see the scene of the crime."

"You are way off course," I said. "The crime scene is not by the chickens."

"I know." She made a face. "This farm is so big. I lost my way."

"You should have come to the house and asked."

She folded her arms, some of her confidence coming back. "Would you have told me?"

"Probably not."

"Exactly. This is a huge story and could make my career. I don't expect a farmer would understand that."

She knew nothing of my career in LA or the fact that I had once been as ambitious as she was, perhaps more. "I think it's time for you to go."

"Fine." She started toward the driveway.

Huckleberry and I followed her all the way down the drive until she reached her car, strategically parked out of view of the farmhouse. We watched as she got in and drove away.

Shaking my head, I picked up Huckleberry and carried him to the farmhouse. I thought it was time Hazel and I headed to the cabin.

It took some doing, but I was finally able to pull Hazel away from my father. "You can sleep in my old room here at the farmhouse if you want to stay here a bit longer," I said. "You might be more comfortable. I only have a sofa at the cabin."

"No, I want to see the cabin! How many kids get to sleep in a cabin in the woods?"

I smiled. "All right, then. Let's go." I didn't mention the reporter to Dad or Hazel. It would have only upset my father and excited Hazel. Neither of them would be able to sleep had they known.

Hazel, Huckleberry, Esmeralda, and I said good night to my father and walked the quarter mile to the cabin. I realized that in the depth of winter, I might want to get out the snow-mobile that was in the barn to make the journey.

We made it to the cabin without issue, and I didn't hear any more broken sticks. I locked the cabin door behind us.

"This is so cool. This is the kind of place I would think the witch from *Hansel and Gretel* lived."

"Thank you. I think." I chuckled. "I hope you don't think I'm a witch."

"No. Although that would be cool if you were." She buzzed around the cabin, which admittedly only took a few seconds.

I went into the kitchen to make some tea and calm down. It had been a stressful day. My grandmother always said tea was the best remedy for everything. She made me drink it for every sniffle and even once for a broken leg. It took me a very long time to appreciate tea on my own after that.

"Hey!" Hazel called from the bedroom. "What's this?"

I set the kettle on the burner and went to the bedroom to see what she was excited about.

In the bedroom, she sat on the corner of my bed holding my grandmother's letter in her hands.

My heart sank. I hadn't even thought about hiding it. "Did you read that letter?"

"Maybe." She cast her eyes down. "Is she talking about dad's friend Logan?"

My stomach tightened.

"Were you going to marry him?" Her eyes were wide. "I never knew that."

"It was a long time ago."

"What about the treasure?" she asked.

"What treasure?" I asked, trying to play dumb.

She waved the letter. "The treasure in here."

I took the paper from her hand and folded it up. "It's just a metaphor."

"A metaphor for what?"

I tucked the letter in my sock drawer. That's where I should have been keeping it all this time instead of in plain sight on the dresser mirror. How could I be so careless? "I don't know. My grandmother liked to speak in riddles at times. It doesn't mean anything."

"It is a riddle, but I think this means you have real treasure here on the farm! Like gold bars or something!"

"You can't tell anyone about this letter," I said a little more sternly than I intended.

"Whoa. You must think the treasure is real!"

I didn't say anything and began rooting through my dresser. I came up with an old T-shirt that would be a perfect nightshirt for Hazel to sleep in.

"You think it's real," she said. "Have you tried to find it?"

"Here's a shirt for you to sleep in. I have a bunch of blankets and quilts we can pile on the sofa to make it more comfortable for you. Do you have any more reading you have to do tonight?"

Her face fell. "You're treating me just like my grandmother would. You won't give me a straight answer."

My heart sank. I held the T-shirt to my chest and sat on the edge of the bed. "I'm sorry. The truth is I don't know if the treasure is real, but I'm hoping that it is because the farm is struggling."

"Have you been looking for it?" she asked with sparkling eyes.

I nodded.

"Then I will look too. We can find it together."

It seemed that my secret was out.

Chapter Thirty-Two

I t took a while to calm Hazel down enough to go to bed after that, but eventually she snuggled into the mountain of quilts and blankets and went to sleep with dreams of treasure hunting dancing in her head. For me, sleep was more elusive. I heard every creak of the house, a tree branch knocking against my bedroom window, and the howl of the wind as cold air traveled across Lake Michigan from Canada.

When morning finally came, I was relieved. I groggily got out of bed on maybe three hours of sleep. I found Hazel and the animals eating breakfast. Huckleberry and Esmeralda enjoyed kibble while Hazel ate cereal straight from the box. I couldn't blame her for doing that due to the state of my kitchen.

"Oh good! You're awake. Are you ready to go look for the treasure?" She beamed.

I sighed. "If you want to help me with this wild goose chase my grandmother put me on, fine."

"Yeah!" She pumped her fist in the air and almost knocked her box of cereal off the table in the process. She caught it at the last second.

"But not right now. Your dad will be here soon to take you to school. We will have to treasure hunt another time."

"Ugh, Shi, you sound so much like an adult."

I started the coffee maker. "I know. I find it alarming too."

Hazel and I decided to do farm chores at the barn until her dad arrived. That way, I could get a jump on the day, and he wouldn't have to come all the way back to the cabin to find his daughter.

Hazel helped me to move some straw bales from the barn to outside of the chicken coop. It was time to change the chickens' bedding.

She let the chickens out of the coop and chased them into the yard. I came out of the barn with a straw bale. I dropped it on the ground just a few feet from the coop.

"You are crazy strong, Shiloh," Hazel said. "You just Wonder Woman-ed that straw bale."

I laughed. "This is the first time in my life that I have ever been compared to Wonder Woman."

Hazel flopped on the hay bale. "Farming is hard work. I told Dad that the last time I was here helping you. I said I probably worked harder than he did." She eyed the chickens. "And they aren't the most cooperative."

Esmeralda jumped onto the hay bale next to Hazel. Hazel hugged the cat. "You are the best kitty ever."

Esmeralda lapped up the praise like it was fresh cream.

"What do you think about sharing Esmeralda?" I asked.

She looked up from where she was scratching the cat under the chin. "We already do, I thought."

I smiled. "We do, but I know that you really want a pet. When you're home, you can keep Esmeralda there, and when you're staying at your grandmother's you can leave her here, if that is okay with your dad."

Her face brightened. "I like that idea! I really want a pet. Grandma is so fussy."

I hid a smile. I agreed with her but didn't say it. I was on thin ice with Quinn's mother as it was.

"It's a deal! Can she come home with me tonight?"

"If it's okay with your dad, you can pick her up after school. We'll have to ask him."

She hugged Esmeralda tight. "We can ask him right now." She pointed. "There's his truck."

Quinn's pickup came down the long driveway. When it rolled to a stop, he got out. Huckleberry and the chickens ran toward him.

"That's quite a greeting."

"You're popular on Bellamy Farm," I said.

He locked eyes with me for a second. "Am I?"

I looked away, regretting my cheeky comment.

"Dad," Hazel said.

I felt my heart skip a beat. I thought for sure that she was going to tell Quinn about my grandmother's note. She surprised me and said, "Sully's going to help me with my history project on local history. He has everything I need."

Quinn smiled. "He would be the one to ask about local history, that's for sure."

"And Shiloh said that Esmeralda can stay at our house when you're home." She danced in place.

Quinn shot me a look. "She did, did she?"

"I said we could ask your dad." I smiled.

Hazel clasped her hand together. "Can she?"

"I'll think about it. I'm too tired to make any decisions right now. Are you ready to go? We need to circle back home before you go to school so you can change."

"Yeah, I just want to go say bye to Sully."

"Hurry up then," Quinn said. His shoulders sagged with exhaustion.

Hazel and Esmeralda, her feline shadow, went into the house.

"Sorry about the cat thing," I said, studying his tired face.

"It's okay. She's been relentless about it for months. I think it's a good idea, but not today. After I drop her off at school, I'm going to bed."

"Long shift?"

"The longest. It's a long time to have to stay awake. We were down a person, so I was up all night on watch." He rubbed his eyes. "It didn't help that my mother wouldn't stop calling."

"About the murder?"

"More about you. She wanted me to deny we were anything more than friends." He was looking at me again with the strange expression.

"I don't know where she got this idea. We're not."

"Is that true?"

I stared at him. "Isn't it?"

He rubbed the back of his neck. "I can't help how I feel."

"How do you feel?" I asked quietly.

"Confused and tired. And maybe so tired that my walls are down, and I will regret saying this later. Right now, I'm not awake enough to care. Logan would want me to be happy," he said. "Even if that means being happy with you."

"With me?" I squeaked.

"Dad," Hazel ran out the farmhouse.

Quinn jumped back three feet from me like he had been shocked.

"I'm ready to go." Hazel picked up Esmeralda one last time and hugged her close. "Can we stop by tonight? Sully said he can help me tonight, and then we can take Esmeralda home for a sleepover."

Quinn raised his eyebrows at me. I was still trying to process what he'd just said. Quinn wanted to be happy with *me*?

"Shi?" Quinn asked.

I shook my head. "Sure. Of course. I'll make dinner too, if you want to come over at six. I promise it will be something better than pizza."

"I like pizza," Hazel said.

"I like pizza too. It's a date," Quinn said.

With his daughter and my father? I didn't think that it qualified as such.

Chapter Thirty-Three

C hesney had class all day, so I was left to my own devices. I could literally do any project that I wanted to on the farm. I typically loved the work, but today, nothing appealed. Added to that was my last conversation with Quinn, which played over and over again in my mind. I needed distraction. Since working on the farm alone the day before hadn't distracted me from worrying over who Mack's grandchildren might be, I knew it would never work to keep my mind off my conversation with Quinn. I had to leave the farm.

For a second night, I had been plagued with nightmares of Kristy going to jail. I had to see her and make sure she was okay. We texted often, but that wasn't enough. I shot her a text and asked if she could meet at the farmers market that morning. She agreed.

As Huckleberry and I drove into town, I thought over the murder and everyone involved. Marshal Chuff had told me to talk to her about the case. I wondered if she would let me see Minnie's tattoo. When I parked my car at the market, I texted her and asked for a photo of the tattoo.

To my surprise, she texted right back. She'd sent a photograph of a black tattoo of a bee. The tattoo was on Minnie's shoulder. The bee was delicate like the tattoo that both Whit and Chesney had, but the picture was different. It wasn't the same tattoo. I let out a sigh. That wasn't definitive proof that the sisters weren't related to Mack, but it was all the proof I needed. I was happy to have it. I had ruled out Tanner and the Stevens sisters, but there were other suspects. Gordon came to mind, despite his physical limitations and his age.

I couldn't shake the conversation I had with Gordon a few days ago. I just had a feeling he knew more about Minnie than he was letting on, and then when Chesney said she had the same hunch last night, I knew there was something to it.

"Are you just going to sit in your car all day? Or talk to me?" Kristy shouted at me.

I blinked, looking up from my phone. Kristy stood outside of my car window. One hand was on the handle of the twins' double stroller. The other held a pair of bolt cutters.

I got out of the car, and Huckleberry followed me. "What are you doing with those?" I pointed at the bolt cutters.

"We are going to break into Minnie's booth, of course."

Of course.

She looked down at her daughters who were cooing and kicking in the stroller. "It will be the girls' first breaking and entering. I'm hoping it will be their last."

"Let's hope so," I agreed and held out my hand. "Let me carry the bolt cutters while you push the stroller."

"Oh, good idea." She handed them to me.

On a non-market day, the farmers market was nearly empty. The only things on the lot were the office trailer and the permanent booths, like Minnie's.

"How have you been feeling?" I asked Kristy as we walked to the far end of the lot where Minnie's booth was. Huckleberry trailed behind, stopping every few seconds to sniff the ground. Sometimes he had delusions of grandeur of being a bloodhound. I would never say that to him though.

"It's hard. I know I'm innocent, but the chief doesn't. He came to my house last night to question me again. The girls were sleeping just down the hall. It was horrible, Shi. The worst thing I've gone through."

"Did he say why he hasn't arrested you yet if he's so sure?"

"A judge won't give him a warrant. It seems the judge is being pressured by Marshal Chuff and her superior to wait. I'm grateful for that."

We stopped in front of the booth shaped like a beehive. It was bright yellow, sunny, and cheerful, nothing like the Minnie I had known. At the back of the booth was the padlocked door.

"I know the police have already looked in here." Kristy gripped hard on the handles of the stroller. "I saw them sniffing around on the lot yesterday, but I have to have a look for myself. Break it open."

I held the bolt cutter to the lock. "I have a feeling Chief Randy is going to frown on this."

"Chief Randy can stuff it as far as I'm concerned."

I closed my eyes and cut the bolt. The padlock tumbled to the ground. Huckleberry gave it a good sniff. I set the bolt cutters down beside it and opened the door. There were three shelves. Each shelf was lined with jars of honey.

Kristy leaned over my shoulder. "What's in there?"

"Honey."

"Just honey?"

I moved the jars around. "It just looks like honey." I ran my hand across the bottom of each shelf. At the bottom of the second one, I felt a piece of paper. "Wait. There's something here." I removed it and straightened up.

Kristy was a good eight inches shorter than I was and stood on her tiptoes. "What is it?"

"A note. How did the police miss this?"

"Read it!" she said. One of her daughters giggled in agreement.

I unfolded the small piece of brown paper. "J—you gave me no choice. When your money ran out so did your time. I'd move along if I were you. G, Mack's friend" I read.

"It's a blackmail note."

I nodded. "But how did the police miss it?"

"I don't know, but it's more proof she's Joan."

"Right, but no clue to who the blackmailer is." The "G" made me suspicious though. There was one "G" it could be, but I still had doubts.

Kristy's shoulder's sagged. "So I'm still the prime suspect." She stared down at her girls.

"We need to give this to Chief Randy," I said. "This puts doubt on you as a suspect at least."

"I'm not sure doubt is enough for Chief Randy."

After I left Kristy at the farmers market, I called the chief, but there was no answer. I left a message saying I had found a note addressed to Minnie. I then called the station and relayed the same message to Connie Baskins, who said that Chief Randy was on an accident call. She promised to relay the message.

With the note in my pocket, I walked to Erie Street, where Minnie had lived. Huckleberry was on his leash and it was a perfect fall day. He seemed to sense the brightness of the day, too, and didn't even fight me on his leash.

When I got there, I saw a moving truck in front of Minnie's small house. Doreen stood in the yard and pointed at the movers, telling them how to put things in the truck. I stopped in the side yard that was a few feet from the hedge separating Minnie's and Gordon's properties, and I almost turned around. Before I could, she spotted me.

She marched over to me. "I'm not surprised you're here."

I could say the same to her, but I held my tongue. "Did the house sell?"

She scowled at me. "No, but it's my job to move Minnie's things out. Most are being donated to charity."

"Does she have an heir?" I asked.

"Let's talk in the back," she said. "The movers don't need to overhear this."

Huckleberry and I followed her to the backyard. She stood next to the hedge with her arms folded. "I don't know why whether or not she has a heir matters to you."

"I just wondered if she had any family."

"*I* was her family."

Before I could respond, she went on, "Maybe she was the person everyone said she was in the past, but the Minnie I knew was my friend, and I'm going to make sure that her things will go to people who appreciate them." She frowned. "My husband told me that you have her bees."

I swallowed. "Just for safekeeping, until they can go to the right person."

"You're the right person," she said. "You keep them. They meant a lot to Minnie, and I know that you'll keep them alive. That's all that matters."

I blinked. "Thank you. I'll take good care of them."

She nodded. "See that you do." She started toward the house and then stopped. "When you make up your mind, take good care of my son too." She went into the small house through the back door before I could say a word.

I stared at the closed door. Did Quinn say something to her about how he felt about me?

"She's a horrible woman, just as bad as Minnie. That must be why they got on so well," a voice said to my right.

Over the hedge, I spotted Gordon on the ground again, weeding the ivy out from his yard.

"What are you doing back here?" he continued. "I thought I told you not to come back."

I stepped around the hedge into his yard in order to see him better. "You said don't come back if I didn't do something about the bees, and look, the hives are gone. They're at my farm."

"Good riddance to them. Every time I looked at them, I thought about Minnie and it made my stomach turn. She did everything that she could to make my life more miserable. Like it wasn't miserable enough with this old body of mine." Slow and painfully using his cane, he struggled to his feet.

Huckleberry began digging into the ivy at my feet.

"You might be an annoyance," Gordon said. "But you have a good dog there."

I ignored his comment. "I wanted to talk to you about Minnie again."

He eyed me. "Why?"

"Because the police think my friend killed her and I know she didn't. I think you might know something."

"I know a lot of things, but that doesn't mean I want to talk to you about any of them."

I pulled the blackmail note from my pocket. "You're G, aren't you? Tell me about Mack DeMarco."

"Where did you get that?"

"It was in Minnie's honey booth," I said.

"I thought she would have been smarter and destroyed all those notes. She told me that she had."

"You're Mack's friend?"

He turned around with fury in his eyes. "Mack was a friend of mine. He had a great life until he got involved with Joan."

I sucked in a breath. "Were you blackmailing her?" I asked.

"So what if I was? She deserved it. She ruined that man and his family's whole life. Not to mention the dozens of people she terrorized by stealing from them at gunpoint. It's karma. She got what was coming to her."

"When did you know Joan was Minnie?" I asked.

"Just a couple of years ago. I spent the last ten years looking for her. I might look old, but I'm good with a computer. I had a PC before you were born. I followed the bees. Bees were always Joan's thing, so I would look online for beekeepers in the region. I knew it was a long shot, but then I got lucky. I found a photo of a woman who looked a lot like Joan at the farmers market in Cherry Glen. I decided she looked enough like her that I would check it out." He took a breath. "I found out where she lived, and when I drove by she was wearing a sleeveless shirt when working in her yard. That's when I saw that tattoo. Mack told me about it once. You could have knocked me over with a feather that my hunch paid off."

"You could have called the police," I said.

"And what good would that have done for me? Mack was dead. There was no putting his family back together."

"So instead you decided to blackmail her?"

"The house next door to hers was for rent. It was providence. I signed the lease that day. The medicine I have to take for my rheumatoid arthritis isn't cheap, and that's just the tip of the iceberg of all the medicines that I have to take. Blackmailing Minnie could solve that problem for me. It's not like I was going out to buy boats with the money she gave me." He said this as if how he spent the money justified the blackmailing.

At the same time, I felt a twinge of compassion for him. By the way he leaned on his cane, it was clear he was in pain. He did need the medicine he used the money for. In any case, blackmailer or not, he wasn't the killer. Seeing Gordon wobble back and forth on his cane, I knew he couldn't strangle anyone, especially not someone as vital as Minnie had been.

Which meant the killer was still out there, and I was out of viable suspects.

"Did you ever meet any of Mack's family?"

"I knew his wife and daughter very well. After Mack died, they fell apart. Both died before they should have. It was a damn shame."

"And his grandchildren?"

"I only met Lynlee when she was very small. She was the youngest, no more than two. I don't know what became of her. She, her sister, and her brother went into the foster system, and that was the end of it."

"Her name was Lynlee?" I asked.

"That's what they called her. Her mother was high at the time, so you can never be sure." He shrugged as if it didn't matter in the least.

"What about the son?"

"Don't know." He hobbled to his back door. "Now, off my property and leave." He went through the back door and let it slam behind him.

Could Lynlee be Lynn Chuff? I tugged Huckleberry away from the ivy. He sighed as if he never wanted to leave.

I felt like I was jumping to conclusions again. Even so, I called Chief Randy. This time he picked up. "What is it, Shiloh?"

I quickly told him about the note Kristy and I found and what I had learned from Gordon.

He sighed. "I had a feeling that old coot was involved in this. I'll have to talk to the DA about what we should do about the blackmailing. No one wants to throw a sick man in prison. I'm surprised you called me," he added. "I thought you'd be telling this to Chuff."

"Gordon is local," I said. "It seemed more appropriate to call you."

"Right you are."

When I didn't say anything, he asked, "Was there anything else, Shiloh?"

I hesitated. I needed a little more clarity on whether Lynlee and Lynn Chuff were the same person. The only person who could give me that clarity was Marshal Chuff herself. "No, no, that was it." I ended the call.

Chapter Thirty-Four

Huckleberry and I went back to the farm. I didn't know what more I could learn in town about the murder. When I drove up the long driveway to the farmhouse, my breath caught when I saw Lynn Chuff and my father sitting at the picnic table by the farm together. Dad laughed at something Marshal Chuff said, and I felt sick.

I parked the convertible and got out. Huckleberry started to get out too. "Stay," I hissed.

The pug gave me a strange look. He knew we were home. He didn't know why I wanted him to stay.

He barked and defiantly jumped out through the driver's side door.

"Huckleberry, get back in here."

He flattened his body on the ground and crawled under the car. I slapped a hand to my forehead. "Huck!" I hissed.

"Shiloh," Dad called.

I looked back at the spot where the pug had disappeared. "Stay," I hissed before walking over to my father and Marshal Chuff.

"Your friend is here," Dad said. "I was just telling her the story of how that old Sherman tank ended up on Michigan

Street." He smiled. "It's not often that young folks want to listen to my stories."

I forced a smile on my face, but every cell in my body hummed. "That's nice, Dad. Marshal Chuff, I'm surprised to see you here."

Marshal Chuff stood up from the picnic table. "Well, I thought I would check on you, Shiloh, before I left. It seems that Chief Randy got his way, and my superiors have called me off the case. They will leave it in his fumbling hands."

I nodded. "I'm sorry to hear that. I know you wanted to see the case through."

She nodded. "I did." She walked toward me. "Chief Randy called me about your conversation with Gordon Elmer. Interesting turn of events that he knew Mack DeMarco. It seems you found the blackmailer and my informant too. Well done."

"Thank you," I said, looking her in the eye.

Behind her, I saw a strange look cross my father's face. Slowly, he stood up from the table, taking hold of his cane. He shuffled toward the chicken coop.

"I found a note that I know now was from Gordon in Minnie's honey booth. How did you and Chief Randy miss it?"

She smiled. "We didn't. How could we when it was stuck on the bottom of a shelf. I don't even think incompetent Chief Randy could have messed up finding that clue. I found it in her house when I searched it before Chief Randy and his officers got there. I knew it was Gordon because there was a list of complaints from him in the same place and in the same hand. That list was signed. My guess is Joan was keeping them to show she was being blackmailed for sympathy if she was ever caught.

"I put it there after the booth had been searched by the police to hurry you along in the direction of Gordon. You seemed to be taking your good old time putting the pieces together. I basically had to give you the answer. I had no idea that it would take you this long to break into the honey booth."

"You knew Kristy and I were going to break into the honey booth?"

She smiled. "I was at the farmers market when the two of you spoke about needing bolt cutters. You never saw me."

"You wanted me to know Gordon Elmer was blackmailing Minnie?"

She nodded and looked pleased.

"It seems that he met the entire DeMarco family, even the grandchildren," I said. "But he met the youngest when she was only two. He wouldn't recognize her even if she was standing right in front of him like you are standing in front of me."

"And what did he say her name was?"

I glanced at my father. He was next to the chickens now. They grazed happily around them, oblivious to the tension in the air. Esmeralda sensed it from her spot by the barn door though; her fur was raised on her back.

"Lynlee," I said. "It sort of reminded me of Lynn."

She removed her gun from the pocket of her puffy coat and pointed it at me. "Me too. I knew I should have changed my name a little more from Lynlee, but it had been my grandfather's middle name and I wanted to honor him."

I couldn't see my father anymore. He must have moved behind the chicken coop. Marshal Chuff wasn't concerned with where he was. She clearly thought he was a hapless disabled man. I knew better.

"Your grandfather? Mack?"

She nodded.

"How did you find out Minnie was here?"

"That was from Gordon." She smiled. "I didn't know at the time that he was blackmailing Minnie and had been for a couple of years. He called into the U.S. Marshals Service tip line and said he was living next door to Joan the Bandit. You would not believe how elated I was. I went into the agency for the sole purpose of finding Joan and making her pay for what she did to my family. It was a great day when that call came across my desk. I begged my supervisor for the case, and he handed it over. No one else was interested in arresting a sixty-something old woman. I wasn't either. I was interested in killing her though."

"Why didn't Minnie just disappear and build a new identity again like she had countless times before?" I asked.

"She said to me, not long before I killed her, that she couldn't leave. She finally had a friend here that was like family. She couldn't leave her friend."

Doreen. I wondered if I should tell Doreen this, assuming I lived to have the chance.

"When I approached Joan on the evening of your festival, she was almost gleeful to see me. She went on and on about how much she loved my grandfather. She said she had no choice but to turn him in, but he was the love of her life. It made me sick. I had no choice but to silence her. Now I will have to silence you too."

"You can't shoot me. Everyone will know it's you."

"Really?" she asked. "I don't think so. I'll shoot you and then your lovely father. I am sorry about that, but no witnesses can be had. Then I will call it in. All I have to say is that I came upon the scene in the midst of my investigation."

"But it's your gun."

She stared at me. "Do you think I'm dumb enough to use a traceable gun?"

I shivered. Clearly, this was something Marshal Chuff had thought about.

"I think you should just give yourself up. Maybe they will be lenient with you after you explain your history with Minnie." I knew that wouldn't be the case.

"I don't think so. Do you know how hard it is for law enforcement in prison? I'm not going there."

"You should have thought of that before you killed Minnie."

"I probably should have, but she brought it on herself, just like you have." She lifted the gun. "Don't worry, this won't hurt. I'm an excellent shot."

There was a cry and then a screeching sound.

Marshal Chuff spun around. "What the—"

The cloud of angry chickens flew at her. My father was behind them, scaring them and waving his cane. The terrified chickens came at her with their claws out, ready to defend themselves. No one who actually raised chickens would call them weak birds, and these chickens were scared and angry. Marshal Chuff screamed as they dug their talons into her arms and legs and even the top of her head. The gun went flying, and I dodged chickens to scoop it up.

Huckleberry was running around the chickens and barking, egging them on.

"Help!" Chuff cried.

"I will after I call your best friend, Chief Randy," I shouted as I shoved the gun in my pocket and made the call.

Dad was next to me. "Give me the gun."

I did what I was told as I was on the phone with dispatch. My father held Minnie's murderer at gunpoint until the police arrived.

Epilogue

You can never leave your past completely behind you. That's what I learned from Minnie's death.

Just like she couldn't leave Mack and what she did to his family behind, I could never leave Logan behind. The same could be said for Quinn about his wife Mariah.

You can't leave it behind, but you can move on if you face it and deal with the repercussions. Minnie never dealt with her past, and it caught up with her. In the end, she paid for it with her life.

It took Lynn Chuff's life too. It became her obsession. What happened to her family because of Minnie took her down a path that affected everything. She chose a career because of it and was driven by it. Revenge was her purpose.

I stood in the middle of the cherry orchard. It was looking better today, even as frost blanketed the Grand Traverse County. When spring came, it would be like a completely new grove.

Hazel and Quinn walked down the row toward me. Each of them carried a shovel. "We are here to plant trees."

I smiled at the wagon of five new trees. It was all I could afford right now, but it was a start.

Hazel ran ahead. "I'm going to check the rows for any changes in the grade." She winked at me. "Signs of digging!"

I swallowed. I knew she was hinting about the treasure. Neither of us had mentioned my grandmother's treasure to her father yet. I doubted it was a good idea to ask a child to keep a secret from her parent, but I reminded myself I never technically asked her to keep this secret specifically from Quinn. It was just understood.

"Changes in the grade? Where did you learn about that?" Quinn asked.

"I know a lot about farming, Dad. Shiloh is a very good teacher." She ran down the row with Esmeralda and Huckleberry close on her heels.

"I know you are," Quinn said to me.

I smiled. "I really don't think she will find anything."

He shrugged. "It's a fun way to spend a Saturday off duty with my daughter and you."

I blushed.

"I still can't believe your father caught a killer with chickens."

I laughed. "And none of the chickens were hurt. Never underestimate a farmer."

"I never will, especially not you and Sully." He looked around with an anxious expression.

"What's wrong?" I asked.

"I'm just keeping a lookout for Hazel," he said.

"She's fine. I think she knows this orchard as well as I do."

"I know." He stepped toward me and stood just inches from me. "I want to apologize for what I said the other morning."

"The other morning?"

"The morning after Hazel spent the night in your cabin."

"Oh," I whispered, not knowing if I was ready to revisit that conversation.

"I was completely exhausted and didn't know what I was saying. I spoke out of turn. I do care about you. That's true, but I'm not at a place to do anything about it."

A pain pinched at my chest. "Is everything okay?"

"I don't think that I'm ready for anything more than friendship with anyone, least of all you." His voice was so quiet, I could barely hear him.

"Oh." My chest felt hollow.

"It's just... I have Hazel to think of too."

I nodded. What he said made sense, but it hurt all the same. I hadn't expected it to hurt.

"I lost my wife two years ago. I loved her. She was such a good woman, wife, and mother. I don't know that I can move on just yet."

"I loved Logan too. It's hard to move on from a loss like that."

"Yes, but you've had more time to heal."

Heal? I didn't know if anyone completely healed from such a devastating loss. "Yes, I have had more time to get used to the idea."

"That came out wrong. I'm sorry."

I shook my head. "No, no, you're right. It's probably a terrible idea. We were doing so well as friends, and Hazel doesn't need any more upheaval."

"That's what I think too." He held out his hand to me to shake. "Just friends?"

I shook his hand. "Friends." Even as I said it, I knew it was a friendship that was now lost.

SHILOH'S
Quick Farm Tips

A problem any gardener or farmer has is how to remove weeds and reclaim land for new gardens or just for a fresh plot of land. When weeds are horribly overgrown, many believe that herbicides and fertilizers are the only answers. There is a better, safer, and organic way to tame your property by snuffing out the weeds with black plastic sheeting. Weeds, like all plants, need light. If you deprive them of that, they will die.

The process is very simple: first mow the area down. It will be easier to cover if it's as flat as possible, then use at least 6-mil black plastic sheeting to cover the ground. You can buy this at any home improvement store, and it usually comes in twenty by one hundred feet rolls. If you are working with a smaller area, cut it to size. Then, lay it down on the weeds you would like to remove and weigh the plastic down so it doesn't blow out of place during bad weather. You can hold it in place with sandbags, concrete pavers, or really any heavy object that you have around that can be exposed to the elements. Leave the sheeting on the weeds for six to eight weeks. The longer the sheeting is on the weeds, the more they will die and decompose. This not only kills them but adds nutrients back into the earth. I have even used this method on poison ivy, and it worked great.

After the set number of weeks has gone by, remove the sheeting, which you can fold up and save to use again later. In my case, I just move it to another part of the farm that needs to be rehabilitated. Now you have a rich patch of soil. Till the soil as soon as you can. That will disturb weed roots that might have survived the blackout, and then plant your ground cover or garden of choice. If you don't plan to garden in that spot, I highly recommend you consider something other than grass, such as clover or another cover crop suitable for your area. Clover and other plants like it help bees and other creatures thrive.

Happy gardening and farming!
Shiloh Bellamy

**Don't miss another farm-fresh mystery
from Amanda Flower!**

Read on for an excerpt from *Farm to Trouble*.

Chapter One

It smelled like home before I even saw it. I caught a whiff of freshly cut hay and plowed earth when I got off the highway and drove down the long country road to the small town of Cherry Glen, Michigan. Huckleberry, my pug, held his flat nose in the air as if he recognized it too. With the top down on my red convertible, the country breeze caressed his small ears. The wind was in my long blond hair—hair that remained blond due mostly to my ridiculously expensive stylist back in Los Angeles.

Just before I crossed the line that marked the town limits, an enormous billboard with a photo of wind turbines on it came into view. *"Support Cherry Glen Wind Farm"* ran along the top of it.

Huckleberry looked at me questioningly with his round brown eyes as we whizzed past pine trees and rolling farms. We weren't in California anymore, that was for sure. Huckleberry was a pug used to palm trees and traffic. He would get none of that in Cherry Glen. Although, like in California, there was plenty of sand. Beyond Traverse City, the closest city nearby, was the Sleeping Bear Dunes along the shores of Lake Michigan. There was more than enough sand there for a beach-starved pug even if the lake water was too cold to touch for nine months of the year.

I drove through the center of Cherry Glen. When I had grown up in this town, it was just a few mismatched buildings made of brick and weathered boards. Today, the downtown was quaint but bustling. Small businesses and shops lined the street. The two largest buildings held Fields Brewing Company, in an old grain warehouse, and Michigan Street Theater. The theater had been abandoned when I was a child. To my surprise, the marquee was lit and proclaimed the upcoming dates for Shakespeare's *The Tragedy of Julius Caesar.*

It was just after seven on a Friday evening in the middle of July. The sun wouldn't set for another two hours, and townspeople and tourists ambled up the new-looking sidewalk. Moms pushed babies and strollers, and school-age children ran in and out of the general store. The tourists, or fudgies as we called them growing up, were easy to pick out from their Michigan-mitten T-shirts and crisp shorts. We called them fudgies because most of them would travel up north to Mackinac Island and the U.P. in search of fudge before heading back down to wherever they came from. They stuck out from the farmers. The farmers wore their dusty jeans and work boots going about their day-to-day.

The town appeared to be thriving. It was nothing like the beaten-down, blue-collar hometown I remembered. Time had been kind to Cherry Glen. I hoped I would find the same at Bellamy Farm.

At the end of the street was the town hall, a modest brick building with a large Palladian window over the front door and a WWII Sherman tank sitting on its postage stamp-sized lawn. The tank had been a gift to the town from a collector who died before I was born. It was the only structure on Michigan Street that looked exactly the same.

I could distinctly remember climbing on the tank as a child with my father looking on. That was over twenty year ago, what felt like a lifetime, and it almost seemed like a memory from a movie I had seen rather than a moment in my own childhood. Despite the town's improvements, it still had the same down-home feel to it, and anyone walking along the sidewalk would take one look at me and know I didn't belong. Didn't matter that I had lived in Cherry Glen for the first twenty-three years of my life. I'd been gone for fifteen years. My capped teeth, blond highlights, red convertible, and portable dog belied that fact. Very few people would know the *new* me, as I cut most of my friends out of my life when I left to recover from what I had lost. In many ways, my father and the land were my remaining ties to this place.

Distracted by the tank, I was driving a little bit too fast. I had been on the road for countless hours and wanted to be over and done with this last leg of the trip.

That was my mistake. I should have slowed down going through the town. It was an afterthought I regretted immediately when I heard the sound of sirens behind me. I would have hoped at thirty-eight years old the sound of sirens behind me would no longer make me jump like a sixteen-year-old with a permit. Sadly, that was not the case.

I looked in my rearview mirror and saw a police officer on a motorcycle coming at me at a fast clip. I shared a look with a bewildered Huckleberry as I pulled to the side of the road. Speeding with California plates through Cherry Glen was a very bad idea.

I watched as the large man climbed off his motorcycle and hitched up his pants. He removed his helmet and laid it on the seat. He wasn't in a hurry to give me a ticket. He wanted me to sweat it out. If how damp my palms felt was any indication, his strategy worked. I wiped them on my skirt and reached for my small clutch next to Huckleberry on the passenger seat.

I had my license, registration, and insurance card out by the time the officer reached me. He was mostly bald but had tufts of hair springing sporadically out of his head. His hair was gray, but he had a wide, black mustache that was still dark, so I knew it had to be dyed. He looked familiar, but it had been fifteen years since I'd left Cherry Glen, so I couldn't quite place how I knew him.

"Well, well, look what the cat dragged in. Shiloh Bellamy. I didn't think we would ever see the likes of you around here again."

I grimaced.

"Remove your sunglasses, please."

"Oh, sorry," I said and took off my aviator glasses. I blinked in the bright sun as the police officer came back into focus. On his chest, a bright silver star read "Chief." Great. Not only did I get pulled over before I reached Bellamy Farm, but it was by the chief of police. What a terrific way to start my triumphant return home. It was time to negotiate, which, as a television producer who had spent most of my career trapped between a studio and directors and actors, I did best. "I am so sorry. I know I was going too fast through town. I wasn't thinking, not that that's any excuse. I'm just in a hurry to get to my father."

"I know all about Sully Bellamy not feeling well. I was the one who took him to the hospital after his last fall." He gave me a beady look when he said that, like it should have been me who took my father to the hospital. I bit the inside of my lip. He was probably right about that. I had wanted to be there, but meetings in New York kept me away.

"Thank you for doing that. My dad always speaks highly of his neighbors. I haven't been around as much as I would like, and I'm grateful to the community for rallying around him." I blinked back crocodile tears.

"You don't remember me, do you?" the chief asked.

I dropped the tears schtick and felt my face redden. This cop looked like he didn't do well with any funny business, so I simply waited.

He hooked his thumbs through his belt loops, and as he did, the gun on his hip shifted. "Chief Randy Killian, but everyone just calls me Chief Randy."

The name Killian immediately struck me—this was Quinn Killian's father. The Killians were a prominent family in the town. And the chief's son, Quinn, had been my fiancé Logan's best friend. I hadn't seen Quinn since Logan's funeral because I packed up the beat-up Jeep I owned at the time and left for California the next day.

I swallowed. I knew coming back to Cherry Glen would remind me of Logan and the guilt I carried over his death. I just didn't know it would be before I even reached my family farm.

"Nice to see you again, Chief Randy." I flashed him my thousand-watt smile—the one that made me believe spending three months' salary on it was worth it. "Again, I'm really sorry about speeding, but you know how my father is unwell, so you can understand my haste. I should have been here yesterday, but I got trapped tying up some loose ends and left later than expected…" I shouldn't be babbling to the police officer about my problems. What he said next proved that.

"You're still getting a ticket, missy. I don't abide by speeding in my town."

The smile clearly didn't work. Away from the bright lights of LA, my veneers were just another waste of money. I handed him my license.

Huckleberry and I sweated in the sun as Chief Randy took his good old time writing up my ticket. As I sat there, I remembered what summer in the Midwest was really like. Hot and humid with no ocean breeze to take the edge off. Huckleberry's tongue hung out as he stared at me. His face bore a look of betrayal, eyes narrowed and nose extra scrunched, as if he was wondering why I brought him to this steamy place. Then again, it could have been gas. You never knew with Huckleberry; he was a pug after all.

Chief Randy came back and handed me my ticket. "You go light on the pedal, all right?"

I nodded dutifully.

"Now, go see your pops. He needs you right now more than you even know." His black eyebrows, which were almost as impressive as his mustache, dipped down in concern.

I wondered what that meant. I knew my father needed

me. He asked me to come back to Cherry Glen to help him with the family farm, and I was here, wasn't I? I'd left my career behind in California.

Chief Randy smacked the side of my car like he would a cow he wanted to move out to pasture and ambled back to his motorcycle. I waited for him to ride away before I pulled out onto the empty road.

I glanced at Huckleberry. "Huck, we aren't in LA anymore."

His eyes rolled into the back of his head, and his long tongue licked his flat nose.

Acknowledgments

As always, thanks to my readers who follow me from series to series. Your support means the world to me.

Thanks again and again to my superagent, Nicole Resciniti, who made my career happen, and to my editor, Anna Michels, and the editorial team at Sourcebooks for their work and support of this series.

Thanks to reader Kimra Bell.

Special thanks to my husband, David Seymour. He supports my writing in every possible way, from traveling to the location, helping me figure out tricky plot points, and being my number one fan. He is the very best.

And to my Heavenly Father, thank you for dreams come true.

About the Author

Amanda Flower, a *USA Today* bestselling and Agatha Award–winning author of more than thirty cozy mystery novels, started her writing career in elementary school when she read a story she wrote to her sixth grade class and had the class in stitches with her description of being stuck on the top of a Ferris wheel. She knew at that moment she'd found her calling of making people laugh with her words. In addition to being an author, Amanda is a former librarian with fifteen years' experience and owns a small farm in Northeast Ohio with her husband.